Ruth Siegel
610 Virginia St.
Vallejo, CA  94590-6144

# THE
# WILD
# CARD

## ALSO BY MARK JOSEPH

FICTION

*To Kill the Potemkin*
*Typhoon*
*Mexico 21*
*Deadline Y2K*

NONFICTION

*Forbidden Fantasies*
(with photographers Mike Phillips
and Barry Shapiro)

# THE WILD CARD

A NOVEL

# MARK JOSEPH

ST. MARTIN'S PRESS
NEW YORK

Please be advised that this is a work of fiction in which the author has exercised the fictioneer's license to rearrange facts for his convenience. Wolfman Jack first broadcast on XERB from Tijuana, Mexico, in 1965, not 1963 as represented in this novel.

"Stay."
Words and music by Maurice Williams
©1960 (Renewed) CHERIO CORP.
All Rights Reserved
Used by permission

www.stmartins.com

Book design by Tim Hall

Library of Congress Cataloging-in-Publication Data

Joseph, Mark.
    The wild card : a novel / Mark Joseph.—1st ed.
        p.      cm.
    ISBN 0-312-26120-9
    1. Poker players—Fiction.   2. Male friendship—Fiction.   3. Death—Fiction.
I. Title.

PS3560.O776 W55    2001
813'.54—dc21

                                                                    2001019171

First Edition: August 2001

10  9  8  7  6  5  4  3  2  1

This novel is dedicated to the memory of my father, Herbert L. Joseph, M.D., who taught me how to play poker.

Thanks, Pop.

Most men love to see their best friends debased; for generally it is on such debasement that friendship is founded.

—FYODOR DOSTOYEVSKI, *The Gambler*

# 1995

# 1

Four miles below Marysville and Yuba City, twin Sacramento Valley towns that face one another across the Feather River, the stream swings gracefully around Shanghai Bend, a broad, sweeping curve whose mineral deposits have attracted miners since the Gold Rush. At the mouth of the bend an unnatural cataract of strange, pitted rocks forms a cascade of shallow waterfalls that drops the river eight feet in a hundred yards. Created by powerful dredges and pumps during the heyday of hydraulic mining in the early twentieth century, the falls at Shanghai Bend prohibit the passage of any craft. The current is swift, the bottom slick and treacherous, and kayakers and canoeists portage their boats around the falls just as miners carried their boats around churning machinery in 1903.

Subject to floods like all rivers in the valley, the Feather has been plugged by dams, constricted by levees and drained for agriculture, yet none of these attempts to tinker with nature has prevented the river from overflowing its banks with alarming regularity. The river is particularly inclined to flood at Shanghai Bend, and every few years the Feather deposits tons of mud and squirming steelhead into the living rooms of a subdivision called Shanghai Bend Meadows.

In 1995 the valley was booming, jobs were being created overnight, and savvy developers promoted nonstop construction of new housing. Thus one morning in late May a backhoe operator began digging a trench between Shanghai Bend Meadows and the east levee. Every year the Feather altered its course, washing out old levees and creating new islands while reducing others to sandbars. The operator was digging in a spot that once had been an island but now was destined to become the backyard of a new house.

In May temperatures in the valley can soar into the nineties, and the operator liked to work fast before the day became unbearably hot. By ten o'clock, the trench was twenty feet long, three feet wide, and four feet deep when she uncovered a human skeleton.

The outline of a rib cage was visible, and two ribs had been smashed by the action of the steel backhoe. Having worked along the river for many years, the operator knew the riverbed was a treasure-trove of archeology. Neither shocked nor horrified, her first thought was that she'd uncovered a Native American burial site, common in the region. That ticked her off because archeologists would be called in, construction delayed, and her paycheck would shrink while the site was excavated. She sat for ten minutes under her hardhat, smoking a cigarette, trying to talk herself into making the bones disappear. Two or three swipes with the backhoe and the lot of reddish-brown calcium would be over the levee and into the river. But the operator was an honest sort, and after thinking it through she decided to do the right thing. She called the foreman who called the developer who called the sheriff who came straight away, took one quick look and called the Yuba County medical examiner.

When the medical examiner arrived, the operator, sheriff, three deputies, and a half dozen construction workers were standing around, looking into the hole as though some great truth were to be discovered there. To the medical examiner, a skilled pathologist, truth was a matter of common sense and forensic science. He jumped into the hole with a small case of tools and a camera, snapped a photo, pulled on a pair of rubber gloves and knelt over the protruding bones with a whisk broom. While carefully brushing dirt from the rib cage, he addressed his attentive audience.

"This *could* be an Indian site," he said laconically, pausing to take more pictures. "Or perhaps a miner who died during the Gold Rush. On the other hand, this might be a godforsaken Okie who came to California to escape the Dust Bowl in Nineteen and Thirty-six and died in the promised land."

Removing soil adjacent to the ribs, he uncovered a fractured cranium and mandible. He photographed the skull, moving in close to capture the small but obvious indentation just above the right temple. Then he exchanged the whisk broom for a smaller brush and delicately removed chunks of clay from the jawbone.

"But it isn't," he declared.

"What makes you say that?" the sheriff asked.

"Silver fillings. Relatively modern dental work."

"Homicide?"

"We have a long way to go, Sheriff, but the skull is cracked."

"Male? Female?"

"Don't know yet, but we will. I'm guessing female."

"How long has this body been in the ground?"

"Don't know that either, but more than fifteen years and less than fifty. That's an educated guess. An artifact would help—clothing, a button, a zipper."

By now it was midday and getting hotter. Sweating, the medical examiner made exploratory stabs with a small spade around the bones and after ten minutes uncovered the only piece of evidence that would ever be found at the site: a single, plastic-coated Bicycle brand playing card, the queen of hearts.

# 2

The phone call from California came late at night when Professor Alex Goldman was alone in his study in Manhattan, cheating at solitaire.

"Hello?"

"Wiz!"

"Hey, Nelson, how are ya? We set up? We gonna play?"

"Yeah, yeah, but listen, Alex, I gotta tell ya, Dean just called. They dug her up."

Dr. Goldman had dreaded this call for so many years, when it finally came he was struck dumb.

"Alex? You there?"

*Pause.*

"Alex?"

"All right, okay."

Dr. Goldman sat up straight in his proper hardback chair, took a deep breath and said, voice deep and husky, "Maybe we can have the big one this year."

"You bastard." Lt. Nelson Lee of the Los Angeles Police Department bristled over the phone line. "All you care about is the fucking game."

Yes, Dr. Goldman thought, all I care about is the fucking game. All I've ever cared about is the fucking game. Our lives are meaningless without the fucking game.

He asked, "Are you in, Nelson, or are you gonna crap out?"

"I'm in. Everybody's in. All the way."

"Everybody?"

"Don't get excited, not to worry, the table is full. Next Friday at the Palace."

"Okay," Dr. Goldman said, calmer. "Good. Very good. See ya."

Dr. Goldman hung up the phone and turned to his computer. He smirked. He had letters to write.

A capsule résumé for Alex Goldman, Ph.D.: assist in the identification of a new subatomic particle as a graduate student, make an an important discovery in the field of plasma physics at twenty-six and parlay the package into tenure in the physics department at his alma mater, Columbia University. Toss in some classified work for the Department of Defense and there you have the good professor as the world knew him, flourishing and seemingly content.

Everyone has secrets, an inner life whose details never appear on a résumé. Among Dr. Goldman's deeply held secrets was a vice, a dangerous obsession, but he maintained such strict control over his compulsion that his family and friends had never glimpsed a different Alex who lurked beneath the urbane academic they saw every day. Neither his wife, ex-wife, nor children of both marriages ever imagined he had a poker jones the size of Nevada.

Dr. Goldman was addicted to poker, a drug more thrilling than heroin. When he looked into himself, rather than into subatomic particles, he knew what he really wanted to do was play cards. Strange and illogical as it may seem, winning a Nobel Prize would shrivel in comparison to destroying a worthy opponent at seven card stud. He had the tools: ruthlessness, a keen ability to observe others, a gift for math, and a phenomenal memory. Nevertheless, in spite of his prodigious talent, his game was cursed. He knew that if he were to sit down and play cards, he wouldn't quit until he lost everything. No matter how good you were, or thought you were, there was always someone better.

Many years before, when he was only eighteen, knowing his passion for poker was irresistible, he vowed to never play again. True to his vow, he avoided casinos and card rooms and friendly games. His father and grandfather, both poker players, had died penniless, each believing one more hand was all he needed to get even. Dr. Goldman had inherited their poker genes along with his grandfather's antique clay chips. It was a heavy legacy.

He kept the chips, thousands of dollars in cash, and a small, leather-bound notebook locked in a safe in his study. Once a year he carefully packed the chips and some of the money, pocketed the notebook, and flew to San Francisco, his hometown, for a weekend of poker with his childhood pals. Only with them could he play cards without his addiction running out of control.

Every June Dr. Goldman and his friends rented a suite in the Sheraton Palace Hotel, stocked it with booze and food and played poker as they had for more than three decades. Sitting around a card table with Nelson Lee, Charlie Hooper, and Dean Studley, whom he'd known since they were kids together in an old San Francisco neighborhood called Noë Valley, he could once again be Alex the wizard of Alvarado Street.

His secret was no secret from them. They knew the Wiz was a poker junkie. That was the way Alex was, in the same way that Nelson Lee was still Crazy Nelson from Twenty-first Street, Dean Studley was the same rum-swilling, dope-smoking outlaw curmudgeon from Elizabeth Street, and Charlie Hooper, fishmonger extraordinaire from Dolores Street, couldn't win in their game if his life depended on it. Charlie always lost just as Alex always won. A patina of age and refinement couldn't change that. They were fifty-year-old men who cared deeply about one another, and who, when the chips were down, would happily slaughter one another at the poker table. They'd played together so long it was difficult to deceive one another, the essence of poker, and their efforts to do so made their poker fests marvelously entertaining. Symbolic bloodletting was the name of their game.

The rustle of fabric, the whir of fans, the murmur of first class. Bustling flight attendants stowed luggage as passengers found their seats and settled in for the long flight. Among the last to board, a tall, ruddy-faced gentleman of fifty came through the hatch in a cloud of tan linen and elegant Panama hat. Just before the Panama disappeared into an overhead compartment, a little girl across the aisle glimpsed the corner of a playing card, a red jack, peeking from the hatband. Curious, she stared as he tilted his seat back and closed his eyes. She could smell his cologne. An imperceptible slit opened between his eyelids and he caught her gazing. Gotcha, he said to himself.

"Fasten your seatbelts, please."

The plane pulled away from the gate. New York lay beyond the tarmac: skyscrapers, rivers and boroughs, wives and children, his adopted home for more than thirty years.

Goodbye, he thought. *Adieu.*

The plane took off. Dr. Goldman took out the leather notebook and began to read. Written in code, a simple transformation cipher, the slim volume consisted of eighty-seven pages of poker wisdom and notes on the habits of players, the first half written in his grandfather's meticulous hand and the rest by him. He read the text in its entirety, reviewing his notes on every game he'd ever played, and when he finished he was transformed. Dr. Goldman no longer existed.

Alex the wizard of Alvarado Street ate a first-class lunch of prawns and steak and took a nap. An hour from San Francisco he woke up and discovered the little girl still staring.

"I saw the card in your hat," she said. "The jack of diamonds."

"You're very observant," Alex replied. "I'm impressed."

"Are you a magician?" she asked.

He smiled, shook out his elegant cuffs, waggled his fingers like a concert pianist, and pulled a deck of cards from his breast pocket. He winked. She smiled. Twisting slightly in his seat, he rolled over his hand and the cards magically spread into a fan. She giggled and her mom looked over. He closed the deck, waggled his fingers, and spread the cards open again. Every card was a jack of diamonds. Her eyes went wide. He winked again and then ripped off a spectacular staircase shuffle, the cards dancing back and forth like well disciplined soldiers.

"Pick a card, any card."

For the next twenty minutes he entertained the passengers in first class with card tricks, warming up his fingers, practicing, letting muscle memory take over. He held the cards in a mechanic's grip, forefingers over the front edge of the deck that allowed him to deal seconds and cards from the bottom, things he would never do in a game but signifying to his satisfaction that his dexterity was still intact. He didn't say much, a little smooth card sharp's patter, letting the cards speak for themselves, and when he finished he gave the girl the deck.

"You really are a magician," she exclaimed.

"No," he replied. "I'm a wizard. There's a difference."

# 3

The boys from Noë Valley now played for much higher stakes than the dimes and quarters they'd wagered as kids. For the last five years the initial buy-in had been two thousand dollars, but this year the price of admission was five grand, serious money for poker, with the possibility of the stakes going much higher. Although the stakes had been raised, a more significant change over the years was the composition of the game. When Alex, Charlie, Nelson, and Dean were teenagers, the game had included a fifth player from the neighborhood, Bobby McCorkle, the one among them whose talent for poker could match Alex's. They hadn't seen Bobby in thirty-two years, since the summer of 1963, the year they graduated from high school. That June Bobby had enlisted in the Army. Expecting to go to Germany to fight the Russians, he'd been sidetracked to Southeast Asia for ten years. When the Vietnam War ended and he didn't come home to San Francisco, his old friends knew why; and when he refused to see them or play in the game, there wasn't a damned thing they could do about it. Bobby had stayed in the Army another ten years until he retired and started a new career as a professional poker player in Reno, a development that only sharpened their desire to have him play in their game. Every year they sent him an invitation, but he never showed up.

Nevertheless, every June they reserved a seat for their missing friend and drank a toast to his good health, but poker with only four players isn't particularly interesting. In 1985, after grousing for years, they decided to fill the fifth chair by inviting a guest to play. Since they didn't allow wild cards in their game, with a little ironic twist they called the stranger the "wild card." The next year they invited another guest, and the wild card became a part of their tradition. They never brought in a patsy; instead, they went to great lengths to find players of formidable skill. Wild cards were either professionals or high-rolling amateurs, and without exception the Wiz had taken them all.

This year's wild card was going to present the greatest challenge yet. Having established conditions that were met—raising the stakes and a clarification of the rules—after lo these many years Bobby McCorkle had agreed to come back and play.

With a fashionable brush cut, gold rings in both ears, and the latest fashions from Milan, Charlie Hooper cut a stylish figure that distracted people from his height, five foot four, his middle-aged paunch, and the jaded wrinkles around his eyes. A true San Franciscan, reckless and neurotic, Charlie worked hard to maintain a reputation as a *bon vivant*, an expensive proposition in a city where the party never stops. As sole heir to the Hooper Fish Company—boats, trucks, icy warehouse, and contracts to supply restaurants and supermarkets—Charlie could afford his flamboyant taste, and he preferred calling for another round of drinks to kicking back and quietly examining his life. Once in a while, at three in the morning after the bars were closed, Charlie couldn't avoid looking inside himself where he contemplated a hollowness like a hidden sinkhole in a river. Charlie shared a closely guarded secret with Alex and the rest of the boys from Noë Valley, and he'd risk anything—his integrity, his fortune, his soul—to protect their secret. This year, when the cards were dealt, he'd find out how much he truly was willing to risk.

The game was the most important event on Charlie's calendar, bigger than New Year's Eve or Halloween, and the preceding week he always became so excited he hardly ate or slept, skulking around his frozen warehouse driving his employees crazy with endless bad jokes—why do people eat so much shark? To get even, hahaha. Ten years earlier, his first domestic partner had been so suspicious of Charlie's annual rendezvous at the Palace that he'd followed him to the hotel, knocked on the door of the suite, and gone bananas at the sight of so much the money. Instant separation. Three years later domestic partner number two used Charlie's weekend on New Montgomery Street as an opportunity for a tryst of his own. That year Charlie lost his buy-in so quickly he went home for more money and caught his partner in the sack with his lover. Another divorce. Ah, well, he never lost his sense of humor and never took anything too seriously, except the game. A lousy poker player more interested in camaraderie than five card stud, Charlie nonetheless hated losing, and with the stakes going up this year—perhaps way up—he was nervous. He could never beat Alex, but he expected Alex to focus on Bobby, the wild card. All he had to do was stay out of the crossfire and concentrate on Nelson and Dean. There you go, Charlie boy, a strategy.

As the only player still living in San Francisco, Charlie took it upon himself to make the annual arrangements. Every year he reserved the Enrico Caruso Suite at the Palace, a deluxe accommodation named for the hotel's most illustrious guest who was tumbled from his bed by the earthquake of 1906. Accustomed to Charlie's special requirements, General Manager Jonathon Sweeny pretended not to hear the word "poker," and every year agreed to install a round card table and overhead light, set up an old-fashioned stereo record player, and hang a set of framed photographs supplied by Charlie.

On this Friday afternoon in June, Charlie was driving through rush-hour traffic on Montgomery Street to check into the suite at five o'clock, meet the caterers, and have everything ready when the others arrived.

It was hot. Once or twice a year cool and foggy San Francisco endured a heat wave that turned the city into instant New Orleans. People wilted on the sidewalks, sagging and sweating with the thermometer stuck at ninety-five. Poor Charlie, the air-conditioning in his new Mercedes had failed and the heat was making him crazy, as if the pending poker game hadn't made him crazy enough, especially this year. Bobby McCorkle, Jesus Christ, after all this time. When Nelson told him about the new construction at Shanghai Bend Meadows, Bobby had no choice. He had to show up for the game.

The past wouldn't stay buried forever.

Rush hour. Commuters jammed the financial district, and the city sweltered in the monstrous heat. As Charlie crossed Market onto New Montgomery, traffic halted him behind a dozen limos and taxis queued up in front of the hotel. Sweaty, sticky heat boiled off the pavement and into the car. A sixty-thousand-dollar-autobahn-burner and the air went belly up. Not that Charlie was superstitious, but it was not a good omen. Things were starting to go haywire. Shanghai Bend Meadows. He shuddered, put the thought away, and demanded of the gods, "Why are we having an impossible heat wave the weekend of the game? Why not last week or next week?"

Charlie fidgeted. Ahead, a young girl in a pink dress escorted by her father emerged from a white limo and skipped through the doors of the Palace. Having checked the hotel calendar when he made the reservation, Charlie knew tonight was Formal Night for the Rainbow Girls.

Immobile and suffocating in his Mercedes, Charlie furiously dialed the car phone.

"Sheraton Palace Hotel. Jonathon Sweeny's office."

"This is Charlie Hooper. Put Mr. Sweeny on the line, if you please. I'm dyin' out here."

The manager's velvety voice came on in a few seconds. "Charlie, how are you?"

"I'm stuck in traffic on New Montgomery and sweating like a week-old cod. Can you send someone out to get the car?"

"Charlie," Sweeny said patiently, "you're a pain in the ass but that's okay. I'll send a valet. Your suite is ready. The caterers are here."

"You didn't let them in, did you?" Charlie demanded.

"No, Charlie. I'm familiar with your protocols."

"Good. I always go in first. That's the ritual."

A uniformed valet knocked politely on the car window. Charlie waved and wiggled the phone.

"Okay, the guy is here for the car. Did Bobby McCorkle check in yet?"

"Let me see. Just a moment. Hang on. McCorkle, McCorkle, no."

Without waiting for the doorman, Charlie grabbed a small valise, a heavy canvas bag, and four large framed photographs from the back seat, handed a twenty to the valet, snatched his parking stub, and barreled into the Palace like he owned the joint, stopping just inside the doors to throw back his shoulders, puff out his chest, and breathe it all in.

The white marble lobby was a sea of foamy chiffon and sparkling satin: Rainbow Girls. The demoiselles and their dads were arriving for an early supper in the Garden Court, the hotel's fancy restaurant. Just what the boys from Noë Valley needed, nubile teenaged girls running around the hotel.

Sweeny was waiting at the registration desk.

"Table set up?" Charlie demanded.

"Yes."

"Caterer upstairs?"

"Yes, Charlie, they're waiting in the corridor. Do you have any luggage?"

"These." Charlie gestured toward the photos and bags.

Sweeny crooked his finger and a bellhop appeared. "Take Mr. Hooper up to the Caruso Suite and make sure he's satisfied with everything."

"Don't drink," Charlie told himself aloud in the elevator. "And don't smoke any of Dean's dope or do any of that shit, because if you do, you'll lose."

"Pardon me?" the bellhop asked politely.

Charlie iced him with a glance.

"What's your name, kid?"

"Andrew, sir."

Charlie stuffed a twenty into the young man's breast pocket. "Andrew, a Mr. Bobby McCorkle is going to check in sometime this evening. When that happens, you come up and tell me."

"Yes, sir. Anything else?"

"You are the soul of discretion, I suppose. Hear no evil, see no evil, speak no evil."

"Oh, yes sir, Mr. Hooper. I know my job."

The Caruso Suite was on the fourth floor in a corner overlooking

Market Street. Carrying the canvas bag himself, Charlie charged down the corridor trailed by Andrew lugging the framed photos and valise. The caterers, Miss Carmen and an assistant, were waiting outside the suite with two carts loaded with comestibles and supplies.

"Hello hello hello," Charlie sang. "Nobody's gone in?"

"Not while I've been here," said Miss Carmen.

"Got the records?"

"Yes, Charlie. I have everything."

Charlie quickly peeked at the carts laden with food and drink and checked out the green felt he would use to dress the card table waiting inside.

"Everything's fine. I'll take it from here. You can go. Thank you."

With a deep breath Charlie keyed the lock and with the bellhop's help pushed the carts through a small foyer and into the living room.

The poker table in the middle of the room was already covered with felt. Alex Goldman's laminated teak chip carousel occupied the center of the table, and another heavy canvas bag lay on a couch. Charlie could hear the fizz of a shower and awful, off-key singing coming from the rear of the apartment.

"Son of a bitch!" he snarled. "Alex, you scumbag!"

He stomped into one of the bedrooms and the bellhop heard riotous shouting and then rowdier laughter. Having been instructed by Mr. Sweeny and tipped by Charlie, the bellhop hung the photos and left.

Alex stepped out of the shower and heard Charlie storming around the bedroom shouting obscenities at the top of his lungs.

"Hi, Charlie," Alex yelled. "How the hell are ya?"

Charlie entered the bathroom and grinned at Alex who stood there, naked and dripping.

"What the fuck, man," Charlie said, shaking his head. "I told you last year if you did it again I'd kill ya. I bribed these fucking people. I told them you'd try some bullshit to get in here first. I knew it. I knew it. I knew it. How'd you do it?"

"I ain't tellin'."

Alex had a small red and blue jack of diamonds tattooed on his left shoulder. Charlie tore off his sweat-soaked Polo shirt and thrust his left shoulder toward the steamed-up mirror. His arm sported the king of diamonds inked into his skin in the same style.

"You're a prick, Alex."

"It's all part of the game, Charlie. Any little edge. You got anything to eat out there?"

"Whatever you want, pal. Alaskan king crab legs. Suckers walked all the way from Anchorage."

Alex slipped on a hotel robe and punched Charlie in the shoulder. "Good to see you, man. You doin' okay?"

"Yeah, sure, the ocean isn't empty yet, but who cares? We're gonna play cards. The rest of the world is bye-bye."

Alex smiled and looked his old friend up and down. "Bobby check in yet?" he asked.

"Not yet."

"He's here," Alex said. "I can smell him."

# 4

This year was going to be special. Nelson hit the bank and the gas station, zoomed onto the I-5, punched the go pedal, and left Los Angeles in a haze of exhaust. Next stop: San . . . Fran . . . Cisco.

To Lt. Nelson Lee of the LAPD, the annual reunion with his old friends up north was all about the party and the stunts he planned months in advance. After all, he was Crazy Nelson and the guys expected something outrageous as his contribution. Genuine outrageousness was hard to come by in California where eccentric weirdness was the norm, but he'd do his best. His briefcase was a Pandora's box of surprises. As for poker ability, he was a wriggling minnow in a school of sharks, and unless he was dealt an exceptionally good run of cards, he didn't stand a chance of cashing in money ahead. Alex—he didn't know if Alex cheated or what, but the guy was a mind reader. And Charlie—Charlie would go nuts and yell and scream and throw cards around in frustration at his failure to beat Alex. Then he'd smoke some of Dean's loco weed and convince himself that losing was hilarious. Dean, the country philosopher, would sit across the table like a teetering sequoia, folding almost every hand while waiting for Alex to drop. When Alex did toss in a hand, timber!—the tree would crash on Charlie's head and Dean would pull in the chips with an acerbic, devastating comment. Nelson wasn't in their league and that didn't bother him one whit.

Five grand, hell. Some years Nelson spent more on the stunts than he dropped in the game. One year he bought into the game with counterfeit hundred-dollar bills, played wildly, lost everything, and then had to pull every string he could when Charlie got busted for passing one of the phony C-notes. Three years ago he'd staged a fake robbery, the one thing the boys from Noë Valley always expected that had never happened. He'd hired Hollywood extras to play bad guys who entered the suite dressed as room service waiters, and then he'd called in a favor to get real SFPD cops to burst in right behind the phony crooks. The boys and the robbers were taken completely by surprise. The gag so rattled that year's wild card, a poker buzzard from Las Vegas named Cookie, that he broke a window and was about to jump from the fourth floor when a cop grabbed him and pulled him back in. Every year it was something: vice cops, fire alarms, flamenco dancers, belly dancers, strippers— this year would be different. He had something special this year, but with Bobby McCorkle sitting in, he expected fireworks aplenty without the goofball diversions he dreamed up.

Bobby McCorkle. By now Bobby was more myth than human being. The Bobby he remembered was only eighteen, the toughest, smartest, best-looking kid at Lowell High School. If Bobby had been normal he would have been varsity quarterback and student body president, but Bobby was half hoodlum and half Lenny Bruce. Oh my god, what times they had; it was a miracle they survived all the screwing around, shoplifting six-packs, hot-wiring cars, and driving drunk. Bobby would go for ideas the other guys wouldn't touch, the wimps. On Saturday nights they drag-raced on the Great Highway, got drunk on China Beach, and hustled three card monte on Powell Street. On Sunday afternoons they scalped forged 49er tickets at Kezar Stadium for money to spend in black whorehouses on Third Street and Pai Gow parlors in Chinatown. Once, stoned, they climbed the south tower of the Golden Gate Bridge and mooned the tourists. Ah god, it was great. They knew what fun was. They invented fun. Rambunctious and full of themselves, testing themselves, finding out who they were, often reaching farther than was possible, they dragged Alex and Charlie and Dean kicking and screaming into the good times. Nelson liked to remember the good times, and he would have preferred never to think about the Feather River, white water at Shanghai Bend, cold beer, teenage madness, and raging hormones. Naturally, he thought about those things all the time.

Radar detectors beaming fore and aft, the speedometer of his '62 Corvette steady at seventy-five, Nelson drove north through the Central Valley, passing oceans of lettuce and white-capped seas of cotton, and after six hours arrived in Oakland just in time to get stuck in Friday evening traffic on the Bay Bridge.

It was hot. Nelson sweltered in the car with the top down and his shirt off. Citizens in Hondas gawked at the vintage Corvette and Nelson in wraparound Italian shades and ten of diamonds tattoo. A panorama of cityscape spread beneath the bridge, and Nelson felt a huge pang of emotional homecoming to his city by the bay. Hills and cliffs, water and steel, Embarcadero, Ferry Building and Market Street cutting a pristine swath through the high-rises. The Palace was right there at Market and New Montgomery, a monument to the Barbary Coast and the earthquake of '06. To the right he could see the swell of Nob Hill and the slope of Chinatown spilling down the flank. He felt like Bruce Lee driving into San Francisco to kick some ass. Nelson was Chinese, a fact he often forgot in L.A. but never here in Old Gold Mountain, the Chinese name for San Francisco.

Maybe he'd come home when he retired in another six years, if he lasted that long. If he made it through the weekend. They were going to play a little cards and then make a decision that would affect them for the rest of their lives.

Evidence. All the original documents were in his briefcase, including the LAPD missing person report from 1963, dental and medical records, county welfare department records, birth and death certificates. At great risk he'd collected them from archives and warehouses throughout Los Angeles County and kept them in a safe deposit box for more than twenty years, just in case. Well, just in case had arrived. The rest of the evidence was locked inside their heads: five men, five heads, five different versions of what happened. To Nelson the issue was cut and dried. As teenagers, they'd taken the easy way out. They'd buried a piece of their lives on an island in the Feather River and then vanished as though they'd never been there. Now, no matter what the cost, they had to do the right thing. If they could agree on what the right thing was. If they could agree on what happened. If they could even *know* what happened. There were many ifs and buts and uncomfortable questions and much more at stake than five thousand dollars—careers, families, fortunes, reputations, and the quaint notion of honor. The consequences of their decision were going to be expensive no matter what they decided, even if the price was no more than their self-respect.

As a kid Nelson had learned from Bobby McCorkle how far out of bounds he could go, and that was pretty damned far. Then, all at once, he'd learned that ethics are self-imposed, and the only real limit to what a person can get away with is self-restraint. Nelson had established and followed strict rules for himself, and he believed he'd been a decent cop. As commander of a street-crime unit in the beach community of Venice, he'd put away his share of vicious criminals and even turned a few into civilized human beings. He'd attacked his vocation with unrestrained zest, but he'd reached his limit. He'd held his breath for thirty-two years, and now he was ready to exhale. With a long sigh of relief or a panic attack? That remained to be seen.

Turning off the first exit from the bridge, he fought traffic to New Montgomery, stashed the car in a garage across from the hotel, pulled on a shirt, grabbed the briefcase, a small suitcase, and a hefty canvas bag, and walked across the street to the Palace.

"Checking in?" inquired the doorman. "Let me help you with those bags."

There was a time in San Francisco when Chinese were not allowed anywhere in the Palace except the laundry and kitchen. Now, rich Asian tourists and Rainbow Girls crowded the lobby. No one afforded Nelson a second glance. His name was in the computer, and a desk clerk politely handed over a key to the Caruso Suite.

On the way up in the elevator he whistled theme songs from old TV shows and fingered several dozen firecrackers stashed in his pocket. He decided to save them for later. Instead, he dismissed the bellhop with a nice tip, opened the briefcase and took out his piece, a Smith and Wesson Model 29 .44 Magnum Dirty Harry special. He pushed open the door to the suite, kicked the canvas bag inside, and then rushed in combat style, crouching, the gun in his hand flashing left and right.

"Hiyaaaaaa! Look out! Look out!"

The cool sound of Dave Brubeck's "Take Five" wafted from the stereo as Nelson shouted and grunted unintelligible noises through the living room, bedrooms, bathrooms, and kitchenette. Unmoved by this display, expecting it, Charlie sprawled on a couch and Alex stood by the caterer's carts stuffing his face with fat crab legs and sourdough.

"Nelson is here," Charlie said lazily. "At least I think it's Nelson. It may be Dirty Harry."

"Nah," Alex said. "It's that other guy, from *Streets*."

"Michael Douglas?"

"Yeah, him."

Nelson duckwalked into the living room, stood up from his crouch, laid the gun on the poker table, unwrapped a cheroot, and asked, "Anybody got a light?"

"It's Clint after all," Charlie said, tossing a box of wooden matches across the room.

"Thanks," Nelson said and lit the cigar. "Hi, Charlie."

"Hi, Nelson."

"Any ghosts in the closets?" Alex inquired.

Nelson grinned. "When did you get here?"

"An hour ago."

"Well?" Nelson asked.

"Well yourself," Alex countered. "Well, *what*?"

"Don't you want to know how I got Bobby to play?"

"Nope," Alex said, grinning with a mouth full of crab. "What I want to do now is eat."

Protected by glass covers, the framed photos were on the wall: James Garner as Bret Maverick, Steve McQueen as the Cincinnati Kid, Richard Boone as Paladin in *Have Gun, Will Travel*, and Wyatt Earp as himself.

"I'm tired of these pictures," Nelson said. "We should get new ones, maybe update a little."

"Fuck that," Charlie said. "In here it's always 1962, the last good year."

"You're nuts, you know that?" Nelson said. "Wallowing in nostalgia like a pig in shit. I bet you still drive around listening to Elvis. Am I right, Charlie?"

"I don't listen to Elvis, honey. I put on polyester and do Elvis," Charlie declared, frantically strumming an air guitar. "Bring your money?"

Nelson dropped the canvas bag on the couch with the others, and tossed five thousand dollars on the table. Charlie picked up a hundred dollar bill and began inspecting it with a magnifying glass he'd brought for that purpose.

"Have some of Charlie's crab," Alex said. "It's good. How are ya?"

"Don't ask," Nelson said, switching on the temporary light fixture. "Let's play cards."

# 5

Dean Studley and his wife Billie lived twenty miles downstream from Shanghai Bend in Verona, a tiny hamlet with one stop sign, a handful of houses tucked along the Feather River, and a much-loved institution: Studley's Machine Shop, Motor Repair, and Rocket Fuel. Dean stood six foot six, weighed two hundred eighty pounds, and wore a bushy Jerry Garcia beard and sweaty sleeveless undershirts stretched over a champion beer belly. Acres of Dean's formidable person were decorated with tattoos: an eagle graced his back, a tiger growled across his chest, "Semper Fi USMC" and "Billie" with a heart adorned his right shoulder, and his left shoulder hosted the queen of diamonds.

A huge, friendly bear, Dean presided over his ramshackle empire with a grand mixture of country wit, Jamaican rum, and very fine *sinsemilla*. Dean and Billie repaired cars and trucks for honest prices, made tractors run like bull elk, and kept patrol cars racetrack ready for ambitious deputy sheriffs from four surrounding counties. Unprejudiced, the Studleys took equal care of the low-grade outlaws who inhabit the California hinterland, tuning Harleys and Camaros for delinquents from Woodland to Redding. When he felt like it and the weather was good, Dean buckled a cocky biker into his cigarette boat, the *Queen of Diamonds*, and unhinged his mind by blasting along the river at a terrifying ninety miles per hour. Three or four times a year Dean and Billie hitched the boat to a truck and went racing. Theirs was a sweet life, but Dean believed it was built on a house of cards, five cards, to be precise: a royal flush in diamonds. Even Billie didn't know about that. She believed he got the tattoo in Bangkok.

From time to time Charlie Hooper drove up to Verona to smoke dope and drink rum, but Dean didn't let him bring his city friends. When Nelson Lee popped in from L.A., usually at three in the morning for a tune-up on his latest Corvette, Dean made sure he didn't bring any fellow cops. Dean and Billie grew marijuana on barges they moved around the rivers and sloughs where no one ever found them. The dope trade earned a fortune that was laundered through the garage and invested in conservative stocks and bonds. Neither greedy nor crazy, Dean sold no weed to locals, and none of his deputy sheriff pals or biker buddies ever suspected the existence of his illicit trade. His carefully selected customers all lived in cities far away, and it was they who'd named his product "Rocket Fuel."

As much as Dean loved internal combustion engines, his true love was the Feather River that flowed past his backyard. No one, least of all Billie, ever questioned his passion for this great movement of water and silt. He swam and fished and buzzed around in his boat, and when rising waters forced a call for help with sandbags on the levees, he was first to volunteer. Dean's strong back and relentless good cheer inspired his fellow volunteers to superhuman feats of levee building. And wherever there was new construction along the river, Dean wandered around the site, shooting the bull with the hardhats and expressing interest in any artifacts dug out of the riverbed.

In the summer of 1963, when they were eighteen years old, Dean, Charlie, Alex, Nelson, and Bobby McCorkle had set out on a voyage in Dean's father's boat, a twenty-seven-foot cabin cruiser, the *Toot Sweet*. Their goal had been to see how far up the Sacramento River they could go, but at Verona they'd taken the wrong fork—Dean could see the spot from his house—and had come up the Feather, mistakenly believing they were on the Sacramento. They'd made it as far as the falls at Shanghai Bend, the end of the line, and since it was almost dark they'd camped on a swampy island with no one around except the river, the mosquitoes, and the long, hot night.

The river had shifted course over the years, and the levees had been rebuilt many times. Now, in the spring of 1995, an extension of Shanghai Bend Meadows was under construction in the spot that had been their campground in the deep boonies thirty-two years earlier. After Dean read the story in the Marysville *Register*, he'd driven over and talked to the hardhats. That night he called Nelson, and Nelson agreed it was time to call Charlie and Alex and then track down Bobby McCorkle and tell him.

The canvas bags were stashed in the boat, and Dean was packed and ready to go. He zipped up a flame-retardant racing suit and walked out on the dock where Billie was securing an overnight bag in a compartment under the bow.

"Billie, you call down to Frisco and arrange a berth?"

"South Beach guest dock. They'll be expecting you. But, Dean?"

"Yes, Billie."

"Why don't you drive down there in the truck like a normal person?"

Short, cute, chubby, blond, and forty, Billie cocked her hands on her hips and looked at Dean like he was nuts. He was, and that was why she loved him. The boat, thirty-eight feet of sleek, black fiberglass, tugged with the current against the lines.

"I ain't normal, that's why. I got a perfectly good boat and I got a perfectly good river that goes where I want to go. You want to go with me?"

"Not on your life, Bubba. Have a good time and don't bring home any diseases."

"Yes, ma'am. Ed Fisher needs his van back in the morning. Can you handle that?"

"No, Dean, I'll be busy shooting up crystal meth and banging the Hells Angels," she said with a hearty chuckle. "Ed can have his van this afternoon if he wants. It's ready."

"You're a sassy old witch, you know that?" he said with affection.

He climbed into the cockpit and started the twin engines. A loud growl burbled from the pipes.

"Don't try to drive that damned thing back if you're hung over, honey. Please."

"Tell you what," Dean said. "You drive down with the trailer on Sunday, and we'll haul it back the easy way."

"It's a deal. You call me Sunday morning if you can talk."

"We just play cards, Billie. That's all."

"Right, and I'm the Queen of Sheba. Good luck. Can I say that? Is it all right to say good luck?"

"Luck has nothing to do with it. This is poker."

He unhitched the lines from the dock and eased away. In the channel he turned to wave, put on his helmet, and, a mile downstream, when the twin Mercury Marine Bulldogs and Arneson surface drives were warm, he opened it up. The engines thundered in his ears, spray hissed along the waterline, and the river uncoiled before him like a ribbon of green felt.

An hour from Verona he slipped through Sacramento at low speed, not wishing to ruffle the denizens of the capital with his wake, then dodged tankers and container ships in the deep water channel to Martinez. After gassing up on the Carquinez Strait, he cranked up the twin V8s and ran flat out at ninety-five miles-per-hour across San Francisco Bay, shooting a roostertail high in the sky, a thrilling, bone-jarring ride that could be heard from Sausalito to Telegraph Hill.

He tied up the *Queen of Diamonds* at South Beach and called a cab. Unlike Nelson, Dean's massive frame, menacing beard, ocean racer's driving suit, and fighter pilot's helmet caused quite a stir in the lobby of the Palace Hotel. The Rainbow Girls giggled and their daddies squared their jaws.

At the desk Dean set down a pair of heavy canvas sea bags, one larger than the other, and boomed, "Studley. Caruso Suite!"

Forewarned, the well-trained clerk contained his amazement, maintained his composure, and handed Dean a key.

"Welcome back, Mr. Studley. Can I do anything for you?"

Dean turned around to face the crowded lobby and grinned at the young girls all dressed up. "I'll take two pink ones and that yellow one over there, medium-rare. Tell them they can leave their shoes on!"

With that he crossed to the elevators and went upstairs.

# 6

A cone of fiery white light hung over the table, waiting. Smoke from Nelson's cigar drifted through the suite, the odor summoning familiar memories of games past. Dick Dale and the Del Tones thumped early '60s surfer music through the stereo speakers, the nostalgic beat of an era before the assassinations, Vietnam, Nixon, drugs, computers, and the fall of the Soviet Union. Outside, street-lights overtook dusk on Market Street as the city geared up for a sultry Friday night.

Alex took a deep breath and let out a sigh, his mind in poker mode with no equations cluttering up his memory. New York was a lifetime away on the far side of the continent, irrelevant. He was in another world now, one that might look like fantasyland—the road not taken—but was in fact the truer, deeper reality. These were his roots—the game, the guys, and all the things they shared. He studied Charlie's glossy black-and-whites of three Hollywood stars and a sheriff, mementos of an ethos that no longer made sense. Our private legends, he thought, forgotten heroes, Paladin and Wyatt Earp the avenging angels, Bret Maverick and the Cincinnati Kid the gamblers. The Kid lost, he remembered from Richard Jessup's novel. He went up against Lancey Hodges in the big game and he lost. How un-American, he reflected, that we should honor a loser.

They heard a rumble in the corridor and Nelson predicted, "Dean's gonna come in and ask what time it is, sure as shit."

"How do you know that?" Charlie demanded.

"He always does. He doesn't wear a watch."

"Twenty bucks," Charlie wagered, the gambling worm twitching in his cerebellum.

Nelson clenched the cigar between his teeth and hissed, "Sucker. You're on."

Alex watched Nelson puff his cigar and flex his chest, confident in his prediction. A strong man, healthy and fit, Nelson held his fear deep and almost inaccessible, perhaps because he dealt with it every day as a policeman. Charlie's terror was as prominent as his tattoo. Even if Charlie won the twenty bucks, he'd lose the head game. If Charlie won, Nelson would slicker him into another silly bet and another until Charlie cracked and agreed to bet on anything. Then Charlie would be mincemeat.

A bellhop with a dolly wheeled in two canvas bags, saying, "The guy said put them in the closet with the others."

"In there," Charlie said.

Dean strolled in, peeled off his racing suit, and parodied a curtsy in Jockey shorts and bulging undershirt. He danced a jig, showing off his tattoos, then flopped in a chair, ripped open a small duffel, and rummaged inside until he found a pair of jeans.

"Hey, Stud, lookin' good," Alex said, giving Dean both thumbs up.

"What time it is?" Dean asked, inverting subject and predicate and flashing a toothy grin.

Nelson was ready with his watch. "Ten after eight," he proclaimed.

"Shit," Charlie said, snatching a bill off his wad. Nelson gave it to the bellhop and sent the kid on his way.

"*Tempus fugit*," Dean quipped, eyes flicking to all points in the room and noticing the money changing hands. A year ago he'd walked out of the Caruso Suite after a weekend of poker and now it seemed as though he'd gone no farther than the lobby bar for a drink. Nothing had changed, neither the photos, the table, nor the guys. He clapped his hands once loudly and bawled, "Let's play cards."

"You don't want to wait?" Charlie asked.

"For what?"

"For Bobby," Charlie said. "What else?"

Dean dug into his bag and found a pair of beat-up old cowboy boots with steel toes and Cuban heels—no-nonsense boots and when he put them on he felt immune to bullshit.

"I been waitin' for that guy longer than I been waiting for Godot," he scoffed. "Fuck that. He may never show. C'mon, fellas. Let's play."

"Ooo, the man is hot to trot," Nelson said. "You been practicing, Deano? Playing a little cards here and there?"

"Wouldn't you like to know, wise guy." Dean cinched his belt under his belly and zipped up his bag. "What do *you* think, Wiz?"

Standing by the caterer's trays, pulse slightly elevated, anxious to play but not wanting it to show, Alex put on tinted glasses and hat and wiped his mouth with a starched, white napkin.

"Thought is no longer required," he said and took a seat.

Alex chain-smoked unfiltered Luckies when he played cards. Now, inside the cone of light with the felt stretching before him like a bottomless green pool, chips snug in the carousel, and cards in unbroken cellophane wrappers, he carefully opened a pack of red spot Lucky Strikes, took out a cigarette, tamped it on the table and lit it.

"We could wait all night," he declared. "The game is on."

Dean plopped down to Alex's left so Alex would have to bet before he did, and this maneuver prompted a wry smile from the Wiz. Nelson took the seat to Alex's right and Charlie to his right, leaving the chair between Dean and Charlie empty.

Each place was provided with a comfortable captain's chair, cup holder, and ashtray. The players fiddled with their chairs, tested the cupholders, and waited for Alex, the acknowledged captain of the table, who said graciously, "Welcome home, Mr. Studley."

"Same to you, Alex. Hello, boys."

"Hey," Charlie said. "If it ain't Mr. Natural his very own self."

"I got something special for you, Charlie, you rotten old faggot. Blow your mind."

"Later later, man. I'm not gonna let you get me all fucked up before we even start. I'm gonna take it easy."

Nelson reached across the table in front of Alex and shook Dean's hand. "Come down in your boat?" he asked.

"Aye, aye. I'm a watery kind of guy."

"I can tell. You smell like the mudflats of Oakland."

Dean laughed. "Beats hell out of the jail stink you carry around, copper. Disinfectant and jism."

"How's your old lady?" Nelson asked without skipping a beat.

"Billie? Billie's just fine and dandy," Dean, expansively spreading his arms. "She blossoms like a sunflower in the summertime."

"Did you tell her anything?"

"Nah. Ignorance is a wonderful thing. We're just gonna play cards, right? That's all she needs to know." Dean stretched and carefully looked around the table. Nobody wanted to talk about the Feather River. Maybe they wouldn't talk until tomorrow or Sunday. He asked Nelson, "How's your new old car?"

"Yellow."

"You paint it?"

"Yeah, the original color. I took it down to the plastic. What the hell."

Charlie cleared his throat and looked at Alex. "Gentlemen," he said, "let's get clear on the rules."

"Let's not and say we did," Dean snorted, and Nelson muttered, "Oh shit, here we go. Fishman, you are one predictable dude."

They all knew the rules would be established by Alex; nevertheless Charlie accused Dean of being an anarchist and started a no-I'm-not yes-you-are pissing contest. Dean often played the lout, but the others knew it was an act. Unnerved by the discovery at Shanghai Bend Meadows, the big man with a heart of gold was trying to disguise his fear with an extra dose of bravura.

"Children, please," Nelson pleaded.

Alex serenely began counting chips, a look of bliss on his face as he made neat stacks of whites, reds, and blues, the traditional hues of an old-fashioned poker game. The smooth clay chips had heft, a weight that registered as money and a feel no plastic could duplicate. A chip tossed into a pot landed with a solid chink and never bounced. One that hit a hardwood floor would break, but the carpet in the suite prevented such mishaps. Nothing could stop Charlie from throwing a handful of chips against a wall, as he had in Alex's parents' garage on Alvarado Street, or Dean from crushing a blue in his fist if he felt like it. It was understood that anyone who broke a chip had to pay Alex its value for that game. Over three generations so many chips had been lost, broken, cracked, stolen, and in one case eaten by Crazy Nelson on a dare, that Alex had sought out a specialty shop that had replicated his grandfather's chips, matching weight and color as closely as possible. In addition, he'd added a stack of black and yellows.

"All right," he said. "Whites are twenty-five, reds are fifty, blues are one hundred, and bumblebees are five hundred American greenback dollars. Buy-in is five thousand."

"Until Bobby gets here," Charlie said.

"We'll decide whether or not to raise the stakes after we've talked to him a while," Nelson said. "Maybe we will and maybe we won't."

"We will," Alex said. "You know damned well we will."

"If we raise the stakes, so will he," Dean said. "If he shows."

"Whatever it takes, we're going to have the game of our lives."

"If it comes to that, you better win, Alex," Dean said. "We're counting on you."

Alex picked up a stack of reds and let them ripple through his fingers, the sound as hypnotic as a Siren's call. "What you get for five grand is twenty-five whites, twenty-five reds, twenty blues, and three black and yellows," he announced. "Help yourself."

No one played banker. Each player put his money into a compartment in the carousel designed for that purpose and counted out his own chips. The four players laid their cash on the table. Twenty thousand dollars, most of it in hundreds, was a lot of bulk paper.

"There's too much damn money," Nelson exclaimed. "It won't fit."

"Here, I got somethin'," Dean said. Grabbing his bag, he pulled out a boxed bottle of 150-proof Jamaican rum and removed the bottle.

"You gonna drink that and play cards?" Nelson squawked. "You're whacked."

"Mind your own fuckin' business, Nelson," Dean snarled and stuffed his fifty one-hundred-dollar-bills in the box. All the money went in, and everyone counted out chips.

"The rules," Charlie insisted. "Let's get clear on the rules."

"How's about no rules, Charlie?" Dean said. "Just play. Fuck rules."

Alex chuckled. Dean was in Oakland Raider mode. In the glory years of the Raiders in the 1970s, Oakland players picked fights on the field to distract opponents. If an opposing player was into the fight, he wasn't into the game, and the battle was half over before it started.

"We'll have to go through this when Bobby gets here," Charlie whined, "so we might as well get it straight now."

"If he gets here," Dean said.

"He will," Alex said.

"You think so?"

"Yes."

"*The rules*, goddamnit," Charlie groaned. "What's the limit?"

"No limit," Dean suggested tersely.

"You're flamin' out of your mind," Nelson shot back. "There has to be some kind of limit."

"Why?"

"Table stakes," Alex said. "The only limit is what you have on the table. You can't go in your pocket or the bank once the hand has started. Okay?"

"Right," Nelson agreed.

"Okay," Charlie consented and they all looked at Dean.

"Ah, you bunch of spoilsports, all right."

"Check and raise?" Nelson asked. "Are we gonna allow sandbagging?"

"No," Charlie said. "We never do that."

"Yes," Dean contradicted emphatically. "That's how they play in casinos. That's real poker. Damned straight, sandbagging allowed."

"How would you know?" Nelson asked.

"Wise guy."

Nelson chuckled and Dean cracked up.

"Bobby wants to play that way," Nelson said. "That was one of his conditions along with the five grand buy-in. I told you that, Charlie. Sandbagging is permitted."

"Okay, okay, check and raise."

"Anything else?"

"A maximum of three raises on any one card."

Nods all around. "Agreed."

"Dealer's choice. No wild cards."

"*Let's play*, for chrissake," Dean thundered and unscrewed the cap from the rum.

"Any more quibbles?" Alex asked, handing Dean a sealed deck of red Bicycle cards. He took a blue deck himself, broke it open, removed the jokers, and began shuffling, a plain gambler's shuffle, scarcely bending the cards. The stiff, new cards felt light in his hands, perfectly sized for his fingers. When the cards were thoroughly melded he announced, "First jack deals," and dealt cards face up to each player in turn until Nelson received the jack of spades.

"First jack, you're the man."

Alex handed Nelson the rest of the blue deck. To speed the game, they alternated red and blue decks as they passed the deal clockwise around the table. Since Alex, sitting to Nelson's left, would deal next, he took the red deck from Dean.

Nelson winked at Charlie, wiggled his fingers like a hypnotist, and intoned in a vibrating basso profundo, "Your eyes are getting sleepy. You're under my spell, and now you're mine," finishing with a wicked, theatrical laugh. "All right," he said, shuffling the cards. "Twenty-five dollar ante, that's one white chip. I don't mind saying these are the highest stakes I ever played for."

"You gonna eat one?" Charlie asked. "Expensive snack."

Nelson smiled. "You got caviar?"

"Yeah, all you want."

"If you come out ahead, Charlie, I'll eat a blue."

"I'll remember that."

Starting with Nelson, the dealer, they anted in turn, each placing a white chip in the center of the table. Nelson passed the deck to Charlie who cut the cards.

"What's the game? What's the game?" Charlie cried impatiently.

Nelson scooped up the deck and held it under Charlie's nose.

"Want to kiss 'em first, Charlie? For luck?"

"What's the game, for chrissake?"

"Blackjack."

"C'mon, Nelson."

"Maybe a little canasta. You know how to play canasta, Charlie?"

"Fuck you."

"Okay, then, seven stud," Nelson declared and began dealing clockwise, flipping each player a card face down, called a hole card, then a second hole card followed by one face up, announcing each up card in turn. "Deuce to Alex, jack to Dean, eight to Charlie, and the dealer gets the big ace. Ace bets twenty-five dollars without looking." Nelson tossed in a white chip, peeked at his hole cards, raised his eyebrows and sighed.

"I call," Alex said, adding his chip to the pot.

"I call," Dean went along. "Charlie?"

"I'm in."

Alex smoked a Lucky and watched the others as each received his next card. Nelson often made gestures that indicated the opposite of his cards. A gleeful laugh meant he had bad cards while a sigh or groan usually indicated good cards. Dean revealed very little and folded early and often. When he stayed in he usually had a decent hand. Not always. He bluffed in streaks. Charlie gave his hand away by silently reading his cards while moving his lips. All Alex had to do was lip-read. Years ago, he'd told Charlie what he did, but he still did it. Too bad for Charlie.

"Deuces paired to the Wiz," Nelson sang out, issuing the next round of cards. "No help for Dean, the nine of diamonds to go with the eight for Charlie, and the dealer gets no help. Alex, deuces bet."

"Fifty dollars."

"I'm out." Dean dropped his cards face down on the table and poured himself a rum.

"Deuces?" Charlie croaked. "You're gonna bet fifty dollars on deuces? I call."

"I raise fifty," Nelson said.

A nice pile of chips occupied the center of the table. As Alex looked around the table, he figured Charlie had a seven and a king in the hole which meant he had three cards to a straight. Nelson was acting as if he had aces paired or even better.

"I fold," Alex said and threw his cards into the center, all face down.

"God *damn*," Charlie swore and dropped a red chip on the pile.

Nelson dealt the rest of the hand, bet his cards, drew Charlie in and won the pot with three aces. Alex smiled. The iceberg was shattered. The game was underway.

# 7

The cable car turntable at Powell and Market was surrounded by tourists, hustlers, pickpockets, and a teenager on his knees dealing three card monte on the brick sidewalk.

"Pick the red jack, the red jack is the winner, pick the red card and win. How 'bout you, mister? Think you can pick the red jack?"

More than thirty years had passed since Bobby McCorkle had planted himself at the foot of Powell Street and taken in the sights. Except for the cable cars and street signs he didn't recognize anything. He watched the kid. The jack of hearts had a bent corner. Three rubes in a row bet five bucks and picked the card with the crease that turned out to be a black king. The kid was good but not that good.

"Hey," Bobby said, crouching down and speaking softly to the monte dealer. "Wanna go fifty? You got fifty?"

"I got fifty, mister. Let's see your money."

"Tell you what," Bobby said. "You got fresh cards?"

"Whaddaya mean?"

"You got the rest of the deck? We can play with any three cards."

"These cards are just fine. There ain't nothin' wrong with these cards."

"Okay," Bobby said and dropped a fifty dollar bill on the pavement. The kid laid down two twenties and a ten.

The kid showed three cards, two black kings and the jack of hearts, flipped them face down, and began mixing them up. The kid was quick but Bobby was quicker. His left hand shot out and grabbed the dealer's wrist while a knife in his right flicked inside the kid's jacket and tickled his chest. It was so fast and quiet no one in the crowd noticed.

"Open your hand," Bobby demanded, "or I'll cut it off."

Five cards fell out of the kid's hand.

"Thank you."

Bobby picked up the hundred dollars and slowly backed away, watching the crowd in case the kid had a confederate. He didn't, and Bobby turned and strolled down Market toward New Montgomery, whistling.

He just didn't give a damn, he said to himself, and that was why he did things like take down a street hustler. It was crazy, that was the word. That was the kind of thing he and Crazy Nelson used to do, and he guessed he just never stopped. Nelson was a cop so it was guaranteed he never stopped either.

Here he was in Frisco again and he could hardly believe it. They had a subway now—he saw the stairs going down—but it still smelled the same, salt air and car exhaust, and the streetcars and cable cars and trolley buses were the same. Sleazy old Market Street hadn't changed, still jammed with junkies, whores, tourists, suits, panhandlers, bums, and goo on the sidewalk. They had all these new stores, Virgin Records and Nordstrom's with pretty windows full of stuff, but Bobby had no use for stuff. As he made his way toward the Palace, he amused himself by picking out the junkies, wondering if they picked him out, too. He didn't give a damn about that, either.

At eight-thirty the lobby was crowded. Bobby stood just inside the door rocking on his heels, taking in the elegant dresses of the Rainbow Girls and the men in tuxedos. He'd like to see those fat cats in a game of seven stud. He was about to light up when he noticed no one was smoking. This was California, after all.

Old friends. Those guys. Alex was what now? A professor or something like that. Alex the genius, Alex the National Merit scholar, Alex with the perfect SAT scores. He always was an arrogant prick. And Dean who joined the Marine Corps and went to Vietnam, he knew, and was at Khe Sanh. He lived up in the boonies somewhere and raced cars or boats or something. Charlie the gay doofus still lived in the city and ran his family fish business, and Nelson was a cop. It was Nelson who'd called him. The Feather

River, he said, they're building a new levee and digging up the old riverbed for a housing development or some crap. Thanks, Nelson, and fuck you and the horse you rode in on. I've only been trying to forget that place for thirty-two years.

He went into the lobby bar and ordered a soda and lime. Nelson said they'd reserved a room for him, but he didn't want to stay at the Palace. Not his style. He wasn't sure he wanted to play cards or even talk to those guys. What for? He'd put Shanghai Bend to rest a long time ago and it wouldn't do him any good to stir up that old shit again. The old feelings, the nightmares. Nelson said they had to talk about it, and maybe they did. But he didn't. Maybe he'd just turn around and go back to Reno.

He looked at himself in the mirror behind the bar. Receding hairline—hell, he was damned near bald. No more pompadour, that was for sure. A little plump in the gut but not too bad. He looked a little closer. Twenty years in the army and not a scratch on him. Ho ho ho, Bobby me lad, the scars are all inside, aren't they? And not from the war, either.

He paid for his drink and found the men's room. The old feelings of hatred and revenge stirred in his guts. Washing his hands he said, "Fuck it," and walked out of the hotel.

# 8

"It's going to cost you three hundred dollars to see the last card," Dean said and gently laid three blue chips in the pot. He was dealing five stud and no one had folded. Each player had one card face down and three up with one more to come.

Charlie leaned over to look at Dean's cards as though they might change if he looked away. Dean had two queens and a three showing.

"Got three queens?" Charlie asked.

"Pay up and find out."

Charlie had the deuce, nine and ten of diamonds face up, three cards to a flush, and was betting as though he had a fourth diamond in the hole. "Okay, I'm in," he said and dropped three blues onto the pile.

Nelson had a pair of sixes and a five. "Three hundred, okay."

Alex had an ace, a seven, and a four showing. "I raise five hundred," he said.

"Got that ace wired?" Dean asked. "Think you're gonna get another one? I see your five hundred and raise you another five."

The pot was the largest of the evening so far. Dean had the queen and three of diamonds, Nelson the six of diamonds and Alex had the ace of diamonds up, reducing the odds against Charlie making his flush. Nelson had either three sixes or two pair, and Dean definitely had three queens.

"Oh god oh god oh god," Charlie prayed and pushed a thousand dollars into the pot.

"Screw this," Nelson said. "I'm out."

"I'll see your five," Alex said. "Roll 'em."

Dean quickly dealt Charlie the four of clubs, killing his flush,

Alex the ace of hearts, making a pair of aces showing, and himself the seven of spades.

"Aces bet," Dean said to Alex.

"One thousand dollars."

Charlie grimaced and threw in his cards out of turn with a groan of disgust.

Dean knew he should raise or drop. It was only nine-thirty, still early, and he didn't want to be buffaloed by Alex. Did the Wiz have the third ace in the hole? Was it worth a grand or more to find out? If he raised, Alex would raise again. Alex was as immobile as the Rock of Gibraltar, calm and relaxed, eyes shaded by dark glasses, smoking a Lucky. Tiny droplets of moisture wetted his upper lip, but that didn't mean anything. Over the years Dean had tried valiantly to find meaning in Alex's tiny gestures, the way he smoked and when he smoked. He hunted for twitches and fidgets, any clue to the cards in his hand. Such a giveaway mannerism in poker is called a "tell." Dean could read Nelson's tells about half the time and Charlie's entire existence was a tell, but as far as he could discover, Alex had no revealing tell. Nothing. Nada. Sometimes Alex had the cards and in other hands he bluffed.

"You're bluffing," Dean said, trying to provoke a reaction. Alex shrugged and folded his arms. Dean looked at his hole card. "Okay, I'll see your thousand and raise . . . no . . . I'm not gonna raise. I call."

Alex flipped over the ace of clubs and raked in the pot.

"This could be a short night," Dean said, standing up to stretch. "Nice hand, Wiz."

"My pleasure."

"I sure ain't doing any good playing straight, so I might as well get loaded." Dean dug around in his bag and came up with a fat joint that he lit and offered to Charlie.

"How you doin', Fishman?" Dean asked. "Wanna smoke some dope?"

"I just can't get the cards. Four cards to a flush and then shit." Charlie shook his head and waved off the reefer. "I swore I wasn't gonna get fucked up, and I'm gonna stick to it. You know what they say."

"No, Charlie, what do they say?"

"Give a man a fish and he can eat for a day. Give him fishing tackle and he can sit in a boat and drink beer all day. Hahaha."

Nelson went over to the carts and ate a shrimp. "Where's our wild card?" he asked.

"You tell us," Dean answered. "You talked to him. You said he was coming."

"I bet he's in the bar downstairs," Charlie said.

"He quit drinking," Nelson said. "He told me he hadn't had a drink in three years."

"Guys get thirsty and fall off the wagon," Charlie said. "Happens all the time."

"As long as he's not sticking needles in his arm, I don't care what he does," Nelson said. "The man was a junkie for a long, long time."

"That really bothers you," Alex said. "Don't be so quick to pass judgment."

"Look, Alex, I got his rap sheet from Reno PD. In and out of rehab and detox, the whole nine yards. I don't give a shit what he does. I've met a million guys like Bobby McCorkle, and I'm around them all the time. I work hard keeping them out of jail rather than trying to put them in unless they fuck up."

"Are you saying Bobby fucked up?"

"No. We're the ones that fucked up. We owe him."

"We know that," Alex said. "That's why we're here."

"He doesn't," Nelson replied. "And maybe he can't be bought off, either."

"The cat was an Army lifer, man," Dean said. "He put in his twenty and got a pension at the ripe old age of thirty-eight. Not a bad gig, but it doesn't pay him anything near what we can offer."

"He'll laugh in our faces," Charlie said.

"No, he won't. He's a loser and he won't be able to resist," Alex said. "After twenty years the Army showed him the door as fast as they could because he was a drunk and had a gambling problem," Alex stated. "The Army didn't know he was a junkie or he would have been gone sooner. You've all seen his service record, two silver stars and one bronze. Look, Bobby went to Vietnam and spent ten years trying to get himself killed. He failed. He tried to drink himself to death and failed at that, too. I suppose he could kill himself with an overdose of heroin pretty easily, but he hasn't. He's tormented by demons and we know what they are and each of us is visited by them sometimes ourselves. This isn't about the war or the Army or anything like that, and we're the only ones who know what it is about. He was our friend, and he's still our friend. We're still the royal flush. We know what we have to do, and we'll just have to wait and see how it goes. In the meantime, let's play cards. It's Charlie's deal."

# 9

One Monday evening in the spring of 1962, seventy-six-year-old Benny Goldman, Alex's grandfather, laid out his best clothes as he did every week, polished and buffed his nails, trimmed his mustache, and slicked back his thick white hair with Brylcreem. Whistling, relishing the ritual, he pressed his one remaining tailored shirt, fastened the sleeves with a pair of gold cufflinks, and slipped on a Sulka tie, diamond stickpin, and blue pinstriped suit. Preening in the mirror he winked and pronounced, "Not bad for a geezer, not bad at all." Thin and compact, no more than five foot five, dressing up made him feel like a giant. He blew on his fingers and rubbed the tips against his lapel. Not for luck. Luck was for suckers.

Benny's room in the Laguna Honda Home for the Aged was scrupulously devoid of sentiment. He didn't need mementos; instead, he had living memories conveniently edited to forget the bad times and remember the good. Long gone were a Bronze Star from the first world war and a winning ticket from the 1949 Kentucky Derby, yet those days stood out like bright stars in the sky of his mind. The medal had represented a day in France in 1918 that Benny would have preferred to forget. Lance Corporal Benny Goldman had endured a frontal assault on a German machine gun position, and when it was over he was the only one in his company still breathing. The Derby was a more pleasant memory. The 1949 Derby had been a lock—that Citation was a hell of a horse, but his winnings from that race and the rest of the money he'd ever won or earned had vanished. Women, booze, cards, horses. Benny didn't go to the track anymore. He was broke except for a small annuity that was doled out by the Home as walking around money. Two hundred a month was nowhere near sufficient for a stake in a real game, but it was more than enough for Monday nights.

Laguna Honda was the penultimate address for many San Franciscans before they moved permanently to Colma, city of the dead, a suburb of cemeteries whose most notorious inhabitant was Wyatt Earp. Life in the Home was stultifyingly dull, and so, to relieve the tedium, every Monday night a party of old men assembled in the lounge for a poker game. A few minutes before seven an attendant covered a large, round table with felt, distributed ashtrays, and arranged Benny's red, white, and blue clay chips neatly into stacks of ten. The game had six or seven regular players and an equal number of kibitzers who occasionally sat in for a few hands.

The game began when Benny took his seat, broke open a new deck, shuffled, and flipped a card face up to each player in turn until the first jack appeared, signifying the dealer of the first hand. Unless he dealt himself the jack, Benny would push the deck across the table and bark, "I'm not ready to play with Wyatt yet, boys, so I ain't plannin' on losin'. Ante up and roll 'em."

The game had strict rules—no sandbagging and no wild cards—and the stakes were low, but the old men took their poker seriously. Benny was a stickler for rules and etiquette. Any player who bet out of turn or dealt a hole card face up had to toss a white chip into the pot. Benny presented a figure so elegant and intimidating that no one dared contradict his edicts.

On this balmy spring night Benny won the first three pots in a row. This was no surprise. None of the other players could shuffle properly, and the cards stuck together from one hand to the next. As often as not, Benny was able to guess the sequence before the cards were dealt. Furthermore, since octogenarians Tom Wilson and George Schilling flashed almost every card they dealt, he could instantaneously verify the accuracy of his guesses. The Monday night game was no challenge for an old hustler like Benny, but he never failed to approach the table with all the dignity due the honorable game of poker. Poker was not about cards, Benny often lectured the codgers. It wasn't even about money. It was about drama, risk, courage, foolhardiness, character, life itself. It was about the essence of being a man.

On the fourth hand of the evening Tom Wilson dealt a game of seven card stud. As was his custom, Benny glanced at his hole cards, gave them a gentle tap, and then carefully watched his opponents for tells that gave away their hands. George Schilling had an ace showing and bet the minimum, a nickel. Everyone stayed in. On the next card George got another ace and bet a dime. Everyone stayed again. By the time the final card was dealt, Benny could read every hidden card on the table.

George's pair of aces were the high cards showing. When George had a good hand, he tugged at his ear and pretended to waffle. "I dunno," he said, reaching for his earlobe. "A pair isn't that good. The bet's a dime." He tossed a red chip into the pot.

Benny had a king and a pair of sevens showing. He figured George for three aces, a pretty good hand.

"See your dime and raise a quarter," Benny promptly replied.

Everyone else folded. George smiled and asked, "What's the maximum?"

"It hasn't changed in five years, George," Benny said. "Fifty cents."

"That's all? Okay, I see the raise and raise fifty cents."

Benny hardly paid attention. For some reason his mind had drifted back to 1918, to a smoking hole in the ground that smelled like a slaughter house. It was raining. The lieutenant was staring at his arm which ended in a bloody stump just below the elbow. Blood was spurting from a severed artery, and the officer bled to death before Lance Corporal Goldman could get a tourniquet on him.

"Benny?"

The rain stopped and the sun shone through the clouds. Citation was the last horse into the starting gate. Churchill Downs glistened in the sheen of rainwater. Benny remembered the taste of whiskey and crushed mint, the flutter of ladies' hats in the breeze, the smell of the track. The smell reminded him of the mud in France. A lot of horses had died in the war.

Something happened. The players were all looking at him, and he knew it was his turn to bet, but his mind went red, then blank. Benny suffered a stroke, fell out of his chair and broke his neck.

It was a mercifully sudden and quick death. Lying on the floor, a freshly minted corpse, Benny clutched his final hole card close to his stylish vest, a seven of spades that gave him a full house, the winning hand.

Benny was buried in Colma in the Jewish cemetery a few dozen yards from where Wyatt Earp rested in peace. Later that afternoon Benny's son David sat down in his living room on Alvarado Street for a man-to-man chat with his eldest son Alex, seventeen, uncomfortable in his new suit and upset by the solemn rituals of funeral parlor and cemetery. All Alex really wanted at that moment was to escape the family and mourn his grandfather in his own way, drinking beer and smoking cigarettes with his buddies.

Oblivious to the mood, Alex's little brothers and sisters ran around the house making a racket. No one shushed them. Women bustled in the kitchen, preparing food for guests who would be arriving soon.

"You all right?" David asked his son.

Alex shrugged. He'd worshipped his grandfather and needed time to reconcile his loss.

"Do you know why your grandfather lived at Laguna Honda?" David asked.

"Because he was old."

"Yes," David agreed, "but Laguna Honda is a place for people who can't afford something better. Your grandfather would've been a rich man if he hadn't been a gambler."

"I thought he always won," Alex protested. "He was a great poker player. He said poker isn't gambling, it's science."

"He was a great bullshitter," David said with a wan smile. "The players at the old folks' home were fish, and he could beat them, no sweat. The problem was, he thought he was better than he was. When I was your age, he'd go to Reno once a month and lose his shirt."

"Like you do now?"

Alex's eyes darkened and he stared at his father with undisguised hostility. Losing his grandfather was bad enough; losing his illusions was almost too much too bear.

"This was his," David said, taking from his jacket pocket a small leather-bound book filled with tiny, precise writing. "He said you were the only one who could understand it, and he wanted you to have it."

He leaned over and handed the book to his son. Alex was a star science student who'd long since surpassed the abilities of his high school teachers. Poker, he thought, was a game of odds and probabilities with a dash of Heisenberg's Uncertainty Principle. He thumbed through the little book, opened to a page at random, and discovered it was written in code.

"Can you read this?" Alex asked his father.

David shook his head. "I don't want to," he said. "I never tried to figure out the cipher."

"It's probably a simple transposition."

It was David's turn to shrug.

"Can I go?" Alex asked.

"There's something else."

David left the room and returned with a cardboard box that contained the old man's personal effects from Laguna Honda. Inside were two unopened packs of playing cards and a polished chip carousel made of beautiful laminated teak and filled with two hundred red, white, and blue handmade ceramic poker chips.

"Maybe you'll do better than we did," David said. "Maybe you can win it all back."

# 10

Some months after his arrival in Vietnam, Bobby started thinking of himself as a psychic fragmentation grenade exploding in slow motion. Boom! Shrapnel! Whistling birds of death, white-hot chunks of rage expanding from his center, ripping mind and nerve, inflicting wounds. By 1995 the shrapnel had burned through three wives, two children, four bankruptcies, and a really nice Porsche. He'd run out of ways to kill himself slowly and gave up trying to do it quick. Only one thing had remained constant, and that was poker. He played cards, and if he wasn't in a self-destructive mood, he almost always won. When he was on the downside of a manic-depressive run through the brambles of his past, he lost. It was a cycle, but that's overstating the obvious.

At the moment of his detonation, before Vietnam, before anything, really, his life had been of a piece, on track, in the groove, daddy-o. He was on his way to Berkeley, and then all at once everything went awry and he started blowing up in slow motion. He'd been eighteen when it happened, and by now, after thirty-two years, the shrapnel had expanded to the limit and was losing momentum. Gravity and friction are implacable.

Hands in pockets, shoes scuffing the sidewalk, shoulders hunched like James Dean, Bobby walked the Tenderloin, the soft underbelly of urban decay that lay just below fashionable Union Square. Massage parlors, bars and cars, downtrodden human dregs skulking around grungy liquor stores. In three blocks seven whores asked him for a date, and an equal number of panhandlers demanded spare change. The girls got a smile and a wisecrack, "Haven't I seen you on Virginia Street in Reno?" and each beggar elicited a "Howdy, pardner" and a buck. The Tenderloin suited his mood. In spirit and decrepitude the district hadn't changed since Bobby had last seen it in 1963.

He found his way by feel from Market Street, not sure where he was headed until he chanced upon Original Joe's Italian Food, steaks and chops, the real thing on squalid Taylor Street. The once elegant Florentine steakhouse was dying just as the neighborhood around it had died long ago. The façade was untouched, last updated in the '50s. Red neon, swinging glass doors, cozy leather booths, an open kitchen with cooks in toques and checkered pants, ancient waiters in seedy tuxedos, and broad-stroked caricatures of long-forgotten dandies on the walls.

Eating a New York medium rare, Bobby was in a time warp. This was where his father brought him after ball games, the swanky place he and Nelson and the rest of them took high school dates for a fancy downtown dinner. The place stank of sentiment and old times and perfectly broiled steaks. Not a single item of California cuisine was on the menu.

"Ah, God," Bobby said, sipping ice water and starting a conversation with himself. "Joe's."

"Do you remember the time that Nelson . . . ?" he started to say.

"Remember?" he interrupted himself. "I was there. Charlie was there. Dean was there. The time in chemistry class when Nelson swiped an ounce of metallic sodium and dropped it in the biology teacher's fish tank. Boom! Instant chum. The night Dean wrecked his Impala in Mel's parking lot. There were seven of us in the damn car, Dean was playing his sax and driving at the same time and he had this flask of gin . . ."

"I remember," Bobby said, savoring the beef. "I remember lots of nights at Mel's and Juanita's in Sausalito and here at Joe's, too. You want cheesecake?"

"I wanna be eighteen again, that's what I want," Bobby said. "Before anything happened."

"Fuck that, man. Don't start that."

"Well, what the hell am I supposed to do? I hate getting old."

"Finish your dinner. You're getting older sitting here."

"Ah, God," Bobby sighed. "What a drag."

Pouring coffee, the seventy-year-old waiter laughed, a sharp bark that caught in his throat and died. Bobby stared at the slice of cheesecake, wedge shaped, creamy, sweet and firm, vulva-like in its richness. A shudder passed through his body, so violent it rattled the table.

"You all right?" the waiter asked. "You're talking to yourself."

"What's it to you?"

"It bothers the other customers."

Bobby looked around the restaurant. "There are no other customers. One guy at the counter, that's it."

The waiter held his hand to his forehead like an Apache scout and scanned the room. "Gol darned if you aren't right. I must be mistaken. You go right on ahead and talk to yourself."

"Hey," Bobby said. "Sorry."

"That's all right. Where you from, son?"

"Reno, but I used to live here, come in here when I was a kid. That was a long time ago."

"Steak good?"

"Still the best."

"You got family here in the city?"

"You're an inquisitive sort. You must be bored."

"Well, you were talking to yourself, so I figured you could pretend to talk to me and no one would notice. I don't mean to pry."

"It's okay. Nah, family's long gone. Everything is gone. All the joints I used to go to, they're all gone except this one. They still got naked women up on Broadway?"

"A few, a couple a places but most a them disappeared like the hippies and the beatniks. I seen 'em all and outlasted 'em all, too."

"Oh, yeah? What's your secret?"

"Joe's steak and a bottle of dago red every day, man. Whaddya think?"

Bobby had to laugh at that.

"More coffee?"

"Just a check, thanks."

Bobby glanced at the bill and left the fifty he took from the monte dealer on the table. Outside, standing on the sidewalk, rocking on his heels, smoking, watching the traffic and the hustlers and pimps, he had the momentary illusion that it was still 1963 and nothing had happened. He blinked and the cruel deception faded.

He walked down Taylor to Market and up Market to Seventh. He knew where he was going now. He walked faster, picking up speed, taking himself quickly to one of the good places.

It was gone. Lyle Tuttle's tattoo parlor on Seventh Street between Mission and Market had vanished. The building that had housed Lyle Tuttle's was a hole in the ground and the Greyhound bus station next door was gone, too, part of the same high-rise development-to-be. Bobby pressed against the Cyclone fence in front of the construction site and laughed. Holy Moley, Lyle Tuttle, king of the tattoo artists. That was a hell of a night. He remembered . . .

"I got an idea," Nelson said.

"Since when does a fuckin' Chinaman have ideas, hey?" Bobby teased.

"What?" Charlie squawked. "What's your idea?"

"Hey, Alex," Nelson said, leaning over the back of the front seat of Dean's Impala. "What's the highest hand in poker?"

"A royal flush."

"And what is that?"

"Well, the highest hand really is a straight flush, five cards in sequence of the same suit, and a royal flush is the highest straight flush, the highest five cards of any suit."

"And they are?"

"The ten, jack, queen, king, and ace."

"And what's the highest suit?"

"Suits don't count in poker. They're all equal."

"Well, which one is the best?"

"What the fuck is the matter with you, Nelson? There is no best. They're equal."

"Yeah," Bobby said, "like a Chinaman is equal to a white man."

"Hey, Kimosabe," Nelson howled. "Fuck you."

"C'mon, Nelson," Charlie prodded, "What's your idea?"

"A royal flush, right? Five guys, five cards, we each get one card tattooed on our arm and we're a royal flush."

"Oh, Jesus, and what the fuck is that supposed to mean?" Bobby said.

"Whatever you want it to mean. If it don't mean nothin' to you, then fuck you."

"Oh. So that's what it means."

"Yeah."

They went downtown, parked the car, and stood in a cluster on the sidewalk in front of the bus station. Lyle Tuttle's was next door. Sailors came from all over the world for a Lyle Tuttle tattoo because he was the best. He was an artist.

"I dunno," Dean said. "My dad'll kill me."

"If he sees it."

"What'm I gonna do, water-ski with my jacket on?"

"So what if he sees it?" Nelson objected. "Is he gonna carve it off your arm? Kick you out of the house? I don't think so."

"It's forever," Alex said. "You know that."

"This is for us," Nelson said. "It doesn't matter what anyone else thinks."

"Anyone got a beer?" Dean asked.

"I heard it hurts," Charlie said.

"Sure it hurts," Alex said. "That's part of the deal."

"You got to hold still, though. You can't jiggle around."

"Like a sissy."

"Like a wimp."

"Like a Chinaman."

"Oh, fuck you. Who do you think invented tattoos?"

"Actually," Alex said. "It was the Polynesians."

"You're fulla shit. They got tattoos in China, in Japan, in Africa, everywhere. The Iroquois had tattoos, and they didn't know jack from Polynesia."

"Well?"

"Well?"

Alex grinned. "Are we gonna stand here on the sidewalk and piss in our pants, or are we gonna go in?"

It hurt. Dean said it hurt the way it must hurt a girl to lose her cherry, and Lyle Tuttle smiled like he'd heard that one before. They picked the suit by asking Lyle Tuttle to cut a deck of cards—Alex had one handy—and it came up diamonds and that was that. Alex spread a royal flush in diamonds face down on the counter over the tigers and wounded hearts and naked women and each picked one. Bobby got the ace.

"You Italian?" Lyle Tuttle asked Bobby.

"No. Irish. Why?"

"Some people believe the ace of diamonds is cursed because a famous mobster named Joe the Boss Masseria was killed playing pinochle with that card in his hand."

"I don't care. We're poker players. As long as it's not aces and eights, it's okay."

It took ninety minutes for each tattoo and they emerged onto Seventh Street at six in the morning. Each of the five young men wore a bandage on his left triceps. The tattoos would be scabs for a day or two...

Bobby's hand went to his shoulder. The ace was still there, of course, still cursed, his only tattoo, the high card in the royal flush. After two or three days the scabs fell away and the five young men full of braggadocio and teenage cool paraded their new tattoos through Mel's drive-in and the Doggie Diner on Van Ness. Ah, man, everything was set up. They were going to be buddies for life, bound together with blood and ink, and then Shanghai Bend, the fragmentation grenade, and monstrous, barely controllable rage.

He'd loved her. It was simple, really, and sudden, like a falling star, and in the next instant, they'd taken her away.

He walked a few yards to the corner of Market and hailed a cab. "Airport," he said, sliding into the back seat.

"Airport it is," the driver replied, making conversation. "Where you flying tonight?"

"Reno."

"I coulda guessed. No luggage."

The cab turned right on Sixth and headed for the freeway. The driver was a woman about thirty, trim, dark-haired, with a hard-ened, citywise gleam in her eye. She glanced at the passenger in the rearview mirror and saw a good-looking man, a little older, no kid, with a pale complexion, dark eyes, and the aura of a guy with something on his mind. He was looking back at her in the mirror, and she thought, Uh oh, here it comes. Wanna fuck me? Wanna have the time of your life, baby?

"It's like a confessional back here, you know?" Bobby said. "Dark and secure, and all I can see is the back of your head and your eyes in the mirror."

"And you're a chainsaw murderer and you want to confess, right?"

Bobby chuckled, his voice dark and hollow. "You'd be surprised."

"You Catholic?"

"Retired," Bobby said.

"Well, you're right," she said. "People like to get things off their chest, and they talk, especially if they never expect to see me again. They say things to a perfect stranger they wouldn't dare say to anyone else. I've been drivin' this cab for eight years, and I've heard sob stories, tragedies, injustice, sex and drugs and rock and roll. It's fifteen minutes to the airport, mister. You can talk all you want."

Bobby leaned over the seat and asked, "How much to take me to Reno?"

She laughed. "Airfare is maybe a hundred bucks if you walk in and buy a ticket."

"I have a ticket but I don't want to fly. How much?"

She stopped at a light, turned around and regarded him closely. "You serious? It's over two hundred miles and I have to come back empty."

"It's exactly two hundred and twenty-eight miles. You ever go that far in your cab? It's gotta make your night. How much?"

The driver calculated time and distance on her watch, saying, "I've gone much farther than Reno, for your information, but you're right. It would make my night. Five hundred dollars in advance."

"How about four hundred?"

"You want to negotiate? Okay, let's see the money, Mr. Passenger, unless you're wasting my time. I won't take your credit card. For a ride outta town like this, it's cash on the line."

Bobby took four hundred-dollar bills from his wallet and fanned them like tail feathers. "Four hundred, take it or leave it."

The light changed and the cab moved slowly down Sixth Street, the driver watching Bobby in the mirror.

"You gonna hit on me?" she asked. "You gonna give me a hard time, ask a lot stupid questions?"

"No. What is this, an interview?"

"This is my office, Mr. Passenger. If I'm gonna drive you to Reno, I want to be sure you're gonna behave. You drunk or coked up or any shit like that?"

"I'm on the wagon. I'm being a good boy."

"Why d'you want to go to Reno?"

"What's it to you? I live there."

She took the money and packed it away in her jeans. "I'm gonna gas up, and we'll be in Reno by two in the morning, about three and a half hours from now. I'm just a driver, not a shrink or a priest. You can talk, but I can't say as I'll listen."

# 1 1

"It's eleven o'clock and all is not well," Nelson said. "We've been stiffed."

"No shit," Dean hollered. "Maybe this is your big surprise, Nelson. Maybe you never talked to him at all."

Nelson pulled a firecracker from his pocket, lit it, and threw it across the table at Dean. Bang!

"What the hell? Watch it."

"I talked to him three times," Nelson said heatedly. "I made the airline reservation and paid for the ticket myself."

"You throw another firecracker at me, Nelson, and I'll toss your skinny ass right out the window."

"Yeah, macho man? Remember what happened the last time you tried to fuck with me?"

"Shit," Dean cursed and then laughed a big laugh that shook his beard and lit up his eyes. "A little tension around the old card table, fellas? I wonder why."

"Just deal the cards," Alex said. "We can work out anything if we play."

Holding the red deck in his hand, brow furrowed in concentration, Dean worked his jaw and leaned over the table. He'd drunk a half pint of rum and smoked a fat joint and was feeling no pain.

"Let's get some broads," he said.

"Whaddya mean, get some broads?" Nelson sneered. "You mean hookers?"

"That's exactly what I mean, dummy. I mean, Jesus."

"For what? Gratuitous sex?"

"Yeah, and any other kind I can think up. Ha!"

"Let's play cards," Nelson suggested. "Roll 'em, Deano."

"Well, it's not all that entertaining with only four players, you know?" Dean said, dropping the deck on the felt. "Alex is winning even faster than usual. I'm down fifteen hundred, Charlie about two grand, and you're down what?"

"I'm up five hundred," Nelson said. "And I want to win some more. Deal the cards, Stud."

Dean stood up from the table and started making a sandwich. Slathering mustard on rye, he hummed a few bars of the Grateful Dead's "Casey Jones" and then said with a teasing lilt, "You really want to play cards, is that it, Nelson? Just play cards?"

"Yeah. That's why I drove up here."

A sly smile from Dean. "Is it?"

Alex's eyes snapped from Nelson to Charlie to Dean. They all had a reason for being there, and it wasn't just cards.

Dean wagged a finger at Nelson. "Want to ante your Corvette?"

"No, no, no. Christ, you're nuts. It's table stakes. The car is not on the table."

"I bet you have the pink slip in your pocket."

"You'd lose."

"You're chickenshit, Nelson. Crazy Nelson, that's a laugh."

"Crazy Nelson is not insane Nelson. You do this every year, Dean. You screw up the game with a lunatic bet because you want to stop playing so some whore can suck your dick."

Laughing, Charlie said, "Hey, Dean, what do *you* put in the pot with Nelson's car? Your boat?"

"Fuck you. That boat is worth two hundred grand. Maybe my truck."

"How about your old lady? Would you put Billie in the pot?"

"And what would you do with her if you won, you old buttfucker? Give her away? I'll tell you what, Charlie," Dean said. "You put in your krautmobile, and then we'll see what I put in."

"The Mercedes?"

"Yeah."

"Too bad. I lease it. I don't own it."

"It's too early for this," Alex said. "Settle down, you guys. Dean, what's the matter with you? Is it Bobby? You want to talk about Bobby now, or play cards or get laid, or what?"

"Look, he's not here and he's not coming," Dean said, his voice hard and flat. "We need a fifth player. Maybe we should call in somebody. Charlie, you must know people in town who'll come and play."

"I dunno." Charlie shrugged, mentally running through his inventory of friends and acquaintances. "It's late, it's short notice, and not many guys keep five grand around like loose change."

"We can call Bobby in Reno," Nelson suggested. "Maybe he never left."

"What kind of place does he live in?" Alex asked, curious.

"A slummy residence hotel right downtown," Nelson answered tersely, as though he were filling in a police report. "Six hundred a month."

"Sounds practical," Alex said, nodding his head. "Makes sense."

"Should we call?" Charlie said. "Maybe we *should* call."

"And what if he's there watching TV at home?" Dean snapped. "What do we say? Where the hell are you? That'd be idiotic. It doesn't matter where he is. He's not *here*. He bailed, and that's all there is to it."

"I disagree," Alex declared, taking off his glasses and snuffing out his Lucky. "He's in the city. I'm sure of it. He just needs to make up his mind to come to the hotel, and it's hard for him. There's just so much baggage, so much crap that's happened in his life. We were all bright boys, right? But Bobby was smarter and better than all of us and we know it. They called me a genius and we laughed at that because we knew who the genius was. Bobby was doing calculus when he was ten, but he flunked math in seventh grade. He just didn't give a shit, that's all. He saw things we didn't see. He understood things as a kid that we'll never understand when we're old men, and it was too much for him. He was fragile in ways that only we can say. But you know what? He'll show."

"Wanna bet?"

"Hell, yes, Dean. A hundred bucks says he'll turn up."

"You're on. Put your money where your mouth is."

Alex pulled a wad of cash from his pocket, furiously peeled off a hundred-dollar bill and slammed it on the table, rattling the chips.

Dean winked and taunted, "Gettin' to ya, Wiz?" He matched the wager while letting his voice drop to a mutter. "He ain't comin'."

"Ooo," Charlie said. "Alex made a side bet. Can't remember the last time I saw that."

"Let's play cards, for chrissake," Nelson insisted.

"What about the broads?"

"What the fuck, Dean," Alex said. "Do what you want. If you don't want to deal, pass the cards."

"Ah, well, what the hell. Okay. Let's play."

He shuffled and the rippling sound seemed to calm nerves all around.

"What's the game? What's the game?" Charlie wanted to know.

"Five draw, jacks or better. That okay with you? Cut, Alex."

In draw poker each player receives five cards, a complete hand, and plays those through one round of betting, including raises. In jacks or better, a player must have at least a pair of jacks to open the first round of betting. After the first round is completed, each player in turn can replace cards—the exact number of discards allowed varies from game to game and with the number of players; in this game one could throw away four cards—and receive new ones from the dealer. A second round of betting follows the draw.

The cards fluttered across the felt like snowflakes, coming to rest in four neat piles around the table. Charlie picked up his cards, moved them around in his hand, put them on the table, fiddled with them, and picked them up again. Nelson puffed on his cigar for a while before snatching up his cards, glancing at his hand, and uttering a yelp of disgust. Alex peeked at the corner of each card one at a time without lifting the ducats from the felt, then arranged them in a fan and left them on the table. Dean spread the cards in his hand and studied them as though they were holy writ.

As dealer, Dean was obliged to say, "Charlie, you gonna open?"

"I open for one hundred."

"I call," Nelson said, matching the bet.

"I raise it to two hundred," Alex declared.

"Think you got a hand?" Dean asked.

"It has potential."

"I see your potential and raise another hundred," Dean said.

"I gotta take a card," Charlie said. "I call."

"I'm in," Nelson said.

"You gonna raise it, Alex?" Dean waved his cards around like notes for a speech. "Come get me, boy."

"I'll see it," Alex said, putting in his chips.

"Cards," Dean recited, asking for discards.

"One card," Charlie said, tossing his discard face down next to the pot, as was proper.

Dean gave him a new card, face down. Charlie grabbed it and wrinkled his nose.

"One," Nelson said and took his card.

"No cards. I'm good," Alex said.

"Standing pat?" Dean inquired.

"You heard me."

"Uh oh, look out, magic is afoot," Dean said. "Dealer takes two cards. You opened, Charlie. Your bet."

"I check," Charlie whispered, eyes riveted to Alex's cards which lay face down, untouched.

"I check," Nelson echoed.

"Two hundred," Alex bet.

Without hesitation Dean said, "See your two hundred and raise you to three hundred."

"Oh, God, I fold." Charlie threw in his cards.

"Check and raise, right?" Nelson looked at Alex, arbiter of rules. "Sandbagging?"

"Right."

"Okay. I see the three hundred and make it five hundred. That's three hundred more to you, Alex."

"Ho ho ho," Alex said. "It's wild and wooly now. You took one card and you must have caught something, Nelson. Okay, here's three hundred and I raise five hundred more. It's seven hundred to Dean."

Thirty-one hundred dollars in chips made a tidy pile in the center of the table. Alex was making it expensive for the other players to see his cards.

"I drop," Dean said.

"You what?"

"You heard me. He's got a pat hand," Dean conceded.

"What do you have?" Nelson wanted to know. "Three of a kind?"

"Something like that."

"It's a thousand to you, Nelson."

"Ah, shit. I fold."

After winning the hand by default, Alex was not obliged to show his cards but the others really wanted to know what he had. Did he have a pat hand or was he bluffing? They would never know. Alex picked up the red deck and mixed in his cards.

"Shit fire," Nelson swore and tossed his cards on the table. One flipped over, the six of hearts. Disgusted, he turned over the rest, a five, seven, eight, and nine of mixed suits.

"I made my straight, but a hell of a lot of good that did me."

"I told you magic was afoot, boys," Dean said, shaking his head. "The Wiz is on a roll. Maybe we should just give him all our money and call it a night."

"Charlie's deal," Alex said and lit another Lucky.

# 1 2

The taxi was speeding across the Bay Bridge, the city a sea of lights in the rearview mirrors, when Bobby started to second-guess himself. His livelihood was playing high stakes poker with amateurs, and twenty thousand dollars was waiting like ripe fruit in the Palace Hotel. The game was no different from hundreds he'd played in, so what was the big deal, that he might lose? It wouldn't be the first time. Was it the wizard? Was he afraid of Alex Goldman? The Alex he remembered was a smug teenager who thought he couldn't lose. Alex was the only player who'd consistently beaten him, but that was a long time ago. As kids they'd been equals, novitiates to the game, but now Alex was a fifty-year-old college professor who played once a year while Bobby was a pro who played every day. If he played Alex tonight, he'd crush him like a cockroach. So, if he wasn't running away from the game, it had to be something else.

He stared through the windshield at the tunnel-like lower deck of the bridge, five and a half miles of steel girders and cars all zooming in the same direction. He felt weird and disembodied, as though he were locked inside a metal cage rushing headlong to nowhere. In the distance the dismal yellow lights of Oakland offered neither solace nor answers to his questions.

Needing a foil to sort himself out, he asked the cab driver, "You play cards?"

"Why do you ask?" Her eyes flicked in the mirror and then locked on the roadway.

"Just curious. That's what I do. I'm a professional poker player."

"Poker only?"

"That's right. No blackjack, no bridge, just poker."

"Must be an interesting life."

"It has its moments, like pushing a hack. What's your name?"

"Driver," she answered quickly, the moniker prepared in advance.

"That's it?"

"That's it."

"Well," Bobby cleared his throat. "Pleased to make your acquaintance, Driver. My name is Bob," and when Driver said nothing, Bobby asked, "Ever been to Reno?"

"Yeah, once."

"You gamble? Play the slots?"

"No."

"Wha'd you go to Reno for?"

"To ski on Mount Rose."

"Ah ha! A winter tourist. Can I smoke in your cab?"

"No."

"Can we negotiate that?"

"No."

"You're not a lot of fun, Driver."

"This is a cab, Mr. Passenger, not an amusement park."

"Sorry. I'll just sit back, shut up, and dream about the old days when a cigarette was just a smoke."

The old days. The game had been born one night in Alex's parents' garage on Alvarado Street. They used a big cable-spool for a table, and those old clay chips, and during that first night they all fell in love with the game. Alex had a book, *Poker According to Maverick*, that explained the odds, told them what a poker face was, described simple strategies (don't stay in if you can't beat the cards you can see), and served as a rule book. They played until dawn that first night and every night for the next week. Simple-minded pop psychologists would call their game "male bonding," but it was more than that. They became part of a history and tradition of card players and gamblers they couldn't exactly define but which resonated deep in their souls. It didn't require analysis. They loved it and lived it and let it sweep them away like the current of a mighty river.

"I call."

"I raise two bits."

"You raise, you son of a bitch? What d'ya got? A straight? Your high card is only the four of spades."

"Pay up and find out, chump."

Smoking cigarettes and drinking beer, they'd played cards and Alex's dad had had the good sense to leave them alone. They could hear Alex's parents arguing upstairs.

"Do you know what they're doing down there? Smoking and drinking and gambling."

"I know exactly what they're doing, and if they weren't doing it here where they're safe, they'd be doing it in the back room of a pool hall on Divisadero Street."

"How do you know that?"

"Because that's what I did when I was their age."

"Well, Alex has to study."

"Don't worry. He's going to be all right. They're good boys. Go to bed."

They were transformed by the game. Alex became the wizard, Charlie the reckless perennial loser, Dean the stodgy conservative, Nelson the party animal, and Bobby—it always came down to Bobby and Alex in a showdown when they had to lay their cards on the table. They were the real players, the fierce competitors— Bobby who played by instinct and Alex the maniac who learned card tricks, read poker books, and studied accounts of famous games by notorious gamblers. They played through the spring and summer of 1962 and as often as possible during their busy senior year at prestigious Lowell High School, finding time for a few hours of cards between family obligations, part-time jobs, and college entrance exams.

In June of 1963 they graduated and faced the inevitable of going their separate ways. Alex was headed for New York City and Columbia; Bobby, who wised up after failing math in the seventh grade, was admitted to Berkeley; Dean had an athletic scholarship to play football up north in Oregon; Nelson was southbound for UCLA; and Charlie, a less than stellar student, was going to live at home, work for Hooper Fish and go to San Francisco City College. Like pollen, they'd been cast to the four winds. With the profound solemnity of adolescence they made a pact to return to San Francisco once a year to play cards, but that was in the rosy future. Meanwhile it was a glorious summer of girls—strip poker, oh boy—and five card stud. Years later, on those rare occasions when Bobby allowed himself to reminisce, he realized that 1963 had been the last year of innocence for them and all of America. Charismatic Jack Kennedy was president and no one had heard of Vietnam or Lee Harvey Oswald. They played cards, went to the beach, got their tattoos, climbed aboard Dean's father's boat and went for a ride up the river.

Boom, fragmentation grenade, and Bobby never went to Berkeley. Instead, the day after their journey up the Feather River he walked into the Oakland Induction Center—he could still remember the smell of disinfectant and sweat—took his physical, stepped across the yellow line and was herded on the bus to Fort Ord just like that. To say he never looked back would be an exaggeration, but he didn't look back often. He didn't look forward much, either, making no plans and living solely in the present, if not in oblivion. He hadn't intended to stay in the army twenty years; every time his re-enlistment rolled around he re-upped because the Army took damned good care of him. The closed world of the military had shielded him from everything but himself—all that cabbage on his chest cut a lot of slack; and when he retired he played cards because that was the only thing he knew how to do except make war and drink and inject heroin into his veins.

Poker had saved him. He wanted to play, exactly why he wasn't sure, and since he couldn't play stoned and drunk he endured withdrawal and detox and kept playing. Occasionally he fell off the wagon and sometimes chipped a little dope, but he stayed clean enough to play a few hours a day somewhere. There is no shortage of poker in America. Poker is the great American game, and anyone can play. Anyone does, and when anyone has a few bucks and thinks he's pretty good, sooner or later he sits down in a clean, shiny casino poker room with Bobby McCorkle. La de da, check and raise, fool. Bobby gobbled up the rubes and made his rent and child support, no sweat. And when he was tap city, there was always the pension check every month.

He was good-looking, always smiling and exuding an unrepentant hustler's charm. Bobby came on slick, sarcastic, bright and brash in a way some women found attractive. In bed, most asked right away about the ace of diamonds tattooed on his arm, and he lied and made up stories about a tattoo parlor in Saigon. If they didn't ask, he saw them again. Three never asked, and he married them. Two had his kids; one lived in Florida and the other in Chicago. It didn't take long for the charm to wear thin, crushed by booze, dope, car wrecks, losing streaks, and white-hot psychic shrapnel. None of the women ever reached his core, a searing morass of trauma and suppressed rage. They only saw the effect, the rolling disaster called Bobby McCorkle. He'd disappear for weeks at a time and then call from New Orleans or Las Vegas saying he was coming home with a hundred grand. When he arrived two weeks later, he had five thousand left and a fresh collection of bruises and tracks. When the women realized he wasn't going to change, they left. None of his wives or girlfriends ever heard a word about the Feather River.

What had happened during one night at Shanghai Bend was the central event of his life, the crucible from which the rest of his days were formed, but he had to admit that he wasn't sure exactly what had happened. He was certain of his responsibility, but in those moments when the memory forced its way into his consciousness and he tried to recall the exact sequence of events, he saw a few pieces clearly but there were blanks. Some gaps had been there the following day because he'd been monstrously drunk. That he knew for sure. Other blank spots were created by his erasing them from his memory. They were just too painful to remember.

It occurred to him that if he stopped ruminating and just let Driver take him to Reno, he might cop some dope and kill himself with an overdose, thus adding a final episode of cowardice and guilt to his repertoire of reprehensible acts. He could take Shanghai Bend to the Reno morgue tonight without ever having uttered those two words to any living person, two words that said his life had run into a waterfall on the Feather River and careened in a new direction, a bearing that wasn't marked on any compass.

Exile on Main Street. Nowhereville. Heartbreak Hotel in downtown Reno, the Biggest Little City in the World. Shark music, can you hear it? Dum dum Dum dum Dum dum. Remember that kid on Market Street, the three card monte dealer? Bobby! You dumb fuck, you're him, trying to get over with a clumsy trick, a little sleight of hand, a cheap hustle.

I'm better than that. I don't cheat. I've never cheated.

Well, whoop dee doo. Want a medal, or a chest to pin it on?

There were advantages and disadvantages to living exclusively in the present rather than the past or future, or some combination as most people do. Zen monks live in the present as do card players, artists, sociopaths, and soldiers in combat. Living in the present is always risky, without security or equity, with no deductible, capital gain, or tax write-off, and since most people practice risk avoidance as a guiding principle, they never experience the present. They may gamble but they rarely risk anything of value. They can't possibly imagine a human being who risks everything every minute on every hand. They'd have a heart attack if they pushed eighty thousand dollars into the pot and said, "I raise." Damn. Bobby had lost that one, but he'd walked away with a thrill that was almost as good as winning. He'd had the balls to make the bet and he got beat, *c'est la vie*. He'd done it before and won, and he'd win again. He was a pro. He knew the odds.

The driver broke into his thoughts by saying, "Open the window and you can smoke. Okay?"

"What a gal. You're terrific. Thanks. I appreciate that. What do you do when you're not driving your cab?"

"What do you do when you're not playing poker?"

"You're a tough lady, you know that? But I'll tell you, anyway. I used to drink, and that filled a lot of time, but since I don't drink anymore, I watch TV. In the winter it's cold in Reno so I go to Vegas and watch TV there."

"And play poker."

"That's right, and play cards."

"It sounds pretty dismal, all that TV."

"Fantasy, young lady, is infinitely preferable to reality, unless you're rich and can make your fantasies come true. Are you rich? I didn't think so. I used to read books, lots of books, but after a while I read everything worth reading. Now I watch TV. My name is Bob, by the way. Got a boyfriend?"

"You weren't gonna ask any stupid questions, remember?"

"I'm just trying to make conversation, that's all. A guy tonight caught me talking to myself. I'll tell you what. You ask the questions."

"Okay. Why were you in San Francisco?"

"For a card game."

"You win?"

"I decided not to play."

"Why not? You a good poker player?"

"I'm a pro. What does that tell you?"

"It doesn't tell me why you didn't play."

"No. Maybe I'm not sure why myself. It's a high stakes game. There's real money to be made in that game."

"Or lost. For every winner there's a loser, right? Seems to me like you're out four hundred bucks."

"I can win that back tonight in Reno, but there's some things in life, you lose them and you can never get them back."

"Oh, yeah? Like what?"

"Innocence."

"Well, gee whiz, Mr. Passenger, you're a genuine philosopher."

Chortling, Bobby rolled down the window and lit a cigarette. "Where are we?" he asked. They'd been on the road no more than thirty minutes.

"Almost to the Carquinez Bridges," she said.

He had to face the men he'd known as boys and together confront Shanghai Bend. He didn't think they could tell him much he didn't know. There was construction on the riverbank and what? They dug up a body. It would take a long time to identify the remains, if that was possible, but let's assume they already had an identification and homicide was indicated but the case was so old there were no suspects. There was an old military adage: Assume is a good way to make an ass out of u and me.

The freeway cut through a hillside that suddenly dropped away in a steep bluff above the town of Crockett. The taxi raced toward the double bridges over the Carquinez Strait, and Bobby could see the lights of the C&H sugar refinery and the dark, swift waters of the strait. In 1963 they'd passed under the bridges on their way up the river in Dean's father's boat. He hadn't come back with the others. He'd walked away from the Feather River and hitchhiked to Oakland and the Armed Forces Induction Center.

"Turn around," he said.

"Pardon me? I'm on the bridge."

"When you get across the bridge, turn around and go back to San Francisco."

"You're a strange one, Mr. Passenger."

"You can keep the four hundred," he said. "I'll take 'strange' as a compliment."

# 13

The room was thick with smoke, the primal vapor of gambling. They were into the game now, concentrating on poker. On the stereo Stan Getz dissected the universe with a saxophone, adding his screed to the sounds of cards scraping on felt, chips clinking in the pot, and the crisp vernacular of the game. The hands were coming faster, the red and blue decks alternating with drill-team precision, and the bets were creeping up.

Around eleven-thirty Charlie won a small pot by catching aces up in seven stud that caused everyone to fold. On the next hand, playing draw, he opened with a large bet and bought the hand when nobody called.

"Winners again," he snickered, gathering up the antes.

On the other side of Bobby's empty chair, Dean's eyes glistened, beady and ferocious. He threw in his cards with a snort of disgust, glaring at Charlie and mumbling, "You prick. Show your openers."

Pleased with his modest winning streak, Charlie flipped over three sixes. "Good enough, tough guy?" he bleated. "No guts, no glory, Deano. You can't *win* if you don't stay *in*."

"The poker gods shouldn't favor puny wimps with lucky cards," Dean declared.

"What's the matter with you?" Alex asked sternly. "You've had a bug up your ass ever since you got here."

Laughing, Dean started to sing, "Old lady river, that old lady river, she just keeps rollin' along."

"Quit yer yappin'," Nelson snapped, dealing quickly. "Same game, jacks or better. Ante up."

Alex thought playing with the boys from Noë Valley was better than not playing at all, but the game lacked the juice injected by the annual wild card. They knew each other too well to generate real excitement. Without a fifth player, the game had a desultory, unbalanced feel that wasn't right. That was why they'd brought a wild card into the game in the first place. The wild card was noble prey, an intelligent victim, a stranger who had to be studied and understood before he could be manipulated, mind-fucked, and ultimately beaten. Poker was a contest of skill and guts and nerve, and that was the challenge Alex craved to satisfy his poker jones. Alas, since there was no wild card, he had to find another way to pump up the game.

The hand was dealt, the cards on the table. Alex let his cards lay on the felt as he watched Dean retrieve his, knowing the bickering had dropped the big man into a funk, priming him for exploitation. Dean moved the cards around in his hand in such a way that Alex knew he had three cards that went together, three cards to a straight or flush or perhaps three of a kind. Meanwhile, Nelson smiled and made pleasurable noises as though he had a good hand, indicating the opposite, and Charlie read his cards while silently moving his lips, saying "Queen" twice. Thinking this was the perfect time to bluff, Alex picked up his cards, glanced at them briefly, and put them back on the table as he always did in draw. He didn't have to bluff. Nelson had dealt him four threes, in all likelihood the best hand he'd see all night.

"I open for three hundred," he said, dropping three blues into the pot. "Charlie's not gonna take another one without a fight."

"I'll see your three hundred," Dean announced without hesitation, "and raise five hundred."

That was it, Alex thought. You don't raise that much on three cards to a flush or straight, but you do with three of a kind.

"Eight hundred to me," Charlie said. "Um, um, um, okay."

Alex winced, thinking playing with Charlie just wasn't fair, but that was poker.

"I'm out," Nelson said. "Too rich for me."

"I'll see your raise and raise another thousand," Alex said mildly, staring at Dean and adding, "No guts, no glory."

"Got another pat hand?" Dean inquired.

Alex cocked his head sideways, looked up at the light, and drummed his fingers on the felt. "Nope," he said, lowering his eyes to face Dean. "Not this time."

"I'll call," Dean announced, and tossed two bumblebees into the pot.

"You don't want to raise again?"

"Go to hell, Wiz," Dean said. "Charlie?"

Charlie waffled, shifting the cards around in his hand. "Shit, I dunno, I dunno. I'm out."

"Okay," Nelson said. "Dean and Alex. Cards, gentlemen."

"I'm good," Alex said. "No cards."

"God damn," Dean cursed. "You said you didn't have a pat hand."

"I lied. Poker is a ruthless game that rewards deception."

"Christ—"

"Dean," Nelson interrupted impatiently. "How many cards?"

"Two."

Nelson peeled off two cards and passed them face down to Dean. "You opened, Alex," he said. "It's your bet."

"I check."

"You're gonna sandbag," Dean snarled. "Alex, you can't raise if I don't bet. I check, too. That's it. Turn 'em over."

Alex flipped over his cards, announcing each one. "One, two, three, four treys and the six of spades. It's not a pat hand. I could've tossed the six."

"Jesus H. Christ, four of a kind. I don't know why I play this game with you." Dean slammed his cards on the table, rattling chips. He stomped over to the stereo and jerked the needle off Stan Getz. "I can't stand this screwball jazz," he steamed. "I want shitkicker music. What d'ya got here, Charlie? Johnny Cash? The Orange Blossom Special? All right."

"Let's have some Elvis," Charlie said. "Elvis was a shitkicker and proud of it."

"Who cares about Elvis?" Dean mumbled. "He's dead."

"Everybody in that record pile is dead," Nelson quipped and then added brightly, "Maybe we're dead. Maybe that's why we're stuck in a time warp playing an antique game with no redeeming social value."

"Ah, bullshit," Dean countered. "Life has no redeeming social value. Life is just life if you have the balls to live it. If you don't, then you might as well be dead."

"Put on anything you like, then sit down," Alex demanded, a little annoyed. "It's my deal."

"Hold your horses, Alex. I just went from winners to losers, an experience that may be beyond your ken."

"Are you in, Dean?" Charlie wanted to know. "Or are you gonna mess around with the records all night?"

"Yeah, yeah, deal me in."

Dean put on Johnny Cash and they played a few more hands with no one catching cards worth betting. The game was like the sea in a squall, turbulent and dank but not really threatening. The big storm was somewhere beyond the horizon. As midnight approached Nelson looked at his watch every few minutes, Alex smoked Luckies, and Dean drank more rum. In normal years the game provided a superb diversion from the stress and anxiety of their lives, but tonight poker could provide only so much distraction from the gritty issue of whether or not Bobby McCorkle was going to arrive, what it meant if he didn't, and what might happen if he did.

"It's not the first time," Nelson reminded them. "Remember, six or seven years ago we had a wild card who didn't show. Just crapped out and you got all pissed off"—he jerked a thumb toward Dean—"he was your guy and you got drunk and dragged some old gal from the bar up here. You wanted to play strip poker."

"I did. With her. In the bedroom."

"You're a horny old toad, you know that?"

"Well, I ain't dead the way you think we're dead. Time warp, my ass. I fuck women. I race my boat. I have a good time and mind my own business, and I sure as shit ain't dead. Not on your—"

"Listen," Alex interrupted. "Maybe we're not dead, but we've always known we were living on borrowed time. When you borrow and borrow and borrow, sooner or later you have to pay and pay and pay."

"No, you don't," Dean declared. "You can croak and nobody collects."

He laughed at his own morbid joke and lit another joint.

"Look," Alex said. "Somebody has to say this. The one thing we were most afraid of has happened. Our worst nightmare has come true. Now, it's up to us, including Bobby, to determine what we're going to do about it. I swear he'll show."

"Who are you, the fucking pope?" Dean asked. "You gonna wave your magic wand and make him walk through the door?"

"Where do you think he is?" Nelson asked Alex. "Maybe he missed his plane. I can call the airline."

"Nah," Alex said. "My guess is that he hasn't been to San Francisco for a long time and he's taking a tour, Noë Valley, Baker Beach, you know, the old stomping grounds. It's hard for him. He doesn't know what to expect from us any more than we know what to expect from him."

"Maybe we should do the same thing," Charlie piped up. "Let's play tourist. Let's forget the game and go to one of the old Irish bars in the Mission. Let's go to the Dovre Club and get fucked up."

"We're here to play cards," Alex asserted, mildly alarmed that the game might be slipping away. "Even if Bobby shows, poker is the main event."

"You're a poker junkie, Alex," Nelson said. "We all know that. You're crazy. And you," he said, pointing a finger at Charlie, "you're losing, so shut up."

"The Dovre Club!" Dean exclaimed with a gleeful laugh. "Hot stuff. All right."

"Shit," Alex said.

"Sorry, Wiz," Dean said, "but we have all weekend. Maybe Charlie can find another player tomorrow."

"Nelson, would you rather play or party?" Alex asked.

"I don't care. If these guys want to go to the Dovre Club and make fools of themselves, I don't give a shit."

"I have an idea," Alex said brightly. "Let's make the game more interesting. Let's raise the stakes to a hundred dollar ante."

"Leave it alone, Wiz," Dean said. "Look, the game isn't working with only four players. That's too bad, but that's the way it is."

"I didn't fly three thousand miles to go bar-hopping," Alex protested, petulant.

"Then why don't you go down to Artichoke Joe's," Dean hissed, naming a well-known local card room.

A look of undisguised horror blanched Alex's face. After a long, long pause he said, "You know I can't do that. I can't even think about that."

Dean immediately regretted his *faux pas* and apologized. "Sorry, Alex. I'm sorry. Really, I didn't mean it."

"Ah, what the hell," Alex conceded. "Every year the game goes haywire one way or another, but usually not until the second night. The wild card usually keeps it interesting until he goes broke."

"You mean until you skin him alive."

"Yeah."

"You've got a fat head sometimes," Dean said. "And if it gets rough, you'd better have the cards."

"Don't worry about it," Alex said. "I used to beat him left, right, and upside the head."

"Except for the last time."

"Don't worry about it," Alex reiterated.

Edgy, inhaling several slow, deep breaths, Alex started doing card tricks to keep his hands busy. For a moment he contemplated going to Artichoke Joe's, sitting down, and never getting up. Maybe he wouldn't lose everything, and if he did, so what? After tonight it might not make any difference.

# 14

The doorbell chimed, followed by a loud rap on the door. They froze. For a moment the only sound in the room was a scratchy old recording of Johnny Cash's ballad of addiction and redemption, "I Walk the Line."

"Holy shit," Charlie squealed, jumping up. "I'll get it."

Dean pointed a threatening finger at Nelson and said, "This better not be one of your stunts."

"I'm pretty sure it is," Nelson replied. "Justice will be served. The star witness is about to step into court, and we get to be our own judge and jury."

"Ain't that the truth," Dean mumbled.

Alex spread the blue deck face up and flipped it over face down, then back and forth, back and forth like a tide. His hands were sweating.

Standing in the corridor was a middle-aged man of medium height, balding, clear-eyed, a little paunchy, and dressed in a tailored English sport jacket, polo shirt, outsized silver belt buckle, flannel slacks, and snakeskin cowboy boots. A diamond-shaped ruby stud brightened his left ear.

"Bobby!"

"Yeah, hello. Charlie?"

"Yeah, yeah, it's me. Thirty years and thirty pounds."

They shook hands and fumbled through the lightest of brotherly hugs.

"Hey, Charlie, all right. How are ya, man? Good to see ya." The voice was instantly recognizable, boisterous and full of hail-fellow-well-met.

"Come on in. We saved you a seat."

"Sorry I'm late."

"No sweat. C'mon."

Charlie ushered Bobby into the living room where Dean and Nelson stood at the table while Alex, resplendent in Panama and dark glasses, remained seated, smoke from his cigarette swirling into the light.

"Hey, Dean, Alex, hey, Nelson. Looks like you boys got yourselves a game going."

"We got a game," Charlie said, the congenial, effusive host. "We got eats, we got seegars and booze and Dean has some dynamite weed. We got everything."

"Well, all right. Sounds good to me."

"Check into your room all right?" Charlie asked, wondering what happened to the bellhop who was supposed to notify him of Bobby's arrival. "They take care of you?"

"I didn't check in, no. I came right up. Nice room, pretty fancy," Bobby answered, pursing his lips, nodding his head, and looking around. Noticing the pictures of Maverick and company he added, "Nice decorations."

"Care for a drink?" Charlie asked.

"Sure. Got a soda and lime?"

"Got everything."

While Charlie hustled into the kitchenette to fix a soda and lime, Bobby stood between the foyer and the card table, arms folded across his chest, slowly nodding his head and looking appraisingly at Alex, Dean, and Nelson. They returned his frank gaze until the long looks became awkward.

Breaking the ice, Dean came around the table to shake Bobby's hand. Grinning, the light making his beard shimmer with rum drippings, his sleeveless T-shirt revealing faded tattoos and munificent belly, he pumped Bobby's arm, saying, "Well, I'll be damned. Good to see you, man, even though you just cost me a hundred bucks."

"How's that?"

"The Wiz and I had a bet. He said you'd show, and it looks like he won fair and square."

"A little action on my arrival, hey?" Bobby said with a nervous smile. "I shoulda guessed. They still call you the Wiz, Alex?"

"It's a time warp in here, Bobby. Nothing much has changed. We just got older, that's all."

"Nice hat, jack o' diamonds."

"I only wear it once a year," Alex said, slowly standing and removing his dark glasses. He walked over, stood for a long moment in front of his long lost friend, and then gripped his shoulders.

"It's been a long time, Bobby. Too long, a lifetime."

Bobby grinned. A rising swell of emotion pushed the two men together and they grasped one another in a strong bear hug. As soon as Alex let go, Nelson grabbed Bobby, slapped him on the back, and was too overcome to say anything more than, "God damn, God *damn*, it's good to see you."

"Hey, Chinaman, you, too."

Embarrassed, almost blushing, Bobby felt as though they were back in Alex's parents' garage, full of swagger, high on life, getting ready to play on a cable-spool. In those days poker had been fun. Now, when he sat down to play every night, he felt nothing. He was neutral. Poker was work, his *métier*, and he'd long since surpassed cockiness or any mindset that interfered with his play. This was different. A swirl of emotions battered him from all directions, and he struggled to maintain his mental balance.

"So you guys do this every year, right?"

"Most years," Alex said. "Sometimes we miss for one reason or another."

"And some years we get so wasted we can't play," Dean said, laughing. "At least I do."

Charlie returned from the kitchen with Bobby's drink, and they endured another long pause until Bobby said, "I went by Lyle Tuttle's tonight, and he's gone. The whole building is gone."

"Still got your tattoo?" Nelson asked.

Bobby's hand went to his left shoulder. "Yeah. It's faded, but I can tell you one thing," he said with a sharp laugh. "I don't look like Dean. You're a walkin' billboard there, boy. USMC. I heard you were in the Corps."

"Semper Fi, dude," Dean said. "I heard you were a lifer."

"Yeah, twenty and out," Bobby said. "How long were you in?" he paused and snapped a mock salute, "Sir?"

Dean smirked and returned the gesture of mutual respect. He wanted to say, "The past is gone and I don't want to think about it anymore," but he couldn't say that because before the game was over the past was going to become the main topic of conversation. Instead he said, "Four years, and that was more than enough. I don't dwell on those times. I got a life."

"You seem to have had a lot of lives," Bobby said, gesturing with his head at Dean's body art.

Dean laughed heartily, his beard quivering and spraying droplets of rum. "Sometimes I use up two or three a day," he said. "I don't give a shit."

Earlier in the evening, while eating at Joe's, Bobby had wished aloud that he wanted to be eighteen again, and suddenly he was, or almost was, as though time had stopped and rolled back to the point where his life had been sheared off and rent asunder. A bond that had been broken was now precariously rejoined. He felt uncertain and a little queasy, and when he decided not to bring up Shanghai Bend immediately, he realized no one else was in a hurry to mention it, either.

Another awkward silence persisted until Alex said, "How about let's play cards. We can reminisce and tell war stories later."

"Right on," Bobby said. "Let's do that."

Standing around grinning foolishly at one another, they were like stardust bouncing aimlessly around the universe. At the poker table their reunion would have a structure that would make it bearable. With a clamber of fussy noise they scrambled into their chairs, fiddled with chips, rattled ice in their drinks, and plinked fingernails against the hotel's fine tumblers.

Bobby took the empty seat and ran his fingers over the felt. "Nelson said you fellas play five and seven stud and draw," he said.

"That's right," Alex replied and rapidly outlined the rules they'd established earlier.

"Sounds like poker to me," Bobby said. "You still playing with chips?"

"The same chips we used in the old days," Charlie said, handing Bobby a blue for inspection. "You don't use chips in your games?"

"In private games it's usually cash, but chips are fine, especially nice ones like these. Five grand, right?"

"Five big ones," Nelson confirmed.

"We don't have a banker," Dean said.

"We never did," Bobby said, turning over the old, flat disk in his hand, triggering a flood of memories. "I remember that."

While Alex counted out five thousand dollars in chips, Dean produced the rum box and Bobby chuckled at the huge wad of bills. He took out a money clip, counted out fifty crisp, new hundred-dollar bills and added them to the box. Alex noticed that Bobby's hands were freshly manicured, the bills turned all the same way, and his manner of counting money efficient and well-practiced. The nervousness in his voice didn't affect his hands.

"Well," Bobby said, arranging his chips in neat stacks, "here we are, a bunch of fat old farts. Except you, Nelson. You look in pretty good shape."

"I work out, go to the gym."

"You live down south, right? That's where you called from."

"Yeah, I live in Hermosa Beach and work in Venice. You ever go to L.A.?"

"I don't come to California very often," Bobby answered, lighting a Winston. "I went to Gardena once."

"The card rooms," Nelson said with a knowing smile. "Oh, yeah."

"It's a living," Bobby said with shrug.

"All right," Charlie said. "Is this a new game? First jack deals?"

"Don't start over on my account," Bobby said. "Carry on."

"It was your deal, Dean," Alex said. "You decide."

Dean shrugged. "It's all the same to me."

"Carry on," Bobby repeated. "As you were, please."

"Okay. Deano's deal," Alex said. "What's the game?"

"Five stud," Dean announced. "Comin' atcha."

The antes clinked into the center of the table, the cards rolled out, and Dean sang the dealer's cadence. "The nine of clubs to the new player, a four to Charlie, another nine to Nelson, an eight to Alex, and a three to the dealer. First nine bets."

Bobby peeked at his hole card and looked up to find Alex studying him like a laboratory specimen. They both smiled.

"First nine bets twenty-five dollars."

# 15

The wait was over, the long hiatus ended. The light over the table seemed a little brighter, illuminating their faces with more energy than before. Cards crackled as they flew across the table; chips dropped into the pot with the sharpness of an axe on pine; the players perched on the edges of their seats, alert and eager, the Dovre Club forgotten, the records ignored, the food abandoned. When it became apparent that the cards for the hand would be nothing special, the unwritten code of competition was temporarily suspended by silent consent because no one wanted to fold the first hand with all of them together. A perfunctory bet of one white chip was made on each card, and Nelson drew a second nine on the last card to win the pot.

"Thank you, gentlemen, thank you, thank you," Nelson said cheerfully, gathering in the chips.

"You're a winner," Bobby said to Nelson as he shuffled the blue deck. "Do you guys still call this Chinaman Crazy Nelson?"

Before anyone could answer, Nelson fixed Bobby with a stony glance, reached under his chair for his .44 magnum and swung it around until it pointed away from the table directly at the photo of Wyatt Earp. "You tell me," he said, sighting down the barrel. "What do *you* think?"

Eyeing the big pistol warily, smelling the clear scent of gun oil, Bobby cleared his throat and said, "I guess some things don't change."

Nelson spun the cylinder, making sure Bobby saw the weapon was loaded, leaned over the table and growled, "You're the only white man who ever called me 'Chinaman' and lived."

Bobby paled, suddenly afraid he'd caused terrible offense. Before he could sputter an apology, Nelson leaned back in his chair and laughed, saying, "No sweat, Kimosabe. Call me whatever you like."

"Put that damned gun away," Dean barked, his voice stiffened with the fiber of command. "You've been living in shit-fer-brains Hollywood too long, Nelson. Nobody gives a rat's ass about your cannon. You ain't Wyatt Earp."

"Oh, yeah?" Nelson said, replacing the gun under his seat. "I'm the closest thing to good ole Wyatt you'll ever have on your side, Studley." Turning to Bobby he asked, "Are you still Bobby these days, or are you Bob or Robert or what?"

"It's Bob to most people, but Bobby is fine. Kimosabe is dandy. I haven't heard that in a long time."

"Hey!" Charlie shouted, his voice rising with complaint. "For chrissake, we know who we are, don't we? What's the fucking *game?*"

"There you go," Alex said. "Thank you, Charlie. It's your deal, Bobby."

"Hear hear, professor," Dean said and Nelson added, "Roll 'em."

"Okay, same game," Bobby declared, cutting off the chatter and dealing with the tidy deftness of a professional. "Five stud."

An amateur holds the deck in one hand and deals with the other, a natural and comfortable way of handling cards. When those two hands belong to a professional, the odious practices of a mechanic— second dealing, bottom dealing, switching, and marking cards—are difficult to detect except by another skilled card sharp. To negate suspicion, an honest pro lays the deck on the felt and snaps cards off the top with one hand, turning cards into projectiles with precise trajectories perfected by thousands of repetitions. In stud, every up card is accompanied by the ceremonial incantation of its value, and Bobby automatically intoned, "A nine to Charlie, a ten to Nelson, a king to Alex, a six to Dean, and another king to the dealer. First king bets."

Alex noticed that Bobby barely looked at the cards, focusing instead on the players. He imagined Bobby's mind working as he soaked up data and built a book on his opponents. When Bobby said, "First king bets," he was looking directly into Alex's dark glasses as though the opaque lenses were as transparent as the smoky air. Bobby was scrutinizing every action and reaction. A poker face wasn't enough. A poker body was more like it.

Alex glanced at his hole card and dropped a blue chip into the pot.

"One hundred dollars on the first king."

"Not for me," Dean said, turning over his card.

Bobby checked his hole card, a second king, and then leaned over the table to stare at Alex's big pile of chips. "Looks like you're the big winner so far," he said. "I'll see your hundred and raise a hundred."

"Good-bye," Charlie declared.

"Likewise," Nelson said.

"I'll see your raise," Alex said.

"Two players," Bobby said. "Next card. A queen to the first king, and a ten to the dealer's king."

"One hundred again."

"I'll raise a hundred," Bobby said.

Alex smiled. "Not going to fool around, are we?" he said. "I'll see your raise and raise another two hundred."

At that moment Bobby realized how much he wanted to beat Alex Goldman, and that was different from merely wanting to win. He was engaged, and in his long, checkered history as a poker player, engagement had been a recipe for disaster. Looking at Alex's cards, he suspected the Wiz either had a king in the hole, in which case there were no more kings in the deck, or he had a queen and was trying to buy the hand.

"I'll call," he said. "There it is, pot's right. Fourth card coming out. Another queen for two queens showing, and a second ten to the dealer."

"Interesting," Alex said. "Very interesting. Three hundred on the queens."

Bobby's two pair, kings and tens, were good enough to beat a pair of queens but not three. His instinct told him Alex had a third queen in the hole, and ordinarily he'd listen to his hunch and fold. Not this time.

"See your three hundred and raise three."

Alex considered the possibility of raising four thousand dollars and blowing the game wide open less than ten minutes after they started. Instead, he took a drag on his Lucky and put three blues in the pot. "Call," he said dispassionately. "Let's see the last card."

Silently chastising himself because he hadn't raised enough, Bobby dealt Alex an eight and himself a third ten, giving him a full house and a lock on the hand.

"Three tens are high," he said and swiftly placed two bumblebees in the center of the pot. "One thousand on the tens."

"Ooo," Nelson warbled. "Gettin' right to it."

"The Wiz has three queens sure as shit," Dean said. "He has a king, and Nelson had the fourth ten. There's only one card in the deck that makes Bobby a winner and that's a king in the hole for a full house. What are the odds on that?"

"It'll only cost Alex a grand to find out," Nelson said with a hollow laugh.

Alex smiled. "You know what they say," he said. "It's better to be lucky than good. I fold. Take it."

Bobby gathered in the pot, thinking both he and Alex had misplayed the hand. If they were going to dance around the past all night, he would've been better off letting Driver take him all the way home. There was no way around it. Serious cards were out of the question until the air was cleared, not of smoke, but of Shanghai Bend.

"Gentlemen," he said, eyes flat and neutral, "this is bullshit. I'm not sure what this is, but it isn't a card game. A week ago Nelson calls on the phone and says a construction crew dug up some old bones on the Feather River. That's all I know, and that got me here. Tell me why I should care, or I'll cash in and go back to Reno."

# 16

Dean squeezed a chip so hard it cracked loud as a pistol shot. Startled, Alex banged a knee against a table leg and all the neatly stacked chips crashed to the felt.

"Damn!"

"Watch it!"

"It's about fucking time," Dean growled. Digging furiously into his bag, he yanked out a month-old edition of the Marysville *Register*, the river town's weekly newspaper, and slapped it on the table.

"If you need a reason to care, you can start with this," he hissed, veins bulging in his forehead.

Page one featured a story entitled "The Queen of Hearts" and a haunting photograph of a skull with a levee and river in the background. Clucking and nodding, Bobby read the brief article and said quietly, "Tell me about the card."

"That was a shock to all of us," Charlie said.

"I'm afraid I tossed the card into the grave, but I never mentioned it," Alex confessed. "That alone could send me to prison."

"That wasn't very smart for a genius," Bobby sneered, flashing a glance of disdain at Alex who smiled in return. Bobby asked Dean, "What else did they find?"

More agitated than the others, Dean was steaming, ready to burst like an overheated boiler. He hunched his chair closer to the table, leaned over on his elbows, thick fists knotted under bushy chin, and turned deliberately from Bobby to Nelson. "You tell him, Lieutenant. What did they find?"

Lighting a cigarette, Bobby caught a glimpse of the photographs of their old heroes and quickly looked away. The images only served to remind him that fear and ghosts were closing in.

"They found nothing," Nelson answered calmly. "The Yuba County Sheriff has a playing card with no fingerprints and a skeleton with a cracked skull that was in the right place, that's been in the ground the right amount of time, and is a female of the appropriate age."

"Have they identified her?" Bobby asked.

"No. They're mystified."

"Will they?"

"Probably not," Nelson replied, shaking his head.

"Why not?"

Nelson hesitated. The answer to Bobby's question was in his briefcase, but he wasn't ready to reveal the documents until he had some indication of how Bobby would react to that information. He looked to Alex for confirmation, not to dissemble but to delay, and Alex nodded.

"Because the evidence will fall through the bureaucratic cracks," Nelson explained. "The Yuba County people are competent, but they don't have the resources to push an investigation very far even with help from the state. They know she wasn't a local girl because they have no unsolved missing person reports from that era in the surrounding counties. It's just not going to happen."

"So what's the problem?"

"We have to do the right thing, Bobby."

"The right thing? The right thing? What the hell is the right thing?"

"That's what we have to decide."

"If they can't identify her, you don't have to do diddly squat. And even if they do, so what? What's to connect her to you?"

Dean spoke up. "If doing nothing is the right thing, then that's what we'll do. In any case, we ran away from it then, but we can't now."

"Why not?"

"It's hard to say, really. Do you believe in redemption?"

"Ha!" Bobby scoffed. "I don't believe in anything. Belief is for suckers. What a load of crap."

"Listen," Dean said, suddenly stern. "We haven't seen you since the night she died. You took off and never came back. Ever since, the rest of us have met every year to play cards, yes, but the real reason we get together is to assure each other that another year of silence has gone by. None of us has ever talked about Shanghai Bend, not one word to anyone, but there was always a joker in this deck, a wild card, an unknown, and that was you. We never knew—and still don't know—if you talked. I'll tell you about belief, and you tell me if I'm a sucker. I believe you've never given away the secret. I believe it because if you *had*, there would've been serious repercussions, and that hasn't happened. But Bobby, right now, I want to hear it from you."

"That's it? That's all you want from me? To know if I shot off my mouth?"

"That's a start."

"I didn't come here to be interrogated."

"And we're not here to question you," Alex said. "It's the other way around."

A glint of understanding crept into Bobby's mind. "You're thinking about turning yourselves in," he said quietly.

"That's right. That's one option."

"That's letting you off easy."

Charlie looked at Alex who shrugged as if to say, we thought it would be like this. Dean's nostrils flared with impatience, and Nelson sighed.

"Bobby," the policeman said. "We think you've always believed that we killed her."

"You're God damned right. I know you did."

"We need to know what you intend to do now that they've dug her up."

Stunned, with decades of rage rising in his throat like bile, Bobby thought he was going to be sick.

"I don't like the sound of this," he said vehemently, pointing an agitated finger at Nelson. "I used to know you, Chinaman, but I don't anymore. You're a cop. Somebody in the boonies dug a body out of the ground, and if I were to say, 'Yeah, these guys killed this girl,' that's it. Case solved, and we all go to jail. To hell with that. I don't have anything to say to you. I came here for a card game."

"What about the Yuba County Sheriff?"

Bobby moved as though he were going to get up and leave.

"Wait a minute, please," Alex said. "There's no reason to be in a hurry. You may have nothing to say, but we do. We're in this together, pal. We're a royal flush, remember? If we hang, we hang together."

"That's right," Nelson said. "I'm not a cop at this table. I'm just the ten of diamonds. My job is on the line here."

"We all have a lot to lose," Charlie said. "Careers, reputations, families, fortunes, the works."

Bobby shook his head. "Why risk it then? You can't bring her back. I can't believe you got me here to tell me you're going to confess. That's really crazy."

"Before you decide we're out of our minds, you need to know what we know," Dean said, the big man's tone quiet, intense, and considerably more sober than earlier in the evening. His fierce eyes scanned the table, looking first at Charlie who nodded and rattled the ice in his drink, at Nelson who raised his eyebrows, and Alex who touched the brim of his hat in salute. Then Dean leaned deep into the table and stared at Bobby who for the briefest instant looked like a deer caught in headlights.

"When you first came in you called me a billboard, and you were right," Dean said, eyes locked on Bobby's every twitch. "I look like I belong in a freak show, but it's a disguise. We're all in disguise, because everything we've done since that night has been an attempt to hide what we did. I live with that every day. Every morning I wake up crazy, split in two. Half of me wants to be so fucking righteous just living is an act of repentance, and the other half wants to be so crazy it doesn't matter what I do. I don't know how to put it into words, but I think you can understand what I mean. You see, Bobby, I live right on the Feather River only a few miles from Shanghai Bend, and I've been waiting all these years for her bones to see the light of day."

Bobby stammered, "Jesus Christ. Why?"

"Isn't it obvious? Guilt. Horrible, convoluted, twisted guilt," Dean said with a shrug that was more like a full body convulsion. "Maybe it isn't obvious because it wasn't so obvious to me at first. I can understand how you, and Alex as well, live far away from where it happened and never want to go there, but I couldn't stay away. When I came home from Vietnam, I couldn't stop thinking about what we did at Shanghai Bend, and I started visiting the river—to fish, at least that's what I told myself. Steelhead, salmon, shad, cat-fish—didn't matter, I was compelled to be there. I got to know a few people, made some friends around Marysville, and, anyway, about twenty years ago there was a major flood that washed out an old mining camp. All of a sudden there were all these exposed skel-etons and it hit me like a ton of bricks. It was only a matter of time before that old river coughed up its most desperate secret, and when that happened, I had to be there. So I found a place, started a business, married a local girl, and waited."

Dean sighed heavily and took a long pull of rum before going on. "We buried her, man, and that was wrong, but I never had the guts to dig her up. I've been waiting for someone else to do it, or the river to do it, like it was fate or destiny, and if it did happen, I wanted to know right away. I had a plan. I was going to kill myself. That's right. I was going to blow my head off with a shogun, but when it *did* happen, and they pulled her out of the ground six weeks ago, I lost my nerve. Maybe that was wrong, too. I suppose so, but there you are. This thing has eaten me alive, and I want to put an end to that."

"Guilt," Bobby said, drawing out the word. "Maybe you *should* blow your fucking head off, Dean."

Dean's linebacker's eyes with flaming whites and bristling pupils bore in on Bobby like laser beams. "After what I just told you, you want to be a smart-ass?"

A tremor swept through the room. Bobby was rocketed back to the instant before detonation, and he took a deep breath to keep from exploding again.

"No, I don't want to be a smart-ass. I want to be smart," he said hoarsely, almost hoping the big man would attack. With the knife concealed in his right sleeve, the fight would be quick and deadly. "I came here to play cards, and now I feel like I should have brought a lawyer. You killed her and buried her so you could have a normal life, and now you feel guilty. Fuck you. See a shrink."

Dean rose half out of his chair, shaking an impassioned fist.

Bobby smiled. "Come on," he said.

"Take it easy, Dean," Charlie said. "Easy, big guy."

Dean sank back into his chair, grabbed one of Alex's cigarettes and lit it. "Shrinks, lawyers, fuck that," he said, voice trembling with contempt. "It's up to us and no one else."

"Look, Bobby," Charlie said, "the only reason for you to trust us is that we trust you. We were all drunk that night, and we're all equally guilty, and we all have everything to lose."

"We've waited thirty-two years for you," Dean said. "Some years we felt betrayed because you never showed, and other years we've just been sad. What we did fucked us all up, not just you. This isn't about you; it's about all of us. If you want to walk away again, so be it, but you already tried running to the other side of the planet, just like I did, and I doubt that worked any better for you than it did for me. What we did, and what it did to us, is in our hearts and we carry it wherever we go. We have a chance tonight to be clean and honest, not with anyone else, not with shrinks or lawyers or any of that, just us here at this table. Hey man, you're the ace of diamonds. When we were eighteen, you were my hero, big, bad Bobby McCorkle. You taught me how to *be*. That's worth something, isn't it? What do you say?"

One way or the other, they were offering him release. "Heroes are accidents," he said with a self-deprecating smile. "I'm a gambler. The only thing I ever did was risk my neck and get away with it, but I guess you can only get away with so much for so long. So what you're really telling me is that if we hang, we hang together."

There were silent nods all around the table. Alex picked up the blue deck, shuffled, and flipped over the top card, the four of clubs, then quickly turned over the following three cards, all fours. The next card was a joker.

"A wild card," he said, lighting a cigarette. "Fancy that."

He picked the joker off the felt and methodically tore it to bits.

"Are you leaving or are you gonna stay?" he asked.

Emotions rioted inside Bobby's head, but in the midst of the chaos one thought stood out: He wasn't going to allow himself to be charged with murder, tried, convicted, and sent to prison, perhaps to be executed for a crime he didn't commit. No doubt lethal injection would end the torture he'd inflicted on himself for the last three decades, but he'd go down fighting. He'd hear them out, and if they truly wanted to turn themselves and him in, no one would leave the Enrico Caruso Suite alive. It would end right there in the Palace Hotel.

"I think it's Charlie's deal," he said. "What's the game?"

# 1 7

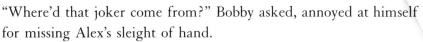

"Where'd that joker come from?" Bobby asked, annoyed at himself for missing Alex's sleight of hand.

Alex made a clown face, snatched off his hat, peered inside and replaced it on his head. "What joker? I didn't see any joker. Did you fellas see a joker? There's no wild cards in this game. Deal 'em, Charlie. Let's play."

He winked at Bobby who leaned back in his chair, pensive, wondering where the next blast would come from in this minefield masquerading as a poker table.

Charlie picked up the red deck and promptly mis-shuffled, sending cards flying in all directions. Dean couldn't resist the urge to needle. "Nervous, are we?"

Charlie twisted in his chair and let fly a vicious backhand in the direction of Dean's head. Reacting swiftly, Dean tilted his chair and Charlie's fingers whizzed by his nose, missing by an inch.

"I know you can't help yourself, Studley," Charlie snarled, "but you don't have to be a jerk all the time."

Dean grinned and let it pass. Bobby saw it was just like the old days, back and forth, teasing and testing. Nothing had changed.

"I don't know if it's nerves or the cards are slick or what," Charlie said, gathering up the deck and shuffling again. He stopped manipulating the cards to fan himself with the deck, saying, "Christ, it's hot in here. The damned air-conditioning must have broken down. I think next year we should play at the Saint Francis, you know what I mean?"

He stood, ripped off his jacket and shirt and, naked to the waist, passed the deck to Bobby. "Jacks or better," he announced. "Cut the cards, if you please."

"You're right. It *is* hot," Nelson agreed and yanked off his shirt.

"I feel like I'm in sweaty old Manhattan," Alex said and removed his glasses and hat and pulled his shirt over his head.

Dean wasn't wearing a shirt, only a sleeveless undershirt that exposed the queen of diamonds inked into his skin. "Four cards to the flush," he said and they all looked at Bobby.

What the hell, Bobby thought, cutting the cards for Charlie. I don't know what they're really up to, but at least there's a chance for a decent game before the shit really hits the fan.

"You guys are fuckin' nuts, y'know," he said. "If you're nuts, then so am I."

He pulled off his jacket and shirt and the splendid ace of diamonds glistened on his shoulder. Without spoiling the occasion with words, they all remembered that this was how they'd played in Alex's garage during those few brilliant weeks when their tattoos were new, when they were indeed a royal flush of glorious young men.

Alex started to laugh and his mirth was contagious. First Dean, then right around the table they all started to laugh and sputter like teenagers. Sniggling, trying to avoid a misdeal, Charlie slowly passed out cards for a hand of five draw and counted them off with a bouncing lilt, "Ah one, ah two, ah three, ah four, ah five, ah one, ah two..."

"Jesus, space cadets," Nelson said. "You all right, Deano? You calmed down?"

"How the hell do I know? All I can see is I'm sitting around a hotel room with a bunch of half-naked lunatics. You're up, copper. Can you open?"

Nelson picked up his cards and said, "I open for fifty."

Still giggling, Alex tossed a blue chip into the pot and said, "I see your fifty and raise fifty."

Dean scooped up a handful of blues and poured them indiscriminately into the pot. "I see the first fifty, the second fifty, and raise five hundred, more or less."

"You can't raise 'more or less' in poker," Nelson objected.

Dean laughed again. "Oh, yeah? You wanna throw another fire-cracker at me?"

"Haha. Not while you're lookin'."

"I call," Bobby said.

"How much is it to me?" Charlie asked.

"Six hundred."

"Okay, I'm in, I'm in. Who wants how many cards?"

They played the hand the way they'd played as kids, reckless and crazy, laughing, as though the game were actually fun. After all, it was only poker, not life and death.

Nelson won the hand with a pair of queens, and they sat there, bare to the waist, feeling silly and a little better.

"What we need is some of that good old rock and roll," Dean hollered. "Da da da da da, back in the U.S. of A. Yeah!"

In an instant the great Chuck Berry was rolling out of the stereo like a steamy night in Memphis. Dean danced around the room, throwing his arms into the air, shouting and singing, "Oh man, oh man! Yeah yeah yeah yeah yeah!"

"Gimme some of that weed," Charlie demanded of Dean.

"Oh, ho ho ho. You ready for that?"

"Hell, yes."

"You're a wild and crazy guy, Charlie."

Chuck Berry broke into "Johnny B. Goode" causing heads to bop and fingers to drum. Dean sat down, rolled a joint, and passed it to Charlie who fired it.

"Rocket Fuel," Charlie breathed.

"The one and only."

"What's that? What's Rocket Fuel?" Bobby asked.

"You're gonna learn all the secrets tonight, dude," Dean said. "I'm a grower and this is the product."

"He's big time," Charlie said. "Or he was."

"This is the last crop," Dean said. "Recent events require prudence in the production of controlled agricultural substances. Too bad, but that's the way it goes. That's just the beginning of what this little episode is going to cost."

"You know about this?" Bobby asked Nelson. "Jeez. You guys are so tight, I guess you must."

"I couldn't care less," Nelson answered. "I didn't become a police officer to throw my friends in jail. Besides, it's just weed. It's not heroin."

This last word caused Bobby to blink rapidly.

"We know about that, too," Alex said.

"What do you mean?" Bobby asked.

"I think you know."

Alex pulled out his wallet and flashed a Department of Defense ID. "Recognize this? I'm sure you do. It's coded class one priority so I can do my own security checks for people who might have access to my classified work. I can obtain a complete dossier on just about anyone, and it's especially easy if the individual in question is or was military."

Alex waited until the meaning of his declaration sank in.

"You've seen my jacket," Bobby said.

"Yes."

"All of it?"

"I think so. I could recite names and dates, but what's the point?"

Bobby's face grew solemn and he said, "I don't know whether to be pissed off or overawed."

"I know, and I wouldn't blame you for being angry, but we had to protect ourselves."

"Against what?"

"Against your giving us away, of course. Look, I have access to your government records, and Nelson has sheets from the Reno police and the Nevada highway patrol, from Louisiana, Arizona, North Carolina, West Germany, I could go on. We know about your addiction, about detox and the car wrecks and all of it. You're sitting here with your shirt off, and I can't see any fresh needle tracks. That's a good sign. Shit, man, we've followed your life all these years, and you scared us to death more times than I can count."

"Jesus fucking Christ. You guys are bouncing me around like a basketball. You work for DoD? I thought you were a professor."

Alex nodded. "I am, and neither Columbia University nor DoD

would be happy to learn I used my clearance and access for personal reasons. They'd be even unhappier if they knew about my involvement with a young girl whose bones were dug out of a riverbed. I'd be disgraced and tossed out on my ear in a New York minute."

"You do classified work?"

"Yes."

"On what?"

"Space-based laser communications for nuclear weapons platforms."

"Wow."

"No, shit, wow."

"That's the price you'll pay for the queen of hearts?"

Alex smiled his most gracious smile, took off his glasses and let Bobby catch a glimpse of Dr. Goldman. He sat up straight, pulled his shoulders back and chin up, and the fact that he was naked to the waist with his white, round, bourgeois tummy exposed only increased the effect.

"Dr. Goldman summers in the Hamptons," he said, deadpan. "Dr. Goldman reads the *Times* and *Journal* and the *New York Review of Books*. Dr. Goldman goes to conferences in Berlin and speaks German. Dr. Goldman knows how to comport himself in a safe room in the Pentagon. Dr. Goldman leads a sophisticated life on the Upper West Side and knows the first names of a dozen headwaiters as well as the names of their children and grandchildren. Dr. Goldman is successful, well-connected, intellectual, and rich."

Alex sniffed, relaxed his haughty manner and became Alex again. "Yes, Bobby, I'd lose my lab and my security clearance. I'm sure my wife Joanna would divorce me, and I'd probably never see my children again, or at least not for a long time."

What Alex didn't say was that the wizard of Alvarado Street didn't like Dr. Goldman very much. He'd rather play cards and think about nothing beyond the next hand.

"How many kids do you have?" Bobby asked.

"Four. Two with my first wife Naomi and two with Joanna. All girls."

"That's a heavy price to pay."

"No foolin'."

"You never told either of your wives anything? Didn't they ask about the tattoo?"

"Sure they asked. Women always ask. Joanna has tried for years to get me to have it removed. I lie. We all lie, make up a story, spin some bullshit, and that's that."

"So you know all about me. That's scary."

"No, not everything, only what's in the paper trail, and we never had any intention of using the information except to keep ourselves informed. We needed to know whether you were alive or dead, where you were, and who you lived with. We're your friends, Bobby, and we're not sitting judgment on you any more than on ourselves. We know the Army sent you to shrinks, and we worried about them. We worried about your being a junkie, because sometimes a junkie will say or do anything to score dope. We know you have two kids. Nelson has one although he's never been married, and Dean may have a dozen, but if he does, he doesn't know about them. He does have the finest wife on the planet, so I hear, but I've never met her."

"You will on Sunday," Dean said. "Billie's coming down to pick me up."

"Sunday's a long ways away. Whose deal? Nelson? What's the game?"

"Seven stud. Ante up."

Each in turn threw a white chip in the pot. Dealing, Nelson called out the cards, "A seven to Alex, a five to Dean, an eight to Bobby, a nine to Charlie, and another eight to the dealer."

"We know about you," Charlie said, "and it's only fair that you should know anything you want about us."

Bobby added it all up and the sum of his thoughts was that his old friends were scary and dangerous, methodically deceitful, and perhaps as crazy as he was. He peeked at his hole cards and said, "All I need to know about you, Charlie, is whether or not you learned to play this game. You're high, nine of clubs. Bet 'em or forget 'em."

# 18

Early on a foggy, wind-swept morning in June, 1963, the twenty-seven-foot cabin cruiser *Toot Sweet* and her crew of five left San Francisco bound for points east. The bay was choppy and all the boys except Dean, the skipper, suffered seasickness until the wind died and the fog burned off. Around ten o'clock as the boat entered the Carquinez Strait, the thermometer started to climb and the party began in earnest with a card game and a few beers—a sure cure for a queasy stomach. The *Toot Sweet* carried two twenty-gallon gas tanks and twelve cases of beer, and one of each was empty by the time the boat arrived in Sacramento around two in the afternoon.

An accomplished boat handler, Dean motored slowly into a marina to take on fuel. A little drunk, a flimsy tri-cornered hat perched on his crewcut, he shouted from the flying bridge, "Ahoy, me bawdies, bringin' her about. Look smart now."

Ready with a line, a red bandana tied around his head, Nelson manned the stern; Charlie, who in those days sported a wispy goatee, stood on the foredeck prepared to secure the boat to the dock. After navigating ninety miles from San Francisco, they felt like hardy mariners, ready for adventure. They were, to use an old phrase, higher than kites.

"Aye aye, cap'n," Nelson hollered as loud as he could.

Charlie sang out, "Easy now. Steady as she goes."

"Ha!" Dean laughed and demanded, "Do you have any idea what that means?"

"Not a clue! Hahaha!"

Bobby and Alex remained below playing five stud in the compact cabin. Hearing Dean bellowing like Captain Bligh, Bobby peered out a port hole and saw pilings sliding by and muddy water slick with kaleidoscopic oil film that dazzled in the bright sunlight. A few small boats were tied to floating docks. Weeds and Cyclone fence and dilapidated metal sheds in varying shades of rust lined the near riverbank.

The boat shuddered as Dean reversed the prop.

"Hmm," Alex pondered. "Maybe we should go up and see what's going on. What's the bet?"

"Half a buck on the four," Bobby said lazily. "You think Dean is sober enough to drive this boat?"

"So far, so good. Let's finish the hand, and I'll go up and smell his breath."

"Like hell! How're you gonna smell his breath when yours already smells like a brewery?"

"Hear, hear," Alex toasted, raising his can of Schlitz. "To the hops."

"To the grain," Bobby replied in kind.

"It's the water!" they both cried out and shared a laugh. They were enjoying heads-up poker while the others ran around the boat like little kids playing pirate. The engine stopped and suddenly the boat was quiet. They could hear little river wavelets slapping against the hull and the pilings of the floating dock. They finished the hand and Alex won for the eighth time in a row.

"Damn, you're a lucky son of a gun," Bobby swore.

Alex winked and said, "It's luck if you think so. I'm going up on deck."

On the bridge Dean tossed the hat aside and clamored to the dock to roust the attendant. He was walking back toward the boat with the gas man in tow when he saw her sitting on a bench near the gas pumps, blond and pretty, forlorn, chin on palms, elbows on knees, tiny suitcase by her side and transistor radio in her lap. She was wearing blue jeans and a pink blouse, and Dean asked the gas jockey who she was. He didn't know. Never saw her before. Fill 'er up?

She was watching him and watching the boat. A young girl on a dock had only a handful of possible reasons for being there, and Dean guessed she was waiting to join someone on a cruise.

"Hey," Dean said, face ruddy and sweating, trying to sound cool.

"Hey, yourself."

"You waiting for someone?"

"Maybe. What's it to you?"

She smiled and he read her as streetwise with her wits on a hair trigger.

"You from around here?" he asked.

"Uh-uh. No."

"Too bad," he said

"Why? Why is that too bad?"

"We could use a little help, you know, a pilot, a navigator."

"I don't know what that is. I don't know anything about boats."

Dean took a long look over the docks and water and the craft afloat around the marina, pointedly drawing her attention to the aquatic nature of their surroundings, and then said, "I suppose it's not as hot by the river as it was wherever you came from. What's your name?"

A string of different names she liked to use flashed though her mind, but because he was near her own age she told him her real name. "Sally," she answered. "Is this your boat?"

Dean turned to look over his shoulder at the white cabin cruiser to make sure she was talking about the *Toot Sweet*.

"I'm the captain," he declared with pride. "My name is Dean."

"What's that mean, 'Toot Sweet San Francisco'?"

"That's the name of the boat. It's sort of . . . French. It means 'Hurry Up' only it's spelled funny."

"So what it says is Hurry Up San Francisco? That's cute. Are you from there?"

"From San Francisco? We're from the city, yeah."

She walked toward him, swaying sexily and asking, "Are you going there?"

"We're headed the other way. We won't be going back for two or three days."

"How many—?" She looked past him and started counting the young men assembling in the stern. She counted three young high school or college guys with crewcuts, one of whom was Chinese or Japanese, and a fourth little guy with a scrawny beard. Savage adolescent horniness dripped out of them like sap.

"Five," Dean said.

"Ooo. All guys? From San Francisco?" If there were five, one was still invisible.

"Yeah, that's right."

"What are you guys? You look like, I dunno, pirates, only I bet you're not."

"We're gamblers," Dean said. "Riverboat gamblers."

She laughed. "My foot. You guys aren't gamblers. I bet you've never even been to Las Vegas."

"So what? We don't need Las Vegas. We have everything we need which is exactly one deck of cards."

She smiled up at the boys who were staring down at her from the after deck. "Do you really have everything you need?"

Watching the girl tease the boys, the gas man hollered, "Hey, kid, you got any money?"

Dean walked down the dock to pay for the gas, leaving Sally looking up at Nelson, Charlie, and Alex. She shifted her pose, placed her hands on her hips, and said, "Hi."

"Hello," Alex answered, trying to sound like an adult. "Who are you?"

"I'm Sally."

"What are you doing down here on the docks, Sally?"

"This is where I got dropped off," she said. "I was hitchhiking."

Alex furrowed his brow and asked, "Hitchhiking from where to where?"

"L.A. to San Francisco."

"Why? Don't you have any money? You can fly from L.A. for twenty dollars."

She considered several answers and considered her interrogator who looked Jewish and smart like a lot of kids from Hollywood. She happened to like wise guys, and so she said, "If I wanted to spend twenty bucks then I wouldn't be here on this dock talking to you, would I? Besides, hitchhiking is fun."

"And dangerous."

"I guess that depends on what you're afraid of, doesn't it?"

"You're running away," Alex stated flatly. "Tell me the truth."

"Yes."

"You're fifteen but you tell people you're eighteen."

"Sixteen."

"Why do you want to go to San Francisco?"

"Why not?"

"Tell the truth."

"I was born there, but I haven't been there since I was three."

"What are you running away from?"

She hesitated. In her view, her story was complex, tragic, and sad, and she wasn't inclined to tell the whole truth to strangers, no matter how attractive or useful.

"A foster home," she said.

"Bad scene?"

"Very bad scene."

"You're a lost soul," Alex pronounced. "And you want the *Toot Sweet* to transport you to paradise."

"Are you a poet?" she asked. "Some kind of beatnik?"

"No," he answered, surprised by the question. "I'm a mathematician."

"Don't mind Alex," Dean said, coming back. "The skinny one is Charlie and the Chinaman is Nelson and Bobby is around here somewhere. Down below. Bobby! Come up on deck, we have company."

In 1963 the epitome of teenage cool was Marlon Brando's eyes, Elvis Presley's hair, a smoldering Hells Angels swagger, and a pack of Luckies rolled up in the sleeve of a white T-shirt. The ace of diamonds suited Bobby like a birthmark. He rose up through the hatch like an angel from below, a can of Schlitz in one hand and a Lucky in the other and Sally caught her breath. Bobby instantly injected a charge into the tableau the way carbonation adds zest to beer. Before Bobby could say a word, Sally fell in love.

"Hey! What happened to the game?" Bobby complained, coming up the ladder and for some reason looking behind him, unconsciously showing off his tight jeans and a rakish, provocative mass of dark hair slicked back in a duck tail. "Are you guys gonna come back down and play, or what?"

He looked down onto the dock, saw Sally and blurted, "Oh, shit."

Her eyes wouldn't let go. They were light blue, the color of a high sky in the afternoon, tinged with cloudy gray around the edges, and he knew she wouldn't be fooled by his carefully constructed façade.

"Bobby," Alex said. "Meet Sally, our little runaway from the city of angels."

And Dean added, "She wants to come with us."

Girls fell in love with Bobby all the time, white girls, Chinese girls, black girls, all kinds of San Francisco girls, and he recognized a world of trouble when he saw it. Whether it was true or merely a fabricated Hollywood tradition, he remembered that women were supposed to be bad luck on boats. He swallowed a mouthful of beer and said, "Hey guys, let's leave her on the dock and get on up the river."

She didn't blink. She smiled and looked away from Bobby and enveloped each of the other boys one at a time in her gaze. Except for Charlie, their pulses raced and their dicks swelled inside their pants. "If you take me with you"—she paused to slide her tongue over her lips—"you won't regret it."

# 19

Every few hands the queen of hearts appeared and transported each player to his private vision of the past. The first time it came up, the red queen spoiled a nine high flush in diamonds for Charlie, and he threw in his hand with a groan.

"Four diamonds and then this. I swear, the card is cursed," he said, exasperated. "The hearts are drops of blood and the queen a taunting ghost."

"Superstitious twaddle," Nelson said to grunts of approval, but for a while no one could win with the queen of hearts in his hand. A little spooked, they continued to play until all the cards seemed freighted with obscure meanings as though the red and blue Bicycles had become tarot decks.

Finally, after the fickle queen ruined a ten high straight, Alex said to Bobby, "You wanted to leave her in Sacramento. Do you remember that?"

"Sure." Bobby closed his eyes and thought, here we go; the opening scenes of this movie play in slow motion with great clarity. "I remember you calling her a lost soul. I was still down below when I heard you and that's why I came up on deck."

"I was just trying to be cute. I had no idea what I was talking about."

"But you were right, and your words were ringing in my ears when I saw her. I thought, holy shit, if she wasn't lost before she met us, her fate would be sealed if she got on the boat. It doesn't matter now if I had a premonition, and I'm not sure it mattered then. You guys decided it was okay. She wanted to go and you outvoted me."

"There was no vote," Dean declared. "I was the captain. I decided."

"That's not true," Nelson contradicted immediately. "There *was* a vote. There was no show of hands but we voted with our dicks."

"Horseshit," Dean insisted.

"Do you really believe you decided by yourself that she could go, Dean?" Charlie's face contorted into a smirk. "My ass."

"That *is* the way I see it, damned straight. Everyone could see she fell for Bobby right away. Her eyes popped, but when you said"—he jerked a stubby finger toward Bobby—"'Leave her on the dock,' I guess she figured, what the hell, and made a play for all of us. If I'd said no, she never would have come on board, but that chick batted her eyes at me and licked her lips like Marilyn Monroe and turned me into a jellyfish."

"That sounds like voting with your gonads to me," Nelson said.

"Chicks know how to do that," Dean said. "Especially that one."

"No kidding," Bobby said sarcastically. "What's the point?"

Before Dean could answer with another angry expletive, Alex interjected. "The point is Dean has blamed himself all these years for allowing her on the boat, and that's not fair. Any of us could've said no, and that would have been that. As it was, only you said no, Bobby. We were eighteen and horny as hell and she was absolutely out of our league. You were the only one who could've said no to a sexy girl like that, and you did, but we didn't have enough sense to listen. You had girls hanging around you all the time, but not the rest of us. We were geeky, gawky teenagers lucky to get a taste of your leftovers. You were way ahead of us on that score and besides, you had that old black magic. That's what I remember."

Nelson grinned and chuckled and said, "Hey, Kimosabe, do you still have it?"

Gimme a break, Bobby thought, and added to himself, whatever it is you're talking about died that night.

The room was so still they could hear the city rumble. Four stories below, the hotel doorman blew a taxi whistle, and a moment later an engine raced in the street, followed by a squeal of brakes. A car door slammed shut and a journey began. Life went on. The city—

the world—was indifferent to their plight. What happened to them meant no more than the turn of a card.

He was fucking her and so drunk he passed out *in situ*. A real high school romeo. And when he woke up she was dead. That's all there was to it. Her skull was cracked, her skin was blue and she was dead.

Charlie drew back the drapes and admired the view up Montgomery Street to Telegraph Hill. He could see his house.

"Ah shit," Bobby said, sensing that if he played along they'd start to tell him whatever they brought him here to tell him. "I never thought about what Shanghai Bend did to you guys. I only know what it did to her."

"Fair enough," Alex said.

Another silence. Alex walked over to the cart and began cracking crab legs, loudly crunching the pink and white crustaceans. "Let's have a little music, what do you say? How about a little Miles Davis?"

"Yeah, yeah."

*Sketches of Spain*. Mellow tones, ancient rhythms, Miles the pure. They listened for a few minutes, and then Nelson asked Bobby, "Do you want to know who she was?"

"I thought she hasn't been identified."

"I said Yuba County hasn't identified her."

"But you have?"

Nelson opened his briefcase and took out the first document. "We knew three things: Her name was Sally, she came from L.A., and she was born in San Francisco. That's why I joined the LAPD, to get access to the right archives. Anyone can get a birth certificate for anybody, so this first document is a formality, and it gives us some important information. Her name was Sally Richfield, and she was born in San Francisco, which is what she told us. This is her birth certificate."

He handed Bobby the stiff, formal paper that registered a live birth at San Francisco General Hospital on May 28th, 1947.

"The rest is straightforward, really," he said. "The only means of identification in this case is dental work. The county medical examiner has X rays of her teeth that he's circulated statewide. A state forensics lab was able to approximate the date of death as between 1961 and 1965. The medical examiner's circular arrived in Los Angeles two weeks ago, and a trainee clerk was sent to look through a warehouse full of old microfiche records of missing persons from that era. The clerk will find nothing because all the records are right here. I took them out of the files twenty years ago, about the same time Dean moved to Verona."

Nelson handed Bobby a sheaf of documents, bulky, old dental X-ray film in manila envelopes, official police reports, and brittle, gelatinous sheets of microfiche. The last document was the Yuba County medical examiner's circular.

"You sure you got them all?"

"I think so. I can't think of anything I overlooked. I got all the duplicates, too."

"So what this means is when they go looking for records, they won't find anything."

"That's the idea."

"So you're home free."

"As far as Yuba County is concerned, they'll never identify her."

"Unless she has family," Bobby said. "Unless there's someone who's always been looking for her."

Charlie coughed, closed his eyes and thought of all the fishes in the sea.

"Is that the ghost that haunts you?" Alex asked.

"One of many," Bobby said, studying the documents. "Her birth certificate lists a mother and father."

"Correct."

Nelson handed Bobby two death certificates.

"Sally's mother died in San Francisco in 1950 when Sally was three. Her father died in Los Angeles in 1962 when she was fourteen."

"An orphan."

"Yes. When her mother died, her father took her to Los Angeles to be raised by his mother in Manhattan Beach. Her grandma became ill with cancer in 1961 and couldn't take care of her granddaughter. She died that year. The dad was out of the picture, a drunken bum—he died of cirrhosis of the liver—and Sally ended up in the care of the welfare department who placed her into a succession of foster homes. None of the foster fathers could keep his hands off her, and she ran away from three foster homes. The last foster family reported her missing *two months* after she left because they wanted the checks to keep coming. They never would have reported her if a social worker hadn't shown up for a routine check. They told her she disappeared the previous day when in fact she'd been gone for two months. I can't account for the first month before we met her. I can only guess."

"So who's left? Friends?"

"Nobody, Bobby. Only us. She had just about the worst luck a human being could have. He mother was a hooker and a junkie and her father was an alcoholic car thief in and out of prison. Her grandmother was an illiterate Okie who came to California in 1935 and worked in an aircraft factory for twenty-five years as a bolt inspector. When she retired, she was almost blind. She couldn't control her granddaughter. Sally was a wannabe surfer girl. She took care of the boys on the beach, and they took care of her."

Taking that statement with a grain of salt, Bobby said, "So she had friends. Beach people. Surfers."

"Maybe you could say that, and maybe not. If she'd had real friends, I don't think she would've tried to hitchhike to San Francisco. She hung out on the beach and stayed for a few days with whoever would take her in. The first two foster homes she ran away from reported her right away. The school authorities declared her a truant, yada yada, and this one social worker knew how to find her on the beach. The last time she was shocked to learn that no one had seen Sally for two months. The surfers were pretty loose, but they remembered Sally. The missing person report was filed on July 22, 1963, a month after we encountered her."

"The social worker. What about her?"

"I know her," Nelson said. "She's a lovely old lady who's long retired. As a matter of fact, she's a card player, a blue-haired demon who plays in Gardena. It's a small world."

"That's it? Nobody else?"

"Just us, Bobby."

"Jesus," Charlie said. "What time is it?"

"Almost two," Nelson said.

"So what do you want to do?" Bobby asked. "Lay it out."

"First we have to find out what really happened," Nelson said. "I'm pretty sure we have five different versions sitting at this table. We need to sort it out."

"And then?"

Alex broke his rule and performed his signature card trick, fanning a deck in which every card becomes the jack of diamonds. He winked and did it again and the entire deck was the queen of hearts.

Alex laughed. "Then we play cards. Even better, we play cards first and sort it all out later."

# 20

Dean hopped into the boat and glanced at Bobby who looked away, muttering, "There goes the game."

"We can still play," Alex said.

"Play what?" Bobby sneered. "Pin the tail on the donkey?"

"She's stranded," Nelson said earnestly. "It wouldn't be right to leave her here, a girl like that. She'll get in trouble."

Gazing down at Sally who stood on the dock smiling up at him like a teenaged vixen, Bobby said quietly, "Let's go inside and talk this over."

Below, Bobby took a seat at the table and waited until the others filed into the cramped galley.

"Nelson is right," he began. "She'll get in trouble because she is trouble. You guys don't see it. She's got you all excited, thinking you're gonna get laid like this was some dirty movie gang bang. You know what? That's bad news because if it happens you'll feel lousy and dirty and cheap. It isn't worth it. And the next thing you know she's running to the cops and we're in jail."

Charlie snickered and Alex rolled his eyes. Across the river a flock of coots thrashed river water into foam and lifted into the sky. Unseen, a train rumbled in the distance. The gas man had disappeared.

"If we don't take her," Alex said, "we'll spend the rest of our lives wondering what might have happened if we did."

"Nothing is going to happen," Bobby said.

"You never know."

"I'll tell you what," Bobby said, suddenly inspired. "Swear you won't touch her, and she can come on the boat. Otherwise, I'm going back to San Francisco right now."

"She's just a broad," Dean said. "Maybe we can have some fun. I'm the captain. It's up to me."

"Shut up, Dean," Bobby snapped. "You're the boat driver, not the captain. We don't have a captain. You swear to leave her alone, or I'm gone."

"Who are you all of a sudden, our daddy?" Dean demanded. "I think you just want her for yourself."

"You swear, or as far as I'm concerned this trip is over," Bobby insisted.

"What if she touches us?" Nelson said.

"You're not gonna let that happen, Nelson. That's what."

"You're serious," Charlie said.

"Damned straight. We've done a lot of shit together, all of us, but taking advantage of some girl who's lost and scared and alone is over the line."

"She doesn't look scared to me," Dean said. "She looks hot to trot."

"Bobby's right," Alex said, placing his hand over his heart. "Besides, we all saw how she looked at him. There's nothing to lose. I swear."

"Me, too," Charlie said with a little laugh. "You know I'm not going to touch her."

"Okay, let's do the right thing," Nelson agreed.

"Dean?"

"Oh, man, it ain't no big deal," Dean said. "All right. Cross my heart and hope to die. Ha! What a hoot."

"You better mean it, you big son of a bitch, or I'll have your ass."

"I'd like to see you try. Who is this guy?"

"He's just being Bobby," Alex said. "Humor him."

Bobby drummed his fingers on the table, fatigued by the constant play of threats and counterthreats. They'd done as he'd asked, yet he considered packing his gear and taking a hike anyway. Something had clicked in his mind and he saw his friends in a new light, as overgrown children with trashy minds and overactive hormones. As pals, a royal flush, they'd run their course and it was time to move on. In a few weeks he'd be in Berkeley strolling through Sather

Gate and pitting his wits against the big brains on Telegraph Avenue. If he bolted, he'd have to hitchhike to San Francisco and explain to his parents why he was there—it wasn't gonna happen. Maybe it would be all right. Maybe the girl would behave and allow the boys to act like gentlemen. He picked up a deck and began shuffling while the others trooped back up on deck.

"Hey!" he heard Dean shouting to Sally, still on the dock. "You coming?"

Sally grabbed her suitcase and radio and scrambled onto the *Toot Sweet* before the boys could change their minds. By teasing them to get aboard, she'd created a ticklish situation. She knew what "You won't regret it" meant to them and hoped she didn't regret having said it, but after one look at Bobby she'd made up her mind to say anything to get on the boat. It had happened so fast, out of the blue, but once she was on the deck, theatrically patting her chest and catching her breath, she saw the boys were merely boys, a species she understood. They were close, one girl and four boys standing in the compact stern of the boat, close enough for her to smell beer on their breath. She made them nervous.

"I'm dealing," Bobby shouted from the cabin, and that's when Sally noticed the tattoos. In 1963, an era of crumbling conservatism when tattoos on middle-class youth were almost unheard of symbols of rebellion, she guessed their defiance was only skin deep.

"You guys are really nice to take me along. I won't get in anybody's way."

"It's a small boat," Dean said. "We can show you around."

Touring the tight spaces of the twenty-seven-foot cabin cruiser, the galley, and forward cabin with two bunks, they tripped over themselves staring at her ripe chest while trying desperately not to touch her. Amused, when the brief tour ended she resolved their confusion by stationing herself on a deck chair on the polished mahogany bow.

Dean started the engine, they cast off the lines, and the journey up the river started anew. Within a few minutes Sacramento was a haze in the southern sky.

They weren't kidding about being gamblers. While the big one drove, the others played poker in the cabin, the crude, exuberant sounds of the game drifting up from below like pungent clouds of smoke.

"Pair of fours bets a dime."

"See your dime and raise a quarter."

"See your quarter and raise another two bits."

"On a pair of fours? You gotta be kidding."

"Put up or shut up, man. C'mon."

"Okay. I see your two bits. Whaddya got?"

"There it is—trips. Three of a kind, the two fours you see, and presto, from the hole, the four of hearts, the whore of farts. Haha."

Upstream from the state capital the river changed color with astonishing quickness. The *Toot Sweet* chugged along, engine generating a pleasant exhaust note, the water reflecting a palette of green from the trees and brambles along the banks. Suddenly, the wake from another boat would rock the cruiser and turn the river into a stream of gleaming metal. Straight down alongside the bow the water was dark green and murky brown speckled with flakes of pure light. Sally remembered from the eighth grade that gold had first been discovered near Sacramento, and as far as she knew it might have been at that exact spot. It looked rustic enough, and she could imagine miners toiling in the sun with pan and sluice box. That made her feel like a pioneer, a circumstance that suited her just fine. She liked Westerns.

Above and behind her on the flying bridge, guzzling beer and indulging in the crudest pornographic fantasies his overheated mind could concoct, Dean was having difficulty keeping the boat in the channel. Suddenly he kicked down the throttle and yanked the wheel to avoid a snag near the eastern bank, almost spilling Sally into the water. She grabbed a handrail and twisted around, shouting, "Hey!"

When the boat suddenly swerved to the left and tilted deep to the right, chips and cards slipped off the table and clattered onto the deck. Charlie fell off his chair and beer cans rattled in the galley.

"Christ. What the hell was that?"

"Dean's so toasted I don't think he could drive a toy boat in a bathtub."

"Well, damn, if this ain't up shit creek without a paddle. Who can drive this tub? Nelson?"

"No way."

"Maybe the broad."

"I don't think so."

"I can," Bobby said, rising from the table and climbing the ladder. "It ain't no big thing."

"Studley," he hollered from the stern, "you can't drive the boat anymore. You're drunk."

Dean drained a can of Schlitz, hooked the empty into the river and firmly grasped the wheel, eyes dead ahead. "Go fuck a duck, McCorkle."

"I'm gonna drive."

"What? You can't do that. That's mutiny."

"That's what it is, yes sir, a rebellion at sea."

"This is my boat."

Bobby stepped up to the bridge and laid his palm on Dean's cheek. "I'll go into the engine compartment and pull the distributor cap and close the gas valve, Dean. Either let me drive the boat, or we drift back down the river all the way to the bay."

"Shit."

"C'mon, man. Go play cards."

Dean took off his tri-cornered hat and dramatically tossed it into the river. Laughing, he abandoned the bridge and, casting a soulful glance at Sally, went below, yelling, "Who wants to play low hole card wild?"

"No wild cards, goddammit!"

Bobby knew next to nothing about boats and quickly discovered that turning the wheel to the left made the stern swing to the right. Furthermore, the current affected the boat's direction. When he pushed the throttle lever, engine noise increased but forward progress as measured by the shore was less than expected. Meanwhile, shouts of glee rose from the cabin as Dean joined the game and attacked the cards with zeal.

The river was mellow, Huck Finn–like in its serenity, and he was alone above deck with a mystery named Sally. She watched him experiment with the controls, gently zigzagging the boat against the current, and after a few minutes she asked, "Do you know how to drive a boat?"

Pretending to ignore the question, he tried to keep a straight face but after a few seconds he cracked a smile.

"No, but I'm learning."

"Should I be scared?"

He laughed, saying, "I'm scared, but if we're going to get up the river, someone has to run the boat."

"At least you're honest."

"No, I'm not," he said. "I lie all the time."

She thought that was cute. "Me, too," she said, and when he said nothing, she asked, "Where are we going?"

"You ask a lot of questions."

"Is that so bad?"

"Another question."

"Why didn't you want me to come with you?"

"Like machine-gun bullets, zow zow zow. Maybe I'll just pull over to the side and put you ashore."

He turned the wheel a little to the right and the stern came around and began pushing the boat toward the river bank. Fifty yards east of the wooded bank a thirty foot levee supported a highway where a semi rolled south toward Sacramento.

She couldn't tell if he was serious, but in case he was, she said, "If you want me to get off, I will. Just tell me why."

Bobby realized that at one level the answer was: Because you're a girl who asks too damned many questions. With that in mind, he said, "This would be a good time to lie, but I'll tell you the truth. There's five of us, see, and we've known each other since we were little, and in a few weeks we're all going our separate ways. We got this boat to have one last adventure together, to go up the river as far as we can go and play cards as long as the money holds out. With you here, well, that makes you the adventure, you understand? And that wasn't the idea. It changes the equation."

"Hmmm."

"Do you understand 'equation'?"

Bobby spoke this last question in such an undertone that Sally had to get out of her chair and climb to the flying bridge to continue the conversation.

"I'm not a dummy," she said. "I'm just trying to get to San Francisco."

"We're going the other way. Those trucks on the highway are going to the city."

"I'm sick of truckers, if you want to know the truth. They're nasty."

"I bet they're not sick of you."

"Are you?"

Bobby had to admit that he liked her feistiness, but liking her only made her presence more complicated.

"You know you drive these guys crazy," he said. "You do it on purpose."

"I just want to get to San Francisco. I told you."

"What's so special about San Francisco? It's just a city."

"I won't know until I get there, will I? I heard about beatniks. Maybe I can be a beatnik."

Bobby cracked up. His high school class had included an inordinate number of baby beatniks, Charlie and Alex among them, who listened to jazz inside the cage at the Blackhawk and flocked to North Beach to hang out in cafes with eccentric refugees from the East Coast who wore sandals and buttons that said Ban the Bomb. Beatniks were interesting, almost as interesting as the hysterical reaction they provoked in some quarters. Sally didn't look like beatnik material to him, but her mentioning the beats hinted that she might be something more than an empty-headed surfer girl. He figured she'd earned a reprieve and steered back toward the middle of the river.

"What do you think a beatnik is?" he asked.

With that question Sally knew she had him.

"I think a beatnik must be everything people don't like," she said. "My grandmother said they're communists. She said they're dirty and against God and the American way and they smoke watcha-macallit."

"Reefer."

"I guess that's it. I don't know what it is."

"What it is is dope, marijuana," Bobby said. "It's illegal."

"I'd like to try it sometime. I'd like to try everything, especially everything you're not supposed to try."

"Oh, boy," Bobby said. "You're jail bait. You know what that is?"

"You keep asking me if I know what things are. I know exactly what jail bait is," she exclaimed in a hoarse voice that startled him with its intensity. "That's what my last foster father called me, the bastard."

"Is that why you ran away?"

She sighed and fished in her jeans for a rumpled box of Newports. Bobby popped open his Zippo, and with the flame came a flash between their eyes.

"Thanks," she said, drawing stylishly on her cigarette. "I was bored. The only really cool people I know are surfers, you know, and, well, they're surfers. All they care about is the ocean and the waves and the beach and, that's all right, I suppose, but for me, I just got bored. I can't even swim." She giggled. "I lived a block from the beach, and every day and all night the waves are sloshing in from I don't where, Japan or Hawaii or someplace, and it was always the same and I got bored. So I left."

"To become a beatnik."

She smiled. "That would be fun, but the truth is I have to find a job. I'll probably become a waitress. It's the only thing I know how to do. I don't care. I want to see the Golden Gate Bridge. Is it beautiful?"

"I don't know," Bobby said as though the idea had never occurred to him, which it hadn't. "I just go across it to get to wherever I'm going."

"I hope it is beautiful," Sally said with a dreamy smile. "It is in the movies."

# 21

At ten minutes to three in the morning a steaming pot of room service coffee occupied the center of the card table. Four miles west, fog rushed through the Golden Gate and into the bay, obliterating Alcatraz and ending the heat wave everywhere except the Enrico Caruso Suite on the fourth floor of the Palace Hotel.

They were telling the story now, slowly, painfully reconstructing a hot summer day in the Sacramento Valley, quibbling over details, adding nuance and interpretation, groping like blind men for some semblance of truth. Bobby's conversations with Sally came back in a rush, and he repeated oddly dated words and phrases he scarcely remembered—*beatnik, Golden Gate Bridge, jail bait*. The more he plunged into long-suppressed memory banks, the more he realized the only thing he remembered clearly was Sally. Once she was aboard the boat, he hadn't paid much attention to anything else.

"You made us swear we wouldn't touch her," Alex said. "Do you remember that?"

They were staring again, inspecting him, measuring his response against an invisible benchmark. Reminded, he started to recall their swearing to keep their hands off Sally—that segment in his memory was fuzzy if not blank.

"If there was any nobility that day no matter how childish or melodramatic, your making us swear was the saving grace," Alex continued. "You called a caucus and made a speech about jumping ship if we didn't swear, and so we did."

"You wanted her on the boat," Bobby said. "You said if we didn't take her, we'd spend the rest of our lives wondering what would've happened if we did. That's a pretty fair irony, as it turned out."

"You got that right," Dean added. "Instead, we've spent thirty years wondering what might have happened if we didn't."

Bobby shook his head. The Feather River had tormented him in many ways, but not that way. "Maybe you did, pal, but not me. What if, what if, that's a waste of time. What if Kennedy hadn't been assassinated? That's bullshit. What happened happened, and you can't change the past."

"If you know what it is," Dean rebuked.

"Don't we?"

"I think," Alex said, lighting a Lucky, "we may be raising questions we can't answer."

"Or asking the wrong questions," Bobby said.

"Okay, what's the right question?"

"*Whose deal is it?*" Nelson roared, drumming a loud conga beat on the felt. "Let's get some money into this game. Come on. Yak yak yak yak yak."

"You ahead or behind?"

"Don't you know it's bad luck to count your money at the table, Charlie?"

"More superstitious twaddle, to use your words, Nelson. Besides, you've been counting your chips all night."

"I'm a do as I say cop, not a do as I do cop."

"Very funny. Ha ha. It's Bobby's deal."

"Five draw, jacks or better."

They tossed in their antes, and Bobby thought his old friends were just too damned cute, too smug, too quick with the sharp remark. He didn't trust their documents or confessions of overweening guilt. Curiously, as they loosened up and discussed the details of their trip—the boat, the river, Sally, and her extraordinary effect on them—the game became less predictable. Perennial losers Charlie and Nelson were winning; Dean, playing erratically, was losing; and Alex was barely breaking even. Ahead, but not by much, Bobby decided to change his style of play and turn up the heat.

He dealt a hand of draw, Charlie and Nelson checked, and Alex opened for five hundred. Dean stayed in and Bobby, with three fives, an ace, and a six, raised a thousand. Alex saw the raise and Dean dropped.

"Now I want some Elvis," he said, getting up to change the record.

Alex took two cards and Bobby kept the ace and took one. The five of clubs. Four fives.

As usual Alex glanced at his hand and left his cards where they lay, then planted his elbows on the table and chin on the backs of interlocked fingers.

"A thousand," he said and placed two bumblebees in the pot.

"See your grand and raise—"

There was a sizzle, a flash, a loud bang, and all the lights in the suite went out. The stereo stopped dead, leaving Elvis six bars into "All Shook Up."

"What the—?"

Charlie rushed to the window and reported, "The lights are on outside. It's not a power failure."

Dean strode to the front door and yanked it open. "Lights in the corridor."

"It's just this suite," Charlie said, picking up a telephone. "I'd better call the front desk. This is too much. Next year we go to the Saint Francis."

Alex stood on a chair and used his lighter to illuminate the light fixture. "This is weird," he said. "Too damned weird." He cautiously tapped the bulb, unscrewed it, and climbed onto the table to examine the temporary fixture installed for the game.

Bobby remained in his seat, calmly watching the Chinese fire drill unfolding around him. Dean came back to the table, dug into his bag, and pulled out the rum box that contained twenty-five thousand dollars.

"What's going on, Deano?" Bobby asked.

"I don't know, but I don't like it. Got to protect this, no matter what."

"Forget the box," Alex said. "Cover the bags, Studley."

"Nelson?"

"You got me. Maybe a short-circuit or blown circuit breaker."

"They're sending up a repairman," Charlie said, hanging up. "The guy says he's going to check the control panel down the hall."

"What the hell?" Alex squinted and poked his face closer to the metal fixture, now blackened and blistered and hot to the touch. "What's this?" He pulled a long, thin wire and tiny microphone away from the device and dangled the contraption in the air. With a long face he announced, "We've been bugged."

"Bugged?"

"Oh, Christ."

Bobby's face went white and he jerked to his feet, his mouth opening to speak but he couldn't bring himself to utter a single expletive. If he stayed in the room another five seconds, he'd explode. Eyes blazing contempt, he grabbed his shirt and coat and hustled out the door and down the corridor past the elevators toward the stairs, pulling on his shirt.

"Bobby! Wait! Oh, shit."

Suddenly realizing what had happened, Alex pointed an accusing finger at the policeman and hissed, "Nelson, you didn't. Oh, Jesus, you did."

"This is your stunt?" Charlie screeched.

"It's just a mike and wire and cherry bomb," Nelson said, laughing. "They're not attached to anything except a timer to make it go bang and cause a short. It went off right on time at three o'clock."

"God *damn*, Nelson," Alex fumed as he climbed off the table. "You freaked him. He doesn't know about the stunts. What were you thinking?"

No athlete, Alex started running clumsily down the corridor just as Bobby disappeared into the stairwell. In shape and much quicker, Nelson quickly passed a huffing Alex, shouting, "Go back to the suite and sit tight. I'll bring him back."

Alex stopped and leaned against a wall, groaning, "Don't give it all away, Nelson. Just enough to get him back."

Leaving Alex wheezing in the corridor, Nelson pushed into the stairwell and heard Bobby tramping down the stairs two floors below.

"Bobby!"

No answer.

"Bobby! I put the mike in the lamp. It was a joke. There's no tape recorder. Bobby! Stop! I can explain!"

"You can't explain shit, Chinaman! Fuck you!"

"It was a joke, Kimosabe."

"Not funny."

Descending the stairs three at a time, Nelson caught his quarry in the empty lobby and gently touched his shoulder. The ground floor of the hotel was so quiet they heard a streetcar rattle by on Market Street.

"Bobby, wait, please."

The plea echoed through the deserted foyers that opened into the lobby. Emitting a primal groan, Bobby pulled away from the brotherly touch but stopped short of the doors. He turned, arms loose at his side, poised and ready, and faced his old friend.

"Wait for what? The cops?"

Breathing hard, Nelson bent over to catch his breath, his words coming in spurts. "No cops . . . No one . . . Nothing . . . at the other end . . . of the wire . . . It's part of our . . . game . . . goofy stunts . . . I do something crazy every year . . . I guess this was the wrong year for this. I'm sorry."

Teetering on the brink of control, hands clenching into fists, Bobby fought a temptation to strike. A disturbing vision of Nelson bleeding profusely onto the white marble floor splashed across his mind. He let it fade. Across the lobby, a lone clerk behind the registration desk was watching.

Standing up straight, Nelson recognized the menace in Bobby's eyes and sensed he'd pushed his old friend too far. Raising his hands, he took a step back, repeating, "It was only a stunt, a practical joke."

"A joke?"

"Yeah."

"On me?"

"On everyone. The guys didn't know. They were just as surprised as you. Look, I knew it was going to be tense during the game, so

I thought I'd create a little fun, you understand? Help lighten up. Looks like it backfired."

The notion of the game being recorded sent a shiver of revulsion down Bobby's spine. A tape could damage them all. Alex had admitted using his security clearance for personal ends; Nelson had described overstepping his authority as a cop; Dean had talked about his marijuana business; and all of them, including Charlie, had talked about Shanghai Bend. Would someone intending to bug the room be so inept that he'd cause a short-circuit in a light fixture? No. Nelson was telling the truth. It had to be a joke. It was too stupid to be anything else. Bobby felt his fear and anger drop away like a suit of wet clothes, leaving him drained and annoyed but no longer on the brink of violence. In spite of an adrenaline edge he wanted to laugh. He lit a cigarette, drawing a scowl from the clerk.

"Some joke," he said, shaking his head. "I had a good hand."

"The breaks," Nelson mumbled.

"I haven't moved so fast in years."

Every sound echoed across the lobby. Phone to his ear, the clerk was still watching them. Nelson scuffed his Nikes on the marble floor creating an eerie screech.

"You used to do crazy stunts all the time," Nelson said, revealing his nervousness by speaking low and fast. "How d'you think I learned? You put a smoke bomb in the school vents and cleared the building so you wouldn't have to take a history test, remember?"

"We're not high school kids anymore, Nelson."

"Sure, and I know it's foolish, but once a year we act like we are. I suppose it's our pathetic way of dealing with"—Nelson paused before adding—"the past."

Bobby choked on a guffaw, thinking his old friends dealt with the past the same way he did, by not dealing with it, ignoring it, denying it, pushing it to the far corners of their minds. They hadn't learned to live with it any better than he had.

"With practical jokes and the game and the bullshit, we've been dancing around the past all night," Bobby said, puffing his Winston and sending a cloud of gray smoke toward the elegant ceiling. "The game isn't going anywhere."

"Excuse me, sir!" The clerk was gesturing frantically from the desk. "There's no smoking in the—"

Bobby turned away from Nelson and spun through the revolving doors onto the sidewalk. Expecting bright lights, big city, he found a ghost town. The bars had closed at two and the city, debauched and spent, awaited tomorrow's hangover. With stomach churning and sweat running down his back, Bobby rocked on his soles, heel and toe, heel and toe, breathing the fresh night air and furiously struggling to slow his thoughts.

What really happened to Sally? The discovery of her grave changed nothing except the psyches of his old friends. They were spooked. The documents, real or forged, made no difference to him. What did make a difference was knowing the boys from Noë Valley had had thirty-two years to prepare for his return, a lifetime to refine a script, but Nelson's stunt had thrown a monkey wrench into their carefully crafted agenda.

Nelson had followed him outside and stood near the doors, hands in pockets. Watching him, Bobby gained control of his thoughts, if not his emotions, and his cunning emerged from the shadows. He had no doubt they planned to fuck him over, but there was a chance Nelson would let slip a telling revelation if he prolonged their separation from the others. The old Nelson, the kid he used to know, fearless Crazy Nelson, had been a loyal friend, a genuine sidekick who called him Kimosabe. That had been great, but he needed to know if the new, badge-and-gun toting Nelson was capable of screwing up his life with cops and district attorneys. Or had the old Nelson betrayed him on the Feather River? Those were the real questions.

A lone taxi, engine idling, waited for a fare in the hotel cab stand. Bobby bent over to peer in, hoping to see Driver. Alas, an old man in a flat cap sat at the wheel.

"Anything open around here?" Bobby asked.

"No, sir, nothing. What're you looking for, sport?"

"What about Twenty-fourth and Church?"

"You want to go to Noë Valley? That's way 'cross town."

"I'm glad you know where it is. What's open out there?"

The driver thought for a moment and said, "An all-night dough-nut shop. Favorite of the police."

"Perfect."

Bobby opened the car door and slid into the back seat. Nelson walked over and looked down at Bobby sitting in the cab.

"So is this it?" the policeman asked. "No good-bye? No hand-shake? No nothin', Kimosabe?"

"Why should I stay? I can go home and wait for a knock on the door."

"There won't be a knock on your door, Bobby, not now, not ever, but we have a lot more to tell you. We're just getting started."

"You want to talk? Okay. Let's take a ride."

"What about the game?"

"The game will keep," Bobby said. "Get in the cab, Nelson."

# 22

A hotel repairman happily pocketed a twenty and exited the suite, leaving a new fixture that illuminated the table with the familiar cone of light.

Dean had passed out and was snoring loudly on the living room couch, Charlie lay on a bed in one of the bedrooms watching a rerun of *I Love Lucy*, and Alex sat at the card table playing solitaire. He laid out a hand and immediately began to cheat, flipping over a buried deuce of clubs. The *William Tell* Overture played on the stereo.

Charlie shouted over the music, "How much will Nelson tell him?"

"Hopefully enough to get him back," Alex shouted in return.

"Dean almost blew it, you know."

"It really doesn't matter, Charlie," Alex said, dropping his voice to a whisper. "In the end, it's just a card game."

# 23

A king of spades painted on the door identified the taxi as King Kab
209. The night had turned balmy, sensuous, fragrant with jasmine.
They rode in silence, Nelson wisely keeping quiet. Bobby opened the
window and let the wind evaporate the sweat on his neck. In the distance the deep bass of a foghorn sounded, and he could feel lifetimes
rolling in with the great Pacific fog bank. Ah, God, he sighed, the
memories searing his mind's eye, warm evenings in Saigon, a silky
night on the Feather River, freezing winters at Checkpoint Charlie in
Berlin, images dissolving one into the next and superimposed on dark
streets that held their own vast stores of secrets.

Bobby knew what terrified the boys from Noë Valley—like revealing tells in a poker game their fear announced itself in blazing
lights from the dark marquee of the Orpheum Theater at Eighth
and Market—*The Secret of Shanghai Bend*—he saw it on the tow-
ering billboards that lined the board boulevard—*Thrills Galore Based
on a True Story*—he read it in the ads on the back of the taxicab's
front seat—*The Curse of the Queen of Hearts*—the lurid promotional
copy of a dime novel, a B-movie, a TV special of the week. *The
truth shall make you free.* Yea, brother, free from what? Bobby had
stepped into the abyss of freedom long ago, and he'd embraced his
freedom like his uniform. The boys didn't have a clue; they were
like civilians or slaves or robots or clones: dumbbells without a fucking clue.

Twenty-fourth Street was a ten minute ride across the deserted
city. As the cab moved away from downtown, the slick new buildings on Market Street gave way to Victorians with bay windows and
gaudy false fronts, the familiar city of Bobby's childhood. Rattling
over the streetcar tracks on Church street triggered his oldest mem-

ories, childhood rides on the J car to explore the mysteries of the fishwharf where Charlie's father operated a fleet of boats, racing around in Dean's Impala, picnics in Dolores Park, making out with girls on dark side streets in the fog—benign, innocent, sentimental memories that Bobby had quashed for many years and was reviving now, bitterly, he realized, in order to pry a secret out of Nelson Lee.

They were deep in the city now, miles from the Palace Hotel and the places tourists visit. As the cab climbed the hill alongside verdant Dolores Park, in the shadows of a pedestrian bridge over the street-car tracks Bobby caught a glimpse of furtive movement, and his infallible junkie's radar detected dope and dope dealers. The innocence of his thoughts vanished in an instant.

Nelson saw the same flash of watchcaps and hooded eyes in the bushes. The policeman smirked and chuckled. It wasn't his beat.

"Do you ever come back here?" Bobby asked as the taxi crested Liberty Hill and dropped into the wide ravine on the east side of Twin Peaks called Noë Valley.

"Sure. My mom still lives here."

"This is us, Nelson. This is where we come from. These streets are the paths of our souls."

"If you believe that, why didn't you ever come back?"

"You really want to know? It was because I was going to show Sally the city, and since she never made it, there was nothing for me here. I couldn't come back and go to Berkeley, just across the bridge, because that was too close. When Sally was taken away, my life exploded. It sounds corny, but my heart was broken. I didn't want to see anyone or talk to anyone or answer any questions. To tell you the truth, I wanted to run away and join the French Foreign Legion, but it was too far away. It was easier to enlist in the army, and that worked out fine. It got me far away."

Nelson became very still in his corner of the back seat. The taxi arrived at 24th and Church, a well-lit corner whose cluster of shops was closed except for the doughnut shop and a laundromat across the street. A black and white patrol car was parked in the bus stop in front of the doughnut shop. Inside, two uniformed cops, the only customers, occupied the rear table.

The meter read twelve bucks. "Can you wait fifteen minutes?" Bobby asked the driver, handing him two twenties. "Get yourself a cup of coffee."

Bobby got out of the cab, waited for Nelson, and led him across the street to the laundromat. It was empty and they were alone.

Shiny new washers and dryers surrounded a large folding table in the center of the bright and spiffy laundry. Cowboy boots clicking on the floor, fingers popping in a quick rhythm, Bobby walked around the table peering into the dryers until he came up with a faded green terrycloth towel. Suddenly, he twisted it into a rope and snapped it at Nelson like they were kids in a locker room. *Whap*!

"Hey!" Nelson protested.

"You people are fucking with me, you know that?" *Whap whap*. Bobby advanced and Nelson retreated around the table. "I hate being played for a sucker, you know what I mean?" *Whap*. "It pisses me off."

Bobby stopped his mock attack, wiped his face and neck with the freshly laundered towel and tossed it into a washing machine. Grinning at Nelson, he fed quarters into the appliance and started the cycle.

"It all comes out in the wash, hey, Nelson?"

"You forgot soap."

"I forget a lot of things," Bobby quipped. "I have a very selective memory."

He walked over to the windows and peered across the street at the doughnut shop. The taxi driver was sitting two tables away from the cops.

"Would you rather talk in front of those cops?" Bobby asked.

"Pass."

"I thought so. You know, I don't think there was a doughnut shop there when we were kids. It was a diner. I remember the grocery store next door because, as we used to say, it was the corner store that wasn't because the diner was on the corner. I'm pretty sure it was a diner, a little restaurant with a counter. Care for a doughnut, Nelson? I could go for a real greasy maple bar myself."

"What do you want, Bobby? You hijacked me across town to our old neighborhood for what? A fit of nostalgia? I'm not sentimental. What are you looking for in a damned Laundromat of all places?"

"What do I want? What do *I* want? I don't want anything. The question is what do *you* want? It's three-thirty in the morning, nobody's around, we're on the old corner where we used to hang out. It's a good place to come clean, don't you think?"

"Come clean about what?"

"You guys are close to panic, Nelson, and it seems like you're afraid of me. You can't be afraid of anyone else because you've got that covered, according to you. Birth certificates, dental records, very impressive."

"We thought we had everything covered at Shanghai Bend, but it got uncovered, didn't it?"

"So what? Dean claimed that was inevitable. Why didn't you leave me in peace? What difference does my being here make? I would have been content to live my life and live with what I live with."

"Maybe you can live with it, Bobby, but not the rest of us. When it was all over and we had to come back without you, we had to lie and say we had a fight over the poker game and you took off. You just walked away and we had no idea where you were. You called your mother the next day and said you were joining the Army, and after that the lies generated more lies and they never stopped. We can't live with that anymore."

"Too bad. You have to play the hand you're dealt."

"That's right, and we were dealt a wild card."

"Me?"

"Yeah. You're crazy. You're a junkie and a drunk and a gambler and completely unpredictable."

"Well, excuse me for stepping off the straight and narrow path of bullshit respectability. You don't like it? Then jump off the fucking bridge, Nelson. This is not my problem."

Tormented, unsure what to say because he felt responsible for the fate of everyone in the Enrico Caruso Suite, Nelson plunged his hands into his pockets and kicked at the floor.

"Look," Bobby said. "This whole thing seems scripted which is fucked if everyone has seen the script except me."

"That's because we talk about Shanghai Bend every year, and you don't. It's new to you, this dredging up the past, going over every detail, trying to find out what happened."

"And you think I know?"

"Do you?"

"I can guess."

"Guesses aren't good enough, Bobby."

"What else is there?"

"You believe we killed her."

"That's right."

"Well? What are you going to do about it?"

Bobby leaned back against a washing machine, flashed his charismatic grin, and lit a Winston. "You've got balls, Nelson, I'll give you that. I think you know what happened. You've always known. I'll tell you something. I had a few hours with a girl named Sally and that's all there was, a few hours—I figured it out, thirteen hours and maybe thirty minutes, and during those few hours she changed me. She saw things I didn't see, and she opened my eyes. She was like a drug and I became instantly addicted. I went to the moon, Nelson, to the galaxies. No shit. I painted the *Mona Lisa* and she was the model. Can you understand me? I loved her. Because of Sally, I became something different, but Nelson, Nelson, that was a long time ago. Sally was—like turning a page and everything suddenly changes from black and white to color. Then, after half a day, she was gone, but I was changed. I took something of her away and that's all of her there is. Your shitty pile of papers isn't Sally. Resurrecting her is not my idea of fun especially when it's done according to your agenda. Like the way you laid out documents, and Dean told his story, and Alex told his story. You planned it."

"You're damned right we planned it, but we're not trying to do a number on your head. We're not trying to get you into any kind of trouble. We want you to listen to what we have to say, and, yes, we've been planning what to say for thirty years. This is a trial, but it's not you who's in the dock, Bobby. Oh, no. It's us. You're the judge and jury."

# 24

Little Eva's "Loco-Motion" rocked out of Sally's transistor radio, beaming a sexy top-forty beat over the placid waters of the Sacramento River. Sally knew the lyrics and the moves, and to Bobby's amazement he was dancing like a choo-choo on the flying bridge of the *Toot Sweet*.

"See, you do it like this," Sally instructed, elbows pumping like pistons, hips swaying like the little engine that could. "Come on, baby, chugga chugga chugga."

Soon there'll be touching, he thought; she'll take my arm or rub her tits against me while she slides by in the confined space. With his head swimming upstream against a flood current of lust, he thought, Jesus, I gotta drive the boat.

"No more dancing," he declared, gripping the wheel tightly. "Go back to your chair or we're gonna have a shipwreck."

Sally bumped him with her hip and said, "Oh-kay," splitting the word into two long syllables. Bobby made her feel safe, and so with a smile and a playful salute, she settled into the chair to watch the river roll by.

In the late afternoon millions of bugs swarmed over the water, raising the fish which naturally multiplied the number of fishermen. Suddenly, guys in outboards sprouted like tules from the river, churning the water and casting lines into schools of shad. At the wheel, laughing and having a grand old time, Bobby waved cheerfully at passing boats and swatted at mosquitoes, often with the same motion.

To Sally, the rural Sacramento Valley struck her as so different from Los Angeles that the only thing comparable to her journey on the river was the Jungle Cruise at Disneyland, an E ticket ride for sure. Fresh water, strange sounds, new colors, bugs, fishermen, an occasional small log floating by, glimpses through levee breaks of vast fields and orchards, rusted farm equipment, swooping red-tailed hawks, the bright yellow of dried grasses on the steeply banked levees. Sally was enchanted; her heart moved. Like Alice in Wonderland, she'd slipped into another dimension. As the *Toot Sweet* made way slowly upriver, her radio added to the unreality by broadcasting Chuck Berry's East Saint Louis boogie and street corner doo wop from Philadelphia. *And to top off the set here's the fantastic harmonics of California's own, the fabulous Beach Boys.* America was cross-pollinating itself on the radio.

Sally snapped her fingers and sang along with "Little Deuce Coupe." The sun was sinking in the west and half the river fell under the shadow of the levee. Ahead, the levees gradually receded several hundred yards to create a flood plain for rice paddies. The setting sun flashed long streaks of red across the water, an alien river on an alien planet. Two hours from Sacramento the last top-forty station faded into static, and when Sally fiddled with the dial, all she could find was hillbilly music from Yuba City. Patsy Cline and Johnny Cash. She turned it off and listened to the boat, the river, and the bugs. The boys in the cabin below had been quiet for half an hour.

"This is so peaceful," she said to Bobby. "You aren't angry anymore, are you?"

"No. It's okay."

The boat was making way slowly now, skirting snags—huge tree limbs that had barreled downstream in the previous winter's storms and embedded themselves in the bottom creating submarine hazards like organic icebergs. Bobby figured if he hit one, the trip was over and he'd turn around and go back toward Sacramento. Unless they sank.

"There's a lot of angry people in L.A.," Sally said, looking up at an angry red sky. "Is it like that in San Francisco?"

"Angry at what?" he asked.

"Oh, I don't know. The system, or because you're black or white or Mexican. Stuff like that."

"I suppose there's people like that everywhere," Bobby said. "I don't know about any system."

"That's because you're part of it and don't know it."

"Oh, yeah?"

"Yeah. You're part of the system, Bobby McCorkle. You toe the line, walk the straight and narrow, don't break any laws, stay in school, and do what you have to do to become a respectable member of society who doesn't rock any boats, especially this one."

"Like hell. I break plenty of laws."

"Oh, yeah? Name one."

"I drink beer, that's one. I know how to hotwire a car."

"Oh, boy. That makes you an outlaw. Hey," she said. "Are you a tough guy?"

"What? Come on."

"Do you get in fights and things like that?"

"No."

"You're lyin'."

"When I was a kid. Not anymore."

"Then why'd you get that tattoo?"

"A tattoo doesn't make me a tough guy."

"Does where I come from."

"Then maybe it's a good thing you left."

"You *are* a tough guy. Tough in the head."

"Oh, yeah?"

"Yeah. You're gonna go to college at Berkeley, right?"

"Yeah."

"I heard of that place. They got a lot of smart people there. You're gonna be all right there."

"How would you know?"

"See? You challenge everything. You don't take nothing for granted and you don't believe anything. That's how I know."

Ahead, the river divided and Bobby didn't know which fork to take. One of life's little conundrums. He asked Sally which way she thought he should go.

"I don't know anything about rivers," she said. "Eenie, meenie, minie, moe, I don't care which way you go."

"Maybe you are a beatnik," he said and yelled, "Dean! I need a map."

Alex emerged from the cabin into the stern, threw up his arms in a gesture of helplessness, and hollered, "Dean threw all the maps and charts overboard."

Bobby blinked, ran his fingers through his hair and shook his head. "That moron," he said. "Why?"

"It's just one of those things, Bobby. He was muttering about being Mike Fink the Riverboat Man and he didn't need any damn maps. Whoosh! Out the window; then he passed out."

"Wonderful. Take a look. The river splits. Which way do I go?"

Alex ascended to the bridge and studied the river ahead.

"Take the biggest one. Go right."

"How's the game?" Bobby asked.

"Dean is wasted and Charlie's seasick. Nelson and I are playing blackjack. Crazy Nelson hit a soft eighteen and got the three of hearts. Can you believe it?"

"Stick to poker, Alex, or that Chinaman will take all your money."

The *Toot Sweet* putted merrily past Verona, and Bobby steered to the right, unknowingly navigating onto the Feather. It looked the same, the banks lined with brush at the base of tall levees, a few trees, and here and there a cornfield or apple orchard in places where the levees opened and offered a peek at what lay beyond. Bobby studied the trees and bushes and realized they had to pull up on the bank somewhere and make camp before dark.

From time to time Sally turned around and smiled. The sun went down and in the twilight, a half mile ahead where the river slipped around an island and curved to the east, Bobby could see a trace of white water, the cataract at Shanghai Bend, the end of the line.

# 25

Foghorns and sirens moaned in the distance, klaxons of danger and distress. Closer, a streetcleaner whirred down New Montgomery, sweeping away bottles, memories, and cigarette butts. Inside the Enrico Caruso Suite the hefty pot from the last unfinished hand was pushed discreetly to one side, protected by Nelson's gun and cuffs. Dean continued to snore loudly on the couch while Charlie, fidgety and sweating, sat at the card table watching Alex cheat at solitaire.

"You look twitchy," Alex commented dryly without looking up from the array of cards. "I bet you never read that book on Zen."

"You wanna talk about Zen Buddhism at a time like this? Jesus. You can play the eight of diamonds."

"No kibitzing! Four in the morning is a fine time to practice Zen. Perhaps I should compose a Tao of Poker. I'm sure it would be a best-seller."

Charlie poured two shots of Dean's rum, passed one to Alex, and asked, "Why do you cheat?"

"I cheat at everything except poker."

"Think they'll come back?"

Simultaneously revealing and concealing a Zen-like fortitude, Alex sighed and resigned himself to answering Charlie's impossible questions. "Nelson will, to collect his piece if nothing else," he said, giving Nelson's pistol a friendly pat. "There's no telling about Bobby."

"What would you do if you were Bobby?"

"Don't be a twit. How would I know?"

"What if Nelson can't talk him into coming back? What if he goes to the cops?"

"Come on, Charlie, take it easy. What are you afraid of?"

"You know damned well. Prison. San Quentin. Lethal injection."

"Ooo, let's be melodramatic, whaddaya say? If it comes to that, you can run away to South America, and if that isn't appealing, you can jump off the bridge. What the hell, you can turn Japanese and slit open your belly. It's considered an honorable way out of an untenable situation. Maybe you can get Dean to whack off your head, just to complete the ritual."

"I'm not gonna jump off the damned bridge, but you better believe I've thought about taking off," Charlie said. "But then what happens to Hooper Fish? I have eighty people who depend on me."

Alex looked up smartly, freezing Charlie with sudden intensity. "Your soul is in jeopardy and you're worried about your business? You have it backwards, my friend. Your employees don't depend on you; *au contraire*, you depend on them. If you disappeared without a trace, you wouldn't be missed. The boats will go fishing, the supermarkets will carve up the catch for the great unwashed, the restaurants will boil lobsters for plutocrats, and the moon will continue to push the tides back and forth. Nothing you do is as important as you think. That goes for you and me and everyone."

"I'm not like you, Alex. I enjoy my life. I'm not bored."

"Boredom is not my problem," Alex replied. "I'm tired. You see my Panama hat? In New York I wear a beret, and I'm tired of looking like a French peasant, *très chic*. What a crock. *Merde*! I'm a straw hat kind of guy. Don't you understand what's happening here? We've been forced to look at ourselves in the mirror. Maybe you like what you see, but I don't unless I'm wearing my Panama. So what? Maybe you can stay the same as you are, if you're lucky. Do you feel lucky, Charlie? You know it's going to come down to one hand, the hand you're dealt and the way you play it."

"You're really crazy, Alex."

"You don't know the half of it, pal, but let me ask you this: If you're so sane and responsible and worried about your employees, why do you play in the game every year? You always lose. If the game continues this morning, you could lose Hooper Fish, and there you are, irrelevant and broke."

"Do you think it'll come to that?"

"I hope so. I like fish. You're not going to bail out, are you?"

"I'm in, Alex. Don't worry."

Charlie trundled off to take a shower and a few minutes later, wrapped in a towel, swept through the suite tuning all the TVs to *The Untouchables*, igniting a cacophony of Hollywood tommyguns blasting well-dressed bootleggers in both bedrooms, bathrooms, the living room, and kitchenette. *Pow pow pow pow pow. Come out of there, Frank. You don't stand a chance.* The noise was so loud Alex didn't hear Nelson and Bobby in the corridor. He looked up and they were standing in the foyer looking wrung out.

Nelson's eyes were guarded, his face blank but tense. Toting a small white bag of doughnuts, Bobby showed no trace of the anger that had propelled him out the door. His spiffy clothes had acquired a few wrinkles. Watching him, trying to read his features, Alex gathered up the cards, tapped the deck square and laid it on the felt. Bobby took his seat and met Alex's gaze.

Nelson went around turning the TVs down to a reasonable volume, pausing to prod Dean. "Wake up, Studley," he demanded, poking the big guy in the shoulder.

"I'm awake," Dean announced from the couch.

"You came back," Alex said to Bobby. "How nice."

"Nelson said this is a trial."

"Oh, it is, but there are many ways to conduct a trial: by fire, by water, by the judgment of your peers, or even the turn of a card."

"I'm in no mood for bullshit, Alex."

"I'm sure that's true for all of us."

"Any more cute tricks like Nelson's stunt with the microphone?"

"Definitely," Alex answered with an impish smile.

"Christ almighty, what the fuck is going on? Are you crazy?"

"Charlie thinks so, but after all, we're only having a card game. Glad you could make it."

Bobby took a deep breath and exhaled slowly. If Alex wanted to be cagey and play games, maybe he really was crazy. He had a lot to lose while Bobby risked only his dignity if they really did get to the truth. He was a man; he'd cried before, but he didn't have many tears left for Shanghai Bend.

"Thirty-two years and counting," Bobby said. "I've run out a patience. What's going on?"

"We owe you," Alex said. "Nelson, did you tell him about the money?"

"No."

"What money?" Bobby asked. "The stake? The twenty-five grand?"

"No, not the stake. We have something for you. Dean, would you care to do the honors?"

"Yo, boss. Comin' right up."

Dean pulled himself off the couch, snorted, farted, groused into a bedroom, and returned with the largest of the heavy canvas bags he'd brought to the hotel. He tossed it on the table.

They were all smiling, grins all around the table except for Bobby who stared at the bag and didn't know what to make of it.

"That's full of dough," Dean said. "It's yours, McCorkle. Take it."

Bobby didn't budge. "Talk to me," he said. "For all I know there's a smoke bomb in this bag, another stupid trick."

"You tell him," Dean said to Alex. "You're the mastermind."

"Tell me what?" Bobby demanded.

"We've all been part of Dean's business for more than twenty years," Alex said. "He grows five hundred pounds of premium marijuana on his barges every year, sometimes a little more, sometimes a little less, and we sell it in L.A., San Francisco, and New York. We've been doing it so long we never actually see it, let alone take possession of it. Dean takes almost all the risk, and so he gets the lion's share of the money. For the rest of us, there's a tidy sum every year to split up, from fifty thousand the first year to a million two this year. Every year when we divide the profits at the annual poker game, we put aside a certain percentage for you, twenty percent to be exact. It's yours."

"You're putting me on," Bobby said.

"Nope."

Bobby blinked. "Why?" he asked.

Alex chuckled and said, "We thought it would make for an interesting card game if we increased the stakes."

"There's a catch."

"No catch. You can take it and leave right now."

"Open it, for God's sake," Charlie insisted, emerging from the bedroom, a bath towel wrapped around his shoulders, eyes red and face puffy but rubbing his hands like he was ready to play. He stood behind Bobby and put his hands on his shoulders. "C'mon, man."

"No smoke bombs, no jack-in-the-box?"

Alex shrugged. "Only one way to find out."

Bobby untied the knots, loosened the laces and poured the contents of the bag onto the table. It was all hundreds in thick packets bound by rubber bands and included several bundles of old silver certificates. It made an untidy but impressive pile on the green felt.

Staring at the money, they were silent for a long moment. In the background the TVs advertised cheap airfares and telephone psychics.

"Tell him how much," Dean growled.

"One million eight hundred forty-seven thousand six hundred, rounded off," Alex recited. "We could've invested it and made much more, but that would have been an accounting nightmare. I'm sure you understand why we stashed it in a safe deposit box every year and left it there. In fact, having so much unexplained cash will be your biggest problem. You can say you won it in a card game."

"A million eight."

"Yup."

"For thirty-two years of silence."

"Yup."

"And continued silence in the future."

"That's up to you. If you want to call the Yuba County Sheriff, we have his number."

"You guys are dope dealers? I can't believe it."

"Oh, we're a regular cartel," Alex said with a chuckle. "Or we were. Rocket Fuel exclusively, no pills or powders or anything else, but it's all over now, done, *finito*. We're not going to push our luck. We've retired. We're filthy rich, and now, so are you. Aren't you glad you came back?"

"Son of a gun," Bobby said, scratching his chin, trying to tear his eyes away from the hill of cash. There had to be a catch, no matter how much they denied it. One point eight million dollars was simply too much money—an unbelievable amount of money—for them to let him simply walk away. Was it a bribe? It smelled like a bribe, but he couldn't be bribed. Money didn't mean to him what it meant to them. If it did, he would've quit playing poker a dozen times when he was ahead with enough to live for the rest of his life. No, the money wasn't nearly enough. For the moment, however, he wouldn't mind playing cards with monopoly money.

"Anyone want a doughnut?" he asked.

"Sure. Whaddaya got?"

"Plain old-fashioned and maple bars."

"Where you been, anyway?" Alex asked.

"We took a little tour of Noë Valley," Nelson answered.

"The old neighborhood is still there, I presume," Alex said, groping the sticky interior of the bag and extracting an old-fashioned.

"It's been gentrified and prettied up but it's the same," Nelson said.

"As long as I was here, I wanted to see for myself," Bobby said with a chuckle, adding, "They're still selling dope in Dolores Park where I used to score hashish."

"Can the nostalgia," Alex snapped. "Are you ready to play cards?"

Dean slid into his seat, reached into his jeans, and pulled out a huge wad of C-notes. "Let's play cards."

"I told you I was in," Charlie said to Alex as he sat down. "I'm in."

Nelson sat down, stashed his pistol and cuffs under the seat, and said, "Let's play a little poker. Bring out the bags."

Alex started to laugh. It began with a jelly roll in his diaphragm and burbled up through his throat and erupted in a brawling, bellowing howl. "Yes!" he shouted, "Yes! Poker doesn't matter unless it hurts. Isn't that right, Mr. Professional? How about raising the stakes just a tad?"

Alex's laughter echoed through the suite, just loud enough to drown out the muffled exhortations of Elliot Ness. *Bust open those barrels, boys. I want to see a river of beer.*

# 26

The first three cards of a hand of five stud had been dealt when Dean's beady, red eyes panned the table and his laughter turned provocative. "I'm gonna raise a buck," he declared. "Any objections?"

Excited, Charlie exclaimed, "No way! What the hell is the point of a limit if you ignore it? There has to be a limit or the game will get out of control."

"Isn't that the idea?" Alex said. "Isn't that why we came up this godforsaken river, to get away from the controls of civilization?"

"You're full of shit, Alex, right up to your brown eyeballs."

*Smack*.

"God damned mosquitoes."

"Gimme another beer. Where's Bobby?"

"He and the broad went off somewhere."

*Smack*.

"I raise a buck," Dean repeated and slapped a dollar bill on the table.

"The limit is two bits," Charlie protested vehemently. "It's always been a quarter. Shit."

"Not anymore. You don't have to play, Charlie."

"Damn right, if you can't play by the rules, I fold. Do you have any idea where we are?"

"Nope, but there's no waterfall on the Sacramento," Dean said. "I know that for a fact. We're on some other river, maybe the Yuba or the American. I dunno."

"I see the buck and raise a buck," Alex said. "Nelson?"

"I'm in. Okay, roll 'em, big daddy."

"A five to Alex no help, a three to Nelson no help, and a six to me for a pair of sixes. A buck on the sixes."

"I raise a buck," Alex said. "You don't scare me by raising the stakes, Dean."

"I'm out," Nelson said.

"I see your raise and raise you back two bucks."

"I call," Alex said. "Deal."

"Another five to you makes a pair and a queen to me. Two bucks."

"See your two and raise five."

Alex had noticed that Dean bet conservatively when he had good cards and wildly when he was bluffing. Raising five bucks called his bluff.

Dean plunged. "I see your five and raise you a case of Schlitz."

"You wanna bet beer? You run out of money? It was your idea to toss the limit, you jerk."

"I raise you a case of beer, motherfucker."

"Jesus, Dean, you really know how to screw up a card game."

"What do you expect from a guy who throws all the maps into the river?"

"I'll see your case of beer. Deal."

"Let's have a brewski before I deal the last card, okay? Hey, Charlie, I got a rule for ya. How about we drink a beer with every card? Ha ha."

"You're doing that anyway, Deano. Is there anything to eat on this boat?"

"Beanie wienie."

Secured against the current with a long rope tied to a stout tree, the boat was pulled partway up a gravel and clam shell beach on a small, wooded island. The boys had planned to erect a tent and set up camp, but because of the bugs the tent remained rolled up and stowed in the forward cabin. The moon and stars and a Coleman lantern provided enough light in the galley to play cards.

"C'mon, Dean, let's see the last card."

"All right. A four to Alex and, ho ho, another queen to me for two pair. I bet two cases of beer."

"Uh uh, cash only, Mr. Studley."

Dean pulled out his wallet, picked out a twenty, and threw it on the table.

"Twenny bucks," he said.

"See your twenty," Alex said, magically producing a roll of bank-notes, "and raise you twenty."

"Holy shit," Charlie said.

"That's all I have," Dean said. "That's gas money to get us home."

"I'll take your marker," Alex said, turning over his hole card, the five of hearts. "Can you beat three fives?"

Dean screamed, "You motherfucker!" and raked the table with his forearm sending beer, money, and chips flying across the galley. Then he cracked up and, laughing and sputtering like a maniac, popped open another Schlitz and chugged it.

Nelson began to sing, "A hundred bottles of beer on the wall, a hundred bottles of beer. Take one down and pass it around, ninety-nine bottles of beer on the wall."

Alex and Charlie joined in. "Ninety-nine bottles of beer on the wall, ninety-nine bottles of beer. Take one down and pass it around, ninety-eight bottles of beer on the wall."

Dean added a baritone, and the bottles came off the wall one by one as the old camp song echoed over the river. Somewhere around the thirty-seventh chorus the pungent odor of burning hot dogs and beans wafted into the air. Laughter, shouts, rollicking crashes and splashes, horrendous off-key singing, the bravura of young men, a cheerful tableau in a buggy paradise.

# 27

At the mouth of Shanghai Bend the levees formed an artificial canyon that concealed all signs of life in the broad valley beyond—no lights, no highway buzz, no vast tracts of lettuce and tomatoes, only the tangled wilderness of a small island that lay close to the east bank.

Picking through the underbrush with a flashlight, Bobby and Sally could hear the cheerful, rowdy noise from the boat over the hiss of the falls.

"Sounds like your friends are having fun, playing cards and whooping it up," Sally said.

Bobby wisecracked, "They're practicing for college."

"If I wasn't here, you'd be with them, wouldn't you?"

*Smack.* "There's a lot of bugs out here," he said. "We're being eaten alive."

"Do you want to go back to the boat?" she asked.

"Nah. There's probably more bugs over there because of the lights."

They reached the tip of the island which afforded a splendid view of the falls. Fifty years earlier, heavy pumps and dredges had gouged tons of clay from the river bottom and formed the cataract, a series of staggered terraces and stunted waterfalls, the deepest of which in June was no more than two feet. Between the vertical drops, whitewater swirled around strange, pitted boulders, the tortured dregs of the last gold rush. Although Bobby knew nothing of hydraulic mining, he could tell the river had been mauled and deformed.

"This place is weird," he said. "Look at those rocks full of holes."

While Bobby tried to figure out what had caused the strangeness of the falls, Sally used the uniqueness of the odd formations to fire her imagination.

"Let's pretend it's the moon," she said gleefully. "President Kennedy says we'll go to the moon real soon, so here we are ahead of schedule. Our rocket ship is right over there, full of drunken astronauts, and here we are visiting the first moon river. Nobody knows the moon has a river except us. We've made a discovery. We're pioneers."

Laughing, she took Bobby's hand and led him to the edge of the water. "I'd jump in if I could swim," she said.

"You really can't swim?"

"I can wade," she declared, kicking off her tennies and rolling up her jeans.

Before Bobby could shed his hightops and socks, Sally splashed into the river, promptly slipped on the slick bottom, and fell on her ass. Delighted, she sat in the inches-deep water and let it run over her like a cool bath.

"I'm not afraid," she said, giggling and speaking to herself in a state of wonder. "It's not like the ocean. It even tastes good."

Awestruck, realizing he was witnessing a moment of liberation, Bobby jammed his wallet in his shoes and jumped into the river next to Sally.

"Maybe I won't go to San Francisco," she said, cupping water in her palms and pouring it over her head. "Maybe I'll stay right here forever."

She threw her arms around him and began kissing him, saying, "Thank you thank you thank you."

"For what?" he stammered. "I didn't do anything."

"You let me stay on the boat so I could come to this magical place."

"You really think it's magic?"

"Sure. Don't you?"

"If it's magic, it might be black magic," he said.

"Places have souls," she said. "Don't you know that?"

She kissed him again, and this time he kissed her back. They were both soaked from head to toe and she trembled as she pushed against him.

"Are you cold?" he asked.

"I'm warming up," she answered with a giggle.

Suddenly they heard banging and crashing in the woods behind them.

"Hey, Bobby! Where the fuck are you, man?"

A beer can clanged off a tree.

"Hey! Yo! Bobby!" Dean's voice echoed off the levees. "We can't play four hands anymore. Charlie won the last hand with a pair of deuces. That's crazy. Where are you, man?"

Bobby and Sally were standing ankle deep in the water and grinning like elves when Dean burst out of the woods.

"There you are," he shouted. "Whatcha doin', man? We got a game goin'."

# 28

They crashed. Recognizing that they were no longer young studs with the stamina to play night and day without a break, Bobby checked into his room, taking his sudden riches with him, while the others flopped in the bedrooms and living room of the suite. They slept through the morning and past noon—dreaming perhaps of the queen of hearts—and roused themselves at a leisurely pace in mid-afternoon.

Dean called Billie.

"How's the game, honey?"

"Interesting."

"You winning?"

"It's not over."

"Hmmm. You still want me to come down tomorrow?"

"I don't know yet."

"You hung over?"

"Yep."

Nelson swam a few laps in the hotel pool. Alex plugged in a laptop and checked his e-mail, deleted all his messages without reading them, and then, as an afterthought, dropped the computer into the trash compactor in the kitchenette and crushed it. Charlie, always the host, ordered breakfast for everyone, coffee, aspirin, a case of beer, and another bottle of rum for Dean. The caterer's carts were cleared away and a stack of room service trays lay outside the door. They didn't talk much. Mose Allison was on the stereo, the shades drawn tight to blot out the useless light of day. The air conditioner whirred away. Brushed clean, the felt glistened under the lamp.

It was four o'clock on Saturday afternoon when the game resumed. Cards from a new deck whistled like bullets over the felt and landed in tidy piles for a hand of draw, Alex dealing. The ante was now a thousand dollars, the new value of a white chip. Reds were ten thousand, blues twenty-five thousand, and a bumblebee chip was worth one hundred thousand dollars. Each player started with a half million in chips, one hundred times the first buy-in.

Two million five hundred thousand dollars in five canvas bags were stacked in a corner of the living room. Even for rich men, the money was enough to make them dizzy. Under his hat, surrounded by a cloud of Lucky Strike fumes, Alex couldn't control his smirk. Finally playing the poker game of his dreams, his eyes flicked around the table taking snapshots. Dean, hung over and sweating, corralled his chips with his arms, coddling them like babies; Charlie was flushed, his face red with wonder at what he was doing; Nelson looked grim and resolute, determined not to lose; Bobby alone was relaxed, leaning back in his chair and toying with a bumblebee chip.

As a pro, Bobby wasn't fazed by mind-boggling stakes, but he knew the others were. They were flat-out crazy to begin with, tortured by guilt and who knows what else, and it occurred to him that perhaps they expected him to inflict punishment by taking all their money. He was happy to oblige.

"It's only money, hey boys?" Charlie said with a nervous chuckle. "We talked about doing this for years, and now that it's happening, Jesus."

"It's just cards and chips," Alex said, not entirely convinced himself. "Can you open, Studley?"

"I open for ten," Dean said, dropping a red chip into the pot.

"Uh oh," Bobby said. "The captain has openers. Okay, I see your ten and raise twenty. Thirty to you, Fishman."

"I'm in," Charlie declared. "Thirty large."

"I fold," Nelson said.

Alex peeked at his cards one at a time—three sixes, the devil's hand. He contemplated his chips and selected two blues.

"Thirty plus twenty is fifty grand."

This time it was Dean who started laughing and sputtering, "It's funny money, fifty thou' on fucking openers. I call."

"Call," Bobby said.

"I'm still in," Charlie said.

"One card for me," Dean said.

Bobby tossed away two cards and said, "Give me two."

"Three," Charlie said. "Make 'em three big ones."

"Dealer takes two," Alex declared. "You opened, Deano. Your bet."

"Ah, shit. I check."

"Me, too," Bobby echoed.

"Fifty thousand dollars," Charlie shouted. "I bet fifty grand, ha-haha."

Alex looked at triple sixes and two new cards that didn't improve his hand. Without a doubt, Charlie caught good cards and had a better three of a kind. He'd call any bet.

"Fold," Alex said, rapping the table sharply with his knuckles.

"I'm gone," Dean said.

"Take it, Charlie," Bobby conceded and tossed in his cards.

Charlie shrieked with joy and stood up to rake in the pot. "I can't fuckin' believe it. Wow. Three eights and I win what? What's in here? One hundred twenty big ones. Thank you, eight of spades. My lucky card."

Alex looked up and saw Bobby smiling at him.

"Nice move," Bobby mumbled under his breath.

"Thank you."

"Ante up for seven stud," Dean announced. "Rolling. Read 'em and weep. A queen, a seven, a ten, a jack, and another ten to the dealer. Queen bets."

"I remember the last time I sat down with you boys," Bobby said as he counted out chips to bet on the queen.

"On the boat," Alex said.

"Yeah, on that damned boat in the middle of fucking nowhere. I was pissed off."

"It didn't show," Nelson said. "You seemed happy to take our money."

"As I recall, you all ran out of money pretty quick, and we started playing for beer."

"Well, we didn't have anything else."

"Except the girl," Charlie added.

"Fifty on the queen." Bobby tossed two blues into the center of the table, clucked his tongue twice, and said, "Yeah, the girl."

# 29

Pulled up on the beach, the boat tilted stern down which meant no level surface anywhere. Drunk as a Hollywood cowboy, Nelson had slipped off the bench and puked so many times they'd kicked him out and made him sit in the stern and hang his head over the transom. Charlie was curled up in the forward cabin, passed out, leaving Bobby, Dean, and Alex still at the table while Sally watched. Miraculously, the little radio picked up Wolfman Jack broadcasting nonstop rock and roll from Tijuana, Mexico, six hundred miles south.

*"That's it, boys and girls, I know you love it, The Rockin' Pneumonia and the Boogie Woogie Blues comin' right atcha from XERB, the world's most powerful radio station. Oh yeah. Now hold onto your hats and put on your dancin' shoes, 'cause we got a request from Bonnie in San Diego for somethin' real special now. My main man, the godfather of soul, the baddest of the bad, Jaaaaames Brown!"*

The galley deck was awash with beer foam and tin-plated steel cans that rattled with a timbre deeper and richer than aluminum, a hearty industrial tune that would soon disappear from the land. In 1963, with America on the cusp of a social revolution, liberation was in the air, in the lively beat of the music, in the desperate yearning of the lyrics. On the *Toot Sweet* Sally was the incarnation of liberation because she'd broken away, every teenager's dream. To her, the scent of freedom was as heady as a bath in *eau de cologne*, and she felt good, a little tipsy from three beers but safer than she'd ever felt with the surfers. On the beach in L.A. a tinge of menace always lurked in the sand dunes. Posturing punks, muscleheads, killer waves. Here, with Bobby and his friends, she felt as though she'd stepped into another world with rules they could make up on the spot. So far, running away was a success.

Sally stood behind Bobby, one arm draped over his shoulders, fascinated by the game. On a hot streak, Bobby was winning hand after hand, taking all of Alex and Dean's money, and when they ran out of bills and coins and started playing for beer he won all the beer.

"You think you're Doc Holliday or what?" Dean taunted.

"Hell yes," Bobby barked and flashed a grin at Sally. "Just like in the movies, hey, babe?"

She winked and laughed and drank a mouthful of beer.

Dean rapped knuckles on his cards and demanded, "Beat two pair aces up, Doc?"

"Dunno. What's it worth to you to find out?"

"A case of that fancy Coors beer from Colorado."

"That stuff is elk piss but okay, you're on." Bobby flipped over the seven of clubs and won again. "Three sevens, sucker. You gonna drive to Denver to get it? I don't think this boat will make it."

"God *damn*!"

Sally had never seen anything as exciting as the boys' poker game. Surfing came close, but that was boy against ocean and this was boy against boy. It was a fight without blows, a war without weapons, and she was bright enough to understand that luck was a small part of this cerebral and emotional game. Right away she caught on to the rules, the sequence of hands, and the concept of bluffing. What else was there? Nuance and subtlety and deceit, and she thought it was the greatest thing since rock and roll.

"I want to play," she said to the boys.

"What? You gotta be kidding," Dean scoffed.

"Aw, c'mon, guys. You afraid?"

"You're a *girl*! Jesus," the three boys exclaimed simultaneously.

No matter how much she cajoled, they wouldn't let her play.

"Maverick's rules," Bobby cited. "Women don't play poker."

"It's in the book, *Poker According to Maverick*, and that's our rule book," Alex said.

"Maverick is full of it. It's just a TV show," she retorted, but they still wouldn't let her play.

"The game is over anyway," Bobby said. "I'm going to set up the tent."

Alex wasn't ready to quit. "What do you mean it's over? We can still play."

"With what? Chips? Chips don't mean dick, and I'm tired of playing for beer we don't have."

"We can play for the broad," Dean suggested.

Bobby screeched, "You want to what?"

"Play a hand for the girl."

"You're sick, Dean."

"Yeah. Ain't it a goof?"

"No, it's a fucked-up, perverted idea."

"Why don't you ask her? Maybe she'll like the idea."

"I don't think so. I don't like the idea."

"You're a chump, Bobby."

"You're drunk, Dean, but that's no excuse to start calling people names."

"Hey, chickee. What do you think?"

"Do I look like a poker chip?"

"Yeah."

"Maybe you need glasses."

"You got a smart mouth for a broad."

"Oh, yeah? You've got a smart mouth for an asshole."

"Did you hear that? Did you hear what this hitchhiking runaway said to me? Shit."

"Shut up, Dean."

"Fuck you. Why do you think I wanted her on this boat?" Dean shouted.

"I thought you felt sorry for her and wanted to be a nice guy."

"Like I said. You're a chump, McCorkle."

Bobby lunged across the table and jabbed Dean hard in the nose, breaking his septum. Blood spurted onto the table and chips. More surprised than hurt, Dean tried to stand up, slipped on the wet deck, and collapsed on the table, bleeding on the cards.

"I'll kill you, you son of a bitch."

"You're too drunk to kill bugs, let alone anybody else," Alex laughed.

"Stop this," Sally insisted. "What is the matter with you people?"

"Dean's jealous and drunk."

"We're all drunk," Alex said.

"That's no excuse for disrespect," Bobby said. "Hell, it's no excuse for any damn thing."

"Listen," Sally said. "You want to play a hand for me? Oh-kay. Bobby will win."

"And what if he doesn't?"

"He will."

"You don't understand poker," Alex said. "Anyone can win one hand."

Sally kicked at the beer cans on the deck, sending one through the hatch where it landed at Nelson's feet, rousing his attention. He looked up, waved meekly and asked, "What's goin' on?"

"Come in and find out," she replied.

She shook her head, violently flailing her hair as though she was exorcising a demon. Outside, the river gods responded to her gesture by conjuring a gust of wind that whistled through the trees and mottled the surface of the water. The boys were mesmerized, nonplussed by having their fantasies thrown back in their faces. Sally snapped back her shoulders, pushed out her chest and lit a cigarette.

"Well, boys?"

"This doesn't sound right to me," Bobby said.

"No? Fine. I have a better idea." Sally leaned over the table and blew smoke in all their faces. "I'll tell you what, guys. You let me play, and whoever wins can do whatever he wants with me, and if I win, I can do whatever I want with any of you."

They were stunned. Nelson stood in the hatch looking confused. Alex's jaw dropped. Dean, still bleeding, muttered, "What a broad," and Bobby slowly shook his head in wonder, thinking, life is full of surprises.

Then Sally leaned over and kissed him. "Don't worry, baby," she said. "How can we lose?"

# 30

"I couldn't believe it," Bobby confessed. "She blew my mind."

Beyond the shuttered windows Saturday disappeared like a day lost to jet lag. A proper summer fog finally had broken the heat wave, sending grateful locals into the bars and tourists strolling through Chinatown. At five sharp the Hooper Fish Company crab boat *Joaquín Murrietta* left Pier 43 to check her traps for the last time that season.

Alex tapped a cigarette on the felt, sniffed it, and touched one tip with his tongue to which adhered a single tobacco flake. The bitter taste caused him to revolve away from the table, and as he propelled the noxious sotweed into the air the professor realized the expression "blow one's mind" was unknown in 1963. A short, fierce, argument inside Alex's head ended with the brutal silencing of Professor Goldman and his pedantic quibbling by the wizard of Alvarado Street. Turning back, scarcely missing a beat, Alex recalled, "When Dean shot off his mouth and yapped, 'Let's play a hand for the broad.' Holy shit! What the fuck! Oh no no no, uncharted territory, big taboo—but not for Sally. She went right with it and turned the whole crazy idea around and blew all our minds."

"We weren't ready for someone like that," Nelson said earnestly. "She was too far ahead of us."

Dean clenched his fists and held them to his eyes as though he were weeping. "Oh, Billie," he moaned. "Oh, God."

Overlooking Dean's histrionics, Alex went on, "That's not quite true, Nelson. Bobby was ready."

All but Dean looked to Bobby who returned their glances with a neutral expression, determined not to put his feelings on display. "I appreciate the compliment, Alex, but Nelson's right. I wasn't in her class any more than the rest of you, not even close," he said quietly, closely eyeing Dean whom the others continued to ignore. Sweating and trembling, the big man appeared ready to erupt from the pressure of reconstructing their voyage on the *Toot Sweet*. Bobby felt equally powerful forces at work inside himself—his mind reluctantly edged closer to the moment of his detonation, the turning point of his life about which these familiar strangers knew nothing. He'd told Nelson a few things in the cab, but how could he explain that Sally had opened a window and allowed him a glimpse of a universe of illumination? And as suddenly as the window had appeared it had been slammed shut—wham, a black hole in time. In the first nanosecond he'd been blinded by the darkness and had spent the rest of his life clawing back toward the light.

"She was the first hippie," Charlie observed. "It took me a long time to figure that out, but I think she wanted to have her Summer of Love a few years early. Whose deal?"

"Ante up for seven stud," Nelson replied, shuffling the blue deck. "We've heard your theories before, Charlie. First hippie, my ass."

"Not me, I haven't heard Charlie's theories, or any theories," Bobby said, curiosity getting the better of him. "You guys have talked about her for years, but I . . ."

Suddenly Dean jumped up, pointed wildly at Bobby, and shouted, "*You broke my nose,* you son of a bitch." Teeth grinding, eyes squeezed tight, head jerking left and right in the throes of intense emotion, he sprawled his huge hands in the middle of the table, leaned over with all his bulk, popped open his eyes, and kissed Bobby on the lips.

Beaming, eyes crazy as an acid dream, he growled, "Thank you, man."

Startled, Bobby recoiled and toppled over backwards onto the floor in a clatter of chair and yelps of surprise. The Enrico Caruso Suite resounded with uproarious laughter, Dean's cackle, Charlie's high shriek, Nelson's giggle, and Alex's belly laugh. Bobby too was laughing, but he wasn't sure at what.

"Christ almighty," he mumbled lying on his back. "What else do I have to put up with to play a little cards?"

Dean rushed around the table and pulled Bobby to his feet, saying, "Every time I see my crooked nose in the mirror I remember what an asshole I was."

"For Christ's sake, Dean, can't we stick to poker without getting all sentimental?" Bobby complained, smoothing out his clothes and no longer laughing.

"Hear hear, let's play," Alex chorused.

"We tolerate Deano because we're used to him," Charlie said.

"Only because the big turd made us rich," Nelson added.

"You're still an asshole, Studley," Charlie taunted. "You haven't changed that much. If it wasn't for Billie, you'd be dead."

"Billie?" Bobby didn't remember who Billie was.

"His wife," Alex said, snapping open his Zippo and furiously lighting a Lucky. "Dean is terrified of Billie finding out about Sally. He's afraid she'll freak out and leave him, but, even though we've never met, from what I've heard I've always thought she'd be more forgiving than that."

"She isn't going to find out unless the world finds out, and then it won't matter," Dean declared ominously.

"Who knows what you say in your sleep?" Charlie teased. "Maybe she already knows."

"Horse exhaust. What a crock."

"You never know, pal. Maybe you're the wild card, Dean. Maybe you always were the wild card."

"Jesus," Bobby muttered, still fussing with his clothes and flexing his back as he sat down. "Damn, I think I pulled a muscle."

"Are you gonna play or throw another fit?" Alex inquired sharply of Dean.

Casting a disdainful sidelong glance at Alex, Dean asked, "You okay, Bobby?"

"Yeah, what the hell, with everything else that's happened in this game, getting kissed isn't the worst of it. Let's play."

Charlie asked, "What's the game? I forgot with all the fuss."

"Pay attention, Charlie, or you'll lose your big stack of chips, which you probably will anyway. Ante up for seven stud," Nelson repeated and after everyone tossed in a white chip, he dealt two cards face down to each player and then one card up. "A ten to Alex, a nine to Dean, a jack to Bobby, a six to Charlie, and a five to me. Jack bets. Bobby, you're boss."

Bobby placed one red chip in the pot. "Ten grand on the jack."

"I fold," Charlie said.

"Too rich for me," Nelson said. "I'm out."

"I'll see your ten and raise twenty-five," Alex said.

"You pricks," Dean swore, breaking etiquette and flipping over his hole cards, a pair of threes. "I'm not gonna get suckered into this with you sharks. I'm out."

"Tough geshitski," Alex said. "Bobby?"

"See your twenty-five. Deal 'em."

"Another ten to Alex for a pair and the three of diamonds to Bobby's jack, no help."

"Oh, man, do you see that? That would've been my three."

"Shut up, Dean," Nelson snapped.

"Fifty on the tens," Alex said.

"Out," Bobby promptly replied, turning his cards face down with a nod to Alex who collected the pot. "Too bad you didn't stick around, Deano. Triple threes might have been good. I think you're spooked."

"What!? I ain't spooked."

Charlie's short, barking laugh spilled into the air, "Hahaha, you're fulla shit, Studley. Everybody's spooked. I mean, we can't play hide and seek with Sally forever. We have to get down to it sooner or later."

An uncomfortable silence descended on the table. Finally, Nelson said, "Nah, let's play cards. C'mon, Wiz, it's your deal."

"That's right, rock and roll, my deal, let's see, what'll we play next?"

"Let's play low hole card wild," a relentless Dean suggested with a gleam in his eye. "Whaddaya say?"

Alex stopped shuffling, lay the red deck on the felt and buried his head in his hands, silently stifling an urge to grab Nelson's piece and shoot Dean between the eyes.

Charlie snarled, "No wild cards, you jerk. Not for this much money."

Shaking his head, Nelson pleaded, "Christ, Dean, give it a rest."

"We used to play low hole card wild," Bobby said mildly. "That's what we played that night."

"Haha," Charlie twittered. "No shit. Maybe that's why we don't play it—"

"We don't play it because it's a lousy game," Alex interrupted vehemently. "It's straight poker at this table, no wild cards, no bullshit."

Sputtering with laughter, Nelson said, "I thought poker was all about bullshit—in spades. Low hole used to be my favorite."

"It's my deal, and we won't play low hole card wild at this table," Alex hissed.

"Ooo," Dean needled. "Watch out for this boy. He's dangerous."

Charlie coughed, Nelson looked embarrassed, and Alex shuffled again, the tension visible in the taught, white tendons in his hands.

He declared, "Seven stud one more time, straight poker. Nelson, cut the damned cards, please."

As Nelson reached for the deck to make the cut, Bobby smiled broadly and said, "Relax, Wiz, a wild card is just a card, y'know. One card of fifty-two, and I know you're on speaking terms with the math, Herr Doktor Professor von Goldman. Wild cards change the odds, but so what? You go with it. You know the numbers backwards and forwards—you didn't have perfect scores on your college boards for nothin'—so what's your problem? You gotta be ready for anything if you're gonna play this game. You gotta be loose."

"Loose," Alex echoed.

"Yeah."

Nelson cut the deck and Alex picked up the cards, clucked his tongue several times, and tilted his hat back on the crown of his head. It was a day for letting things go. He remembered the little girl on the plane and then thought of his children who'd never met the wizard. He thought about the letters of resignation that waited in his suitcase, brief missives addressed to his department chairman at the university and supervisor at the Department of Defense. Equations flashed across his mind's eye, significant issues of time, space, the motion of particles, the speed of light, the essence of being— useless junk, quickly replaced in his memory with odds for seven card stud low hole card wild. Bobby was correct. He knew the numbers.

"I guess we should listen to the pro, right, boys? I mean, he knows what he's talking about, that's for sure," he drawled and adjusted his hat low on his brow. "You're right, Bobby, a card is just a card, a slip of stiff cardboard covered with ancient mystic symbols, hearts, clubs, diamonds, spades, the king with his sword, and the knave who wields a stealthy knife. A wild card, though, that's high concept, illusion and deception taken to another level."

With a flourish Alex fanned the cards, cut them, cut them again, and pushed the deck over to Nelson for another cut.

"There's no point in being a dogmatic fool," he said. "You called it, Stud. Down and dirty, here they come."

# 31

*"Aw right, baby, it's time to git naked, git crazy and boogie aw night long with the Wolfman, 'cause we all just animals in the moonlight howlin' at the big pizza pie in the sky. Now I'm gonna lay a little Maurice on ya. Stay just a little bit longer, baby, and maybe maybe maybe you'll learn the Wolfman's secret of life in the insane lane. Aw right."*

The little radio buzzed, Wolfman Jack howled and Maurice Williams and the Zodiacs pumped out their immortal song of teenage desire, "Stay." Sally stood close behind Bobby, gently pressing her belly against the back of his head and moving her hips to the slow beat of the erotic ballad.

"You sure you wanna do this?" Bobby asked her.

Eyes closed, nodding her head, Sally quietly sang along with the Zodiacs. *"Well, your daddy don't mind, bopbop a wahwahwaaah, and your mommy don't mind, bopbop a wahwahwaaah, if we . . ."*

"If we're gonna do it," Bobby said, clutching the deck and twisting to wink at Sally, "it has to be low hole card wild."

"Oh, shit."

"Oh, no."

"Oh, *yeah*."

"Alex thinks low hole card wild is strictly for morons," Nelson snickered. "You definitely qualify, Studley. You never win."

*Smack.* "Damn bugs."

*"Please please please please please, tell me that you're going to . . ."*

"Explain this game to me," Sally asked, snapping to attention.

Dean guffawed and blurted, "I wish someone would explain this damned game to *me*."

"You explain it, Alex. You're so logical," Bobby taunted. "We know how much you love it."

"What's it called again?" Sally asked.

"Low hole card wild," Bobby said.

"Low hold card wild," she repeated like a mantra. "Low. Hole. Card. Wild."

A fish jumped and landed near the boat with a loud splash. "It sounds . . . exciting," she said, drawing out the last word. Droplets of sweat surfaced on her upper lip.

Nelson danced a little jig, wailing, "It's a crazy game for crazy people and that's why it's Crazy Nelson's favorite game. I'm gonna wake Charlie up; he can't miss this action. *Charlie*! Get your butt outta the sling."

The song ended—"*come on come on come on and stay, ooo, la de da*"—the Wolfman spieled platter chatter, and Sally crouched down next to Alex and looked at him with fawn's eyes. "Tell me the rules."

"You've been watching us, so I guess you understand regular poker, the sequence of the hands and all that, straights and flushes?"

"I think I do, yes."

"Okay," Alex began. "It's actually called seven card stud low hole card wild because you deal it like seven stud. Everybody gets two cards face down and one up to start and you bet, then three more up, one at a time, and you bet on each one, and then the last card down and a final bet for a total of seven cards, three down and four up, and the best five make your poker hand. The three down cards are called hole cards, and the lowest hole card in your hand is wild, and all like it in your hand are wild. A wild card can represent anything you want. If you have a pair of tens and a wild card, say a five, the five becomes a ten and you have three tens. The wild card is a chameleon, a magic card that can make your dreams come true and then break your heart. It can be part of a flush or straight and even give you a royal flush which can lose in this game to five of a kind, or even six or seven of a kind. In seven stud low hole card wild everything is turned upside down and crazy. It's poker for lunatics, at any stakes. Everyone has a different wild card and you don't know what any of them are, except yours, and you can't be sure of that because what happens in this game, and this is the dirty, evil, wicked part, what happens is, say you have two sevens on the first two hole cards, making sevens your wild card, and a queen up, and you think you have three queens, but on the last card you get a three which is lower than a seven and now the three is your low hole card and that's your wild card and you only have three sevens. Get it?"

"I think so," she said with a gulp that provoked an outburst of laughter from the boys.

"Don't kid yourself," Alex said, giving Sally a friendly but patronizing pat on the hand. "Nobody gets it right away. One other thing. An ace in the hole can be high or low, and you decide if it's your wild card. It doesn't have to be. Here, let me show you."

Alex shuffled the deck and laid out a demonstration hand for two players, dealing each imaginary player two cards down and one up.

"Okay, the first hand shows a deuce up and the second an ace up, so one player has a pair of deuces or something better, and the other at least a pair of aces, because each has a wild card in the hole."

He turned over the first pair of hole cards, a deuce and an eight.

"This guy's low hole card is a deuce, which is as good as it gets, especially because he has one up and it's wild, too. He has three eights. Let's see, we'll turn over the other guy's hole cards, and he has a pair of nines in the hole to go with his ace showing, and this guy knows his last card may be lower than nines, in which case he'll have three nines which is a good hand in regular poker but not good enough to win in this game with five or six players."

He swiftly dealt the rest of the hand, and the second player lucked out, paired his ace, keeping the nines wild and giving him four aces. His opponent received a flurry of low cards and ended up with his original three eights. "See what I mean? It can be confusing."

Sally laughed and said, "Let's just play and see what happens."

Alex squeezed around the table, making room for Sally, and she sat down and began casually collecting the cards.

"We have to bet something," Charlie said. "Otherwise everyone just stays in and you might as well deal all seven cards at once."

"Got any ideas?"

"Strip poker," a leering Dean suggested.

"No way," Bobby said. "Don't be a creep."

"I have some money," Sally said.

"So do I, everything I won from you guys," Bobby hastened to say. "We're the only two players."

"Wait a minute, I have some dough," Dean announced, digging in his pocket.

"What? You been holdin' out on us, man?"

"I got twenty bucks."

"You owe me that, you scumbag," Alex spat. "You owe Bobby, too."

"Well, ain't that just a bitch," Dean scoffed. "Haw! I'm in."

"That isn't your money, Dean. You owe everybody."

"Go to hell, Alex. This is a new game." Dean slammed the double sawbuck on the table, rattling the chips and beer cans.

"We can divide twenty bucks four ways, that's five each and we can all play," Nelson suggested.

"Yeah."

"Yeah."

"Ah shit, all right. Count out some damn chips."

"Who's gonna deal?"

"Let Sally deal," Bobby said. "It's her ass on the line."

"What? C'mon," Dean protested. "She doesn't even know how to shuffle."

"So what?"

Rubbing eyes puffy with sleep and alcohol, Charlie appeared, asking, "What's going on?"

"Low hole card wild, my man, with a kicker in the pot," Dean replied.

"Sally wants to play," Bobby said.

"A girl? That's against the rules."

"We have new rules," Sally said with a cheerful smile. "The winner gets whatever he wants from me unless I win, and then I get whatever I want from whoever I want."

Blinking rapidly, Charlie rubbed his eyes again and stared at Sally while his comprehension grew in increments. Finally he said, "Whose crackpot idea was this?"

"Mine," Dean and Sally said simultaneously.

"Well, I don't have any more money and I'm fucked up. I'm going back to sleep."

"No, no, no, no, no, you have to play. Everybody has to play," Nelson insisted. "Dean was hiding twenty bucks and if we divide it four ways, we're all in. Sit down."

"There isn't any room."

"Stop making with excuses, Charlie. Scoot over, Dean," Nelson ordered. "Siddown."

Charlie complied and wedged himself onto the bench that formed an L around the table, mumbling, "You should rename this boat the *Sardine Can.*"

Alex counted chips, distributed neat stacks of whites, reds, and blues, and gestured toward the deck already in Sally's possession.

"Your game, your deal. Give everyone one card face down, then another one, then one face up."

"Shuffle first?"

"Yes."

Sally picked up the cards and executed a perfect cascade shuffle, a type of shuffle sometimes seen in bridge but rarely in a poker game. The cards rippled in her hands in consonance with the gurgling river. "Like that?" she asked unable to contain a smirk.

"God *damn,*" Dean swore. "Would you look at that."

"Hey, we got a player here," Alex chortled. "You've played before."

"Hearts," she said, shuffling again, her eyes flicking up to follow a mosquito. Instinctively, they all followed her glance away from the cards while she continued her patter. "I used to play hearts with my grandma and she taught me how to shuffle. She taught me a lot of things. Somebody get that bug."

*Smack.*

"You ever play poker?" Nelson asked.

"When the game is over, you tell me," she answered and dealt the hand, singing out the cards the way she'd observed. "A deuce to Charlie, a six to Nelson, a nine to Alex, a king to Bobby, a seven to me, and another nine to Dean. Bobby bets."

"A quarter on the king."

"So now I put a blue one in?"

"Yes, or two reds and a white."

"Okay."

"Want me to tell you what I'm gonna do if I win?"

"No."

"I'm gonna—"

"Shut up, Dean. You don't have to be crude."

"Oh, yeah? Maybe I do. What if you win, Alex? What'll you do?"

"Throw your ass in the river, wise guy."

Everyone stayed in. On the next card Charlie paired his deuce and bet a quarter and everyone stayed in again with nothing showing. On the fifth card Charlie caught a third deuce, and before Sally could finish dealing the round, Charlie bolted from the table, rushed to the stern and vomited over the side of the boat.

"Charlie?" Alex hollered.

"He's drunk and fucked up, but he's got winners," Bobby declared. "No one is going to beat four deuces or better."

"Maybe, maybe not," Dean contradicted, and when Charlie returned but didn't sit down, he said, "Your bet, Charlie."

Charlie reached across the table and flipped over his hole cards, the fourth deuce and an ace, giving him five aces in five cards, the best hand they'd ever seen.

"I win," he said simply.

"Charlie wins? Charlie?"

"Charlie wins the broad?"

"Charlie the *queer*?"

Flabbergasted, Bobby turned to Sally and said, "What are you going to do?"

With the most innocent sweet smile she answered, "That's up to Charlie."

Charlie took a deep breath, looked at his friends and at Sally and said, "You all know what I am, so I give her to Bobby. That's the only thing that's fair."

Bobby howled like the Wolfman, and Alex laughed loud enough to give himself a stomach cramp. Everyone hooted except Dean who screeched, "Just wait one fucking minute."

Bawling with laughter, Sally tried to speak, failed, pointed at Charlie, and then at the rest of them, and finally said, "You all knew?"

"How could we not know?" Alex replied. "I've known Charlie since kindergarten. I don't care if Charlie likes boys instead of girls."

"What about the rest of you?"

"We're not three dollar bills," Dean answered. "Only Charlie."

"Speak for yourself, Studley."

At that Nelson and Alex jumped on Dean and began cooing and kissing him, prompting a wrestling match as he struggled to throw them off, rocking the boat and once again rattling the beer cans.

"This isn't fair," Dean howled, his nose bleeding again. "I think we should play another hand."

"Be quiet, Dean," Alex shouted over the tumultuous squabbling, silencing everyone. "We had an arrangement here, an agreement. We played one hand like we said we were going to do, and Charlie won fair and square. That's it. The deal was the winner could do anything he wanted, and a deal's a deal."

"Yeah, but Charlie ain't gonna do shit. Bobby gets the goodies."

"So what?"

"It isn't fair."

"Quit whining or you'll get popped right in the kisser again."

"You wanna try it, Wiz?"

"You ain't so tough, Mr. Football Star."

Alex launched a roundhouse fist that Dean blocked with a meaty forearm, and their efforts spilled both boys onto the deck in a racket of beer cans, tumult, grunts, hubbub, good-natured wrestling, more spilled beer, and a frantic Little Richard screaming on the radio, *"Keep A-knockin' But You Can't Come In."*

"This is *gross*," Charlie shouted to no avail. "This is supposed to be a poker game, but it's becoming something else."

"*Stop it*," Sally yelled, voice ripe with command. "No more fighting, Jeez, not while there's money on the table. You'll spoil the fun," she said brightly, winking again at Bobby. "Let's turn up the music and play another hand."

Nelson grabbed Dean and pulled him off Alex, shouting, "You're gonna sink the boat if you keep messing around. *Cut it out.*"

Bobby threw back his head and laughed. "The lady is callin' all the shots, so let 'er rip. Deal 'em, girl, down and dirty."

# 32

*"Are you rockin' tonight? Are you cruisin' in your fine automobile with your plastic Jesus on the dashboard and your baby right beside you, sittin' real close, drinkin' your Royal Crown and makin' the scene, baby? What's that? You say you got no money, got no gas, no sweetheart, no fine automobile with no plastic Jesus on the dash? You still okay, baby 'cause you always got ROCK AN' ROLL. Here's a brand new beach party tune that's gonna make you feel good wherever you are. This is XERB, the world's most powerful radio station, and the Chantays with 'Pipeline.' Aw right."*

Sally scooped up the cards and shuffled several times with her fancy shuffle. Oblivious, Dean played air guitar, sliding his hands down the neck of an imaginary Fender Stratocaster while Nelson chugged another beer, Charlie closed his eyes and dozed, and Alex scratched his ass and fiddled with his chips. Only Bobby was paying attention to the deck in Sally's hands because she'd dealt the first hand of low hole card wild right-handed and now was holding the deck in her right and preparing to deal with her left. Before he could blurt, "She's ambidextrous!" in one smooth motion her left hand passed over her right, concealing the deck from all eyes except his, while her right thumbnail flicked the second card from the top, sliding it forward a quarter of an inch. The moving left hand snatched the wrinkled and soiled red card in a flash and dealt it to Dean. With the same motion the next one underneath went to Nelson and then the top card to Bobby.

He blinked, glanced at Sally whose face was pinched with concentration, and then peeked at his card, a deuce. Returning his gaze to her hands, he watched her deal him the second card from the top for another deuce in the hole, and then, singing out the next round of cards—"A king to Bobby, a four to Charlie, a seven to Nelson, a six to Alex, a queen to Dean, and a nine to me"—she brazenly dealt Bobby the king from the bottom of the deck. Boggled, Bobby scanned the table for a reaction but there was none. No one else had noticed her legerdemain.

"King bets, I think," she said in all innocence. "Is that right, just like last time?"

"You got it," Alex said, casually surveying the table.

Mesmerized, looking at his hole cards, a pair of deuces, and the king of hearts staring at him like a red devil, Bobby's heart fluttered as he stammered, "Um, uh, okay, the king bets two dollars."

"That's over the limit," Nelson protested.

"What limit? In a game like this?" Alex retorted. "What difference does it make?"

"I'm out," Charlie said without looking at his cards. "No more hanky-panky games for me."

With a shrug Nelson tossed in eight blues. "I gotta stay."

"I know when the cards are running against me," Alex said, disgusted. "I'm out. Is there any beer left? I might as well drink myself to death."

"Some big-time card player you are, Wiz, you chickenshit. I'm in," Dean said. "I'm gonna win and then, you and me, little runaway. They wrote a song about you, you know that?"

" 'Long Tall Sally?' That's not about me. I'm too short."

"Naw. 'My Little Runaway.' You know that song by Dion and the Belmonts?"

"What the fuck is a Belmont?" Nelson demanded. "That's what I want to know."

"Who gives a shit?" Charlie said, lolling his head and looking ready to upchuck again. "Anyway, it's by Del Shannon, not the Belmonts."

"I'm in," Sally said, putting in her chips and dealing the next round of cards. "A three to Dean, a ten to Nelson, another king to Bobby, Charlie and Alex are out, and an eight to me. Looks like the kings bet again."

"Adios, Kimosabe, good-bye," Nelson said before Bobby could bet.

"You've played before," he added with a gesture of his head toward Sally.

She smiled and said, "Only for fun."

"I bet another two dollars."

"Shee-it, the poker gods must love you, boy. I quit," Dean bellowed and tossed his cards in the air.

Bobby leaned back and stretched as much as he could in the tight quarters. The tiny galley reeked of beer and sweat. The river gurgled, the mosquitoes buzzed, the radio blared. Alex caused a commotion by pushing everyone out of the way as he slid out from behind the table, went outside, and jumped off the stern into the shallow water. Dean started methodically crushing beer cans on the galley counter as though he were a pile driver. *Crack. Crack. Crack.*

Bobby hunched over the table and said, "It's just you and me, Sally."

"Two dollars?"

"Yes, eight blues."

"Okay, that's all I have left."

"Put it in and deal the rest of the cards."

"Why bother?" Nelson asked. "You're both gonna win."

Giggling nervously, Sally passed out the rest of the cards and Bobby won with four kings, a lesser hand than Charlie's five aces but still impressive. Sally's aces and eights came in second best. Awestruck, Bobby not only failed to reveal what he'd seen, he was speechless. More than a cheat, she was a wonder, possessed by genius, and he felt privileged to have witnessed her work. Her only flaw was that he'd seen her do it, but he'd bet that had been no accident.

Grinning, she wrapped her arms around Bobby's neck. "You win, baby. I'm all yours—" and to Dean "—fair enough?"

"Ah, shit. Are all these dammed things empty? Anybody find a full one, let me know, will ya? My daddy always said life wasn't supposed to be fair. Nothin's fair."

*Crack.*

Slowly exhaling a deep breath, Bobby gathered the cards into the deck, turned them over face down, and shuffled. With a " 'Scuze me," Charlie returned to the cabin, lay down, and went to sleep.

"Well?" Dean said to Bobby.

"Well, what?"

"You gonna get on with it? Whatcha gonna do?"

"Oh, man, we're not gonna put on a show, Dean. Just cool it."

Sally picked up the radio and wandered out on deck where she tapped her feet in time to "The Duke of Earl," still on the charts after forty-one weeks. Only Alex in the water could see that she folded her arms around herself and trembled. Alex thought she was trembling because she was cold, which was odd because it was almost eighty degrees that night at Shanghai Bend, but she was shaking from fear that Bobby would say something and provoke another ruckus, from anticipation of what was going to happen next between her and Bobby, and from the exhilaration that comes from cheating at cards and getting away with it.

The falls whispered their song from the other end of the island. Without another word Bobby slid away from the table and into the forward cabin. A moment later they heard grunts and commotion and the hatch on the forward deck popped open. Bobby sprouted through and dragged the heavy, rolled up canvas tent onto the deck with a series of violent jerks. With a heave he pushed and kicked it over the side onto the beach.

"Sally!" he hollered.

"See you later, guys," Sally bid the rest of the boys, gathered her suitcase and radio, and disembarked from the *Toot Sweet*. On shore she picked up one end of the tent and silently followed Bobby into the woods.

# 33

The cards were cut and Alex held the deck in his hand ready to deal low hole card wild when Bobby decided to tell them something he was certain they didn't know.

"She cheated," he said flatly, adding, "She was a mechanic and a good one at that."

"What!?" Charlie squealed.

"She *what*?" Dean roared.

"You guys dug into her life, got your documents and everything, but you didn't learn that, did you," Bobby said, the edges of a smug smile quivering at the corners of his mouth.

Nelson threw up his hands in a gesture of disbelief. "Come on. That's ridiculous."

"Is it? Remember her fancy shuffle?"

"Sure. She said she played hearts with her grandmother."

"Yeah, right," Bobby said, picking up the red deck. "Remember Alex's demonstration hand?"

"Of course."

"Watch."

Bobby flipped through the cards and laid out a replica of Alex's demonstration hand.

"You can see the first player has deuces as wild cards and the second player wins with four aces, nines wild. There are a lot of aces and deuces on the table."

He could see the light dawning in Alex's eyes, but the others remained unconvinced. He gathered the cards, shuffled in Sally's manner, cut the deck, and rapidly dealt the next hand exactly as she had, six players with the winner holding an astounding five aces in five cards, Charlie's hand.

"Voilà."

"All the right cards were there in the first hand," Alex said. "The ace and deuce of hearts, all of them. It's true."

"God *damn*!"

"I didn't see how you did it," Charlie said.

Bobby scooped up the cards, shuffled nervously and said, "You're not supposed to. It took me seven years to learn that trick, but she could do it when she was sixteen, and I believe she invented it on the spot. If she'd lived to play for real money, she might have been one of the great ones, but we'll never know, will we?"

The sting in Bobby's tone cut deep into their shame and guilt, except for Nelson who shifted into cop mode and exclaimed, "This is outrageous. Let me get this straight. She cheated and you knew about it? Where's that at, Kimosabe? You could have planned it with her when you were out by the falls."

"Very good, Lieutenant. I understand you have to ask, but no, it didn't happen that way. I had no idea she was capable of stacking the deck and planting a hand until I saw her do it."

"When?"

"On the very next hand. She was dealing seconds and pulling cards off the bottom, flick flick flick so slick it was greased."

"You didn't tell us."

"No, sir, I most certainly did not. There was no way in hell I was going to blow the whistle. I mean, I was the beneficiary, right? She was cheating on my behalf, if not for herself. I was in absolute awe, and that's what I meant when I said she blew my mind. She just blew me away, man, like nobody before or since."

Wham, the darkness. Bobby blinked rapidly and steeled his mind to remain in control of his body. He went on, "If she'd quit after the first hand, I might never have figured it out. You said she played with our heads, but Alex, she did it with the cards. We didn't stand a chance."

"So why'd she deal me the winning hand?" Charlie asked.

"Damned if I know, but she could tell you were gay. How? Got me. In those days you acted straight, and nobody knew about you except us. For God's sake, Charlie, not even your parents knew. It wasn't like today. And then along comes Sally out of nowhere with insight I can't fathom, and she had us pegged the minute she stepped onto the boat and saw our tattoos. Dealing Charlie the winning hand and knowing what he would do was a game so out of our league, all of us, you never knew until now that you were had. Believe me, I've spent a thousand sleepless nights wondering what would have happened if I'd said something, but we'll never know."

"So it wasn't fair, after all," Dean mumbled.

"Not even close. Like your daddy said: nothin's fair. Look, if she was the queen of hearts at sixteen, maybe if she were alive today, forty-eight years old, she'd be fat and grotesque, smoke too much and have an addiction to the ten-twenty Texas Hold 'Em table at Binion's Horseshoe in Vegas."

"I've seen plenty of them," Nelson said.

"We all have. I make my living off of them."

"Ever catch one dealing seconds?" Alex asked.

"I leave that to the pit bosses. Not my business. Besides, in casinos the players don't deal. Only dealers deal for just that reason."

"What about private games?"

"Like this one?"

"Yeah."

"I walk out. It's happened a couple of times, not very often. Good players don't need to cheat; but for some people, it's their nature."

"Like Sally?" Dean asked.

"Damned if I know."

"Are we gonna play or what?" Alex demanded.

"Wild thing," Charlie sang, a little giddy. "You make my heart go ring a ding ding."

"Ante up."

A wave of revulsion surged through Bobby like a tide. The room began to spin like a time machine, jerking him into the past, and he remembered how much he'd wanted to kill them. Before Alex could deal the hand, Bobby stood abruptly and swept the table with cold eyes.

"I'm taking a break," he announced and walked out of the suite and down the corridor to his room.

# 34

Lying on a hotel bed, eyes closed, a canvas bag containing $1.3 million for a pillow, he remembered the hand as if they'd played it only a few minutes ago.

Holy moley, she was dealing seconds. What happened took no more than five seconds, so fast that in order to understand it he'd stretched the rapid events into a series of slow, frame by frame images. Scooping up the cards from the previous hand, sorting them, cutting them into the deck, the shuffle that looked impressive but only shuffled half the cards, the cut, the thumbnail chewed and ragged under a coat of chipped, red polish, the motion separated into the pass, the snatch and the deal. Sally had wrought a clinic in sleight of hand, a moment of perfection, a masterpiece, and over the years he'd compiled a long list of superlatives that celebrated her achievement but couldn't answer the only important question: Why did she cheat? Why had she given him that last card, the king of clubs for the winning hand?

He hadn't asked and therefore didn't know the truth but could only guess, a futile yet unavoidable exercise. Did she do it because she could or because she was a natural anarchist who hated rules? That was a good one. She made her own rules, but they were rules nonetheless. To succeed, cheating at cards required the precise timing and discipline of a concert violinist, so that wasn't the answer. Sometimes he thought she did it for the thrill, the big jolt, the delicious home run feeling that came from working a scam and scoring. He'd known scumbags of that ilk. He could say to himself, well, she was a hustler and a cheat, anathema to every principle he'd ever held, and all his other thoughts about her were delusions. He'd never cheated at cards in his life. Once in the army he'd caught a soldier cheating in a barracks poker game and had almost beaten him to death. Why was Sally different? Because she was a girl, a sweet young thing who did it for fun? He didn't know. There were no easy answers. All he knew for certain was that he'd loved her so much in half a day that he'd used up his lifetime quota of love.

He hadn't loved the army or Vietnam and he'd hated the war. He didn't love poker, either—he needed it and that was different. He'd tried to love his wives, but he'd chosen women not for their own qualities but because they'd superficially resembled Sally, short blondes with quick wits. The marriages were doomed, and he didn't really know his children. Oh, Christ. He'd loved Sally and one of those bastards killed her. Maybe all of them. He'd been cheated, all right, but not by the queen of hearts.

Do the right thing? What the hell was that? Take the money and walk out? Kill them all and then stand off the cops in a fucking hotel room? He'd be on TV, oh boy. At any time over the years he could have learned where they lived, and killing them would have been easy. Long ago in another life he'd been skilled in weaponry and the ways of violent death. That was the nature of war, but he was no longer a warrior. He was just a card player who wanted justice for a girl long dead; he wanted them to pay, not simply with blood or money—he wasn't a fool; he'd take the money—but with their hearts. First, he wanted the truth, and he hoped he'd be able to stand up to it, deal with it, learn from it, and find release.

He wanted to see the light, if only for a moment.

He remembered her touch, the softness of her lips, her delight in his body.

He cried himself to sleep, and dreamed.

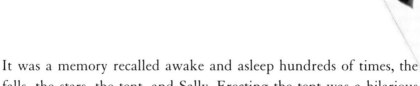

# 35

It was a memory recalled awake and asleep hundreds of times, the falls, the stars, the tent, and Sally. Erecting the tent was a hilarious fiasco, fumbling in the dark, the poles collapsing twice in heaps of canvas and laughter before they got it right.

"Some Eagle Scout you are, city boy," she cracked.

Finally pitched twenty feet from the cool, black river, the tent sloped slightly downhill at the edge of the woods overlooking the strange rock formations and hissing falls. To this one-note melody Bobby added a primitive beat by whacking steel with a flat granite saucer. Sally knelt beside him, gently holding the stake while he struck sparks.

"Steady . . . steady . . . okay." Bobby wiped a trace of sweat from his forehead. "That's the last one," he said, brushing his hands together, workmanlike. "I think it'll hold."

They remained kneeling side by side for a long minute, breathing the heady perfume of the great valley. The moon had disappeared behind the levee, and the only light was starlight from the universe revolving overhead.

"Do you think we'll be in San Francisco tomorrow?" she asked, almost in a whisper.

"We don't have to be back for another couple days. You in a hurry?"

"I was, but not now."

Not shy, Sally threw an arm around his neck and held him tight. Planting a big kiss on his forehead, she pressed against him cheek to cheek and looked straight up at the Big Dipper. Bobby's attention was focused much closer than distant heavenly bodies. An inch from his lips, the downy hair on her arm was too close to resist. He licked her sweat, tasting her, and felt so dizzy he thought he'd swoon.

"I bet you know the names of the stars," she said.

He thought: I don't want to bet; I don't want to think, I just want one hundred million years of biology to work its simple magic.

"Which one is Andromeda?" she asked.

Bobby glanced up at the blizzard of stars and explained, "Andromeda is a galaxy. Most stars don't have names, like Polaris, the North Star. They have numbers."

"Numbers? Bobby, stars have souls. Everything comes from stars, even people, especially people. People are stars that can talk. That's what we are, the eyes and ears and voices of our star, the sun."

Twisting sideways, he gazed into the silky face so close to his, unsure how to respond to this description of the cosmos never mentioned by Oppenheimer or Heisenberg, his favorite physicists. With no warning, at a moment when he was most vulnerable, Sally's handful of words peeled away everything he thought he knew and precipitated the first spiritual experience of his eighteen years. Bobby's consciousness bounced from gonads to brain and his mind opened like a sunrise.

"People are stars? You're a star?"

"Yes, and so are you, and we can talk to other stars, but they're so far away, it takes a long time before they talk back. It makes as much sense as talking to God."

At that moment Bobby fell in love.

"You're not so far away," he said.

She giggled.

"How'd you come up with that? Talking to stars?" he stammered.

"I don't know," she breathed with a nervous laugh. "I heard it from some people on the beach. They were Hindus or Buddhists or something." Then she said, "I'm a virgin."

Taken aback, his mind reeling as his thoughts retreated to the swollen blood vessels between his legs, he blinked in surprise and said, "You could've fooled me."

"Sure, that's easy," she said with a grin. "I fool people all the time. I lie and tease and make up stories because I'm not an honest person,

Bobby, at least until now. I think I told my first lie the day I learned to talk, and why not? Everything everyone ever told me was a lie, and they're all liars except you, and I only met you today. That doesn't matter because I don't think you'd ever lie to me, so I'm telling you the truth. I don't want to lie to you or be a tease, and I don't want to be a virgin anymore, either." She giggled again. "Are you nervous?" she asked, tickling his ribs.

"Yes," he admitted.

"See? You can't lie any more than I can. I'm nervous, too. I'm scared to death."

"You weren't nervous at the card table."

"Maybe you didn't see, but I was."

She reached behind her into her bra strap and came out with the ace of hearts.

No longer surprised by being surprised, he mumbled, "Jesus, you're too much."

"You can never have too much of a good thing," she said, laughing.

"Sally, you—"

Putting her finger to his lips, she whispered, "Don't say anything, you didn't see anything, just believe that I wanted you to win and you did. There now, that's one fine tent, ready and waiting like a little house in the wilderness."

The breeze carried the faint sound of the boys rollicking drunkenly on the boat at the other end of the island.

"Do you think they'll leave us alone?" Bobby wondered aloud.

"I don't care," she said, pushing through the opening of the tent. When he hesitated, she urged, "Well, come on."

Sally turned the radio on softly. Inside the tent it was dark and smelled of canvas and must. He heard Sally rustling close to him, unrolling a sleeping bag. Suddenly he smelled her powerful odor of lemony Jean Naté cologne, river mist, and ripe young woman. He felt woozy and high, and as he lay down, reaching for her, he felt the skin of her belly, warm and aquiver. She'd already unbuttoned her shirt and unhooked her bra, and she pressed his hand against her breast. He could feel her heartbeat, and her intense heat sent colors rocketing through his brain, infrareds and ultraviolets and colors without names. He felt as though the stars had burned through the tent and bored inside his head. A supernova exploded only a few light-seconds away, and Bobby felt himself being drawn into the primeval light, the source of life itself.

He kicked off his shoes and tore at the buttons on his jeans. Wolfman Jack reached across the ether and played a rock and roll love song.

"Oh, Bobby," Sally said. "Star light, star bright, first star I see tonight, wish I may, wish I might, grant this wish—"

# 36

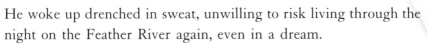

He woke up drenched in sweat, unwilling to risk living through the night on the Feather River again, even in a dream.

"Stars that talk, Christ," he uttered aloud, laughing at himself, pleased the dream hadn't robbed him of his sense of humor. "Jesus, I'm still talking to stars."

Awake, he could remember their lovemaking and what it felt like, the tug of her cherry, her forceful, determined pelvic thrust that burst the membrane, her tiny scream of exultation, legs locking behind his back and how they both came and came all night, their entire bodies convulsing in a prolonged orgasm of cosmic, perfect sex—but he couldn't really capture the reverie of his few hours with Sally unless he was asleep; then, as often as not, the dream went on too long and turned into a nightmare.

Sometimes he saw her hovering lifeless underwater staring blindly at the fishes; other times she was a cheerleader fucking the football team in the locker room with Alex, Charlie, Dean, and Nelson in shoulder pads and jerseys. Once in a while he and Sally rose fresh and bright the next morning, returned safely to San Francisco and lived happily ever after. When that cruel version of the dream woke him up choking and sobbing in rage, wives and girlfriends always thought he was having a nightmare about the war. He never told them otherwise.

As time went by the nightmares disappeared for as long as a year, yet for reasons he could never discern they always returned, and he suffered until he stopped the horror with booze and dope. In the beginning, disguising his condition in Vietnam was easy; crazed, drunken junkies were indistinguishable from crazed soldiers who were stone cold sober. After the war, the army took care of its own,

smothering and concealing the foibles of Sergeant McCorkle, genuine hero, for ten years until he retired. When the nightmares descended on Bobby McCorkle, civilian poker player, he binged, often
for months until he was sick or broke or both. Tap city—reduced
to living on his pension—he dried out, cleaned up, and started playing cards until the cycle started anew. Although he believed in the
power of the game to keep him alive, in his heart he didn't feel his
life could change, and he wasn't convinced he wanted it to change.
He lived on the brink of oblivion because he liked it. Playing for
keeps gave him a thrill. He'd come to San Francisco with the frail
hope that hearing the truth from his old buddies would end the
nightmares. No such luck. Lying on the bed in the Palace Hotel he
shouted, "Wrong!" and laughed at himself again.

After listening to bullshit for twenty-four hours, his slim flask of
hope had run dry. Knowing the exact cause of Sally's death could
only make the nightmares worse. The truth—that elusive bugaboo—
was that the boys from Noë Valley were afraid of their dirty little
secret, millions of dollars worth of afraid, but a fat bag of money
would only buy him a few months until he spent it or gave it away
or lost it in Biloxi. Alex and the rest were pathetic bastards who
believed money could buy respectability and solve their problems.
The sad part was that in their world they were usually right, but
he didn't live in their world. Money couldn't solve his problems or
significantly alter his life. He, not Alex, was supposed to have been
the professor, and he easily could have become a cop like Nelson or
run a business like Charlie or even lived as a quasi-outlaw freak like
Dean. As it happened, it didn't turn out that way, and he couldn't
blame his choices on them any more than he could chart his life by
the stars. Neither karma nor fate nor destiny nor any other form of
nonsense was responsible for his life. He was. Every time he sat
down he had to play the hand he was dealt. One time the deck was
stacked against him and he lost. Sally, with all her skills, never got
to play her cards, forever aces and eights, the infamous dead man's
hand.

If there was anything to chastise himself about that night, it was
that he hadn't exactly fallen asleep in the tent—he'd passed out dead

drunk. In the middle of the night he'd gone back to the boat for more beer, found Charlie and Nelson asleep and Alex still playing five stud with a sulking, glowering Dean. No one had said anything. He'd simply grinned and shrugged, grabbed a six-pack and split. At that point his memory faltered. He remembered fragments of more sex, more drinking, and more talk before he passed out. When he woke up a few hours later four of the six beer cans were empty and Sally was dead.

Her lungs drew no breath; her heart was still; she didn't sweat or see or talk to the stars, and when Bobby saw her blue and bleeding, his head began to implode like a dying star. In an instant he was taken from the most wonderful night of his life, the zenith of his existence, to the worst moment he could imagine. In a flash his future evaporated like river mist in the morning sun. The fuse was lit, the detonation only seconds away—

He got off the bed, splashed cold water on his face, opened the well-stocked minibar and stopped his hand an inch from a bottle of tequila. Poker, he reminded himself. You can't play when you're loaded, and there's a ton of money to be won. He drank a can of tomato juice instead.

There was no salvation for Bobby McCorkle, poker player from Reno, but justice had to exist for Sally, the runaway who talked to the stars. *Star light, star bright, grant this wish I wish tonight.* Would dragging Alex, Dean, Nelson, and Charlie into court provide justice? Legal proceedings would destroy their tidy lives and embarrass their families, but they'd have expensive lawyers who knew how to blur the line between guilt and innocence. The scumbags would plea bargain, negotiate, post bail, file motions, hire experts to delay and obfuscate until in the end their clients would walk away poorer and humiliated but free. No justice there. What else was there? He could kill them, but ritual execution would be nothing more than vengeance. Revenge was for fools, bad movies, and the Count of Monte Cristo, and killing them would say more about him than about them. He was no angel of vengeance. Hell, he was no angel of any kind.

He locked Sally away in the corner of his mind where she lived like an eternal flame, smelling good, shining bright, smiling like an oracle. His mind steady, he ordered a club sandwich from room service, took a shower, and ate the sandwich. Then he toted the bag stuffed with C-notes down to the front desk and checked it into a lock-box.

The lobby was busy and through the glass doors he saw swirls of fog blowing down New Montgomery Street. Frisco. The wicked city beckoned, her devil-may-care attitude on full display in the sexy clothes of the women, the smiles of the men, the profound understanding of a people who lived directly atop an earthquake fault and didn't give a damn about anything except the party that wouldn't stop until bang! The Big One. Six miles straight down the great fissure shifted a fraction of a millimeter, and Bobby felt it in his soul. The earth moved! God damn! Bobby breathed it in and liked it and let it enhance his mood. Out of sight around the corner a lone guitar player sang the blues.

*Oh lawd oh lawd, baboom baboom. Oh lawd oh lawd, baboom baboom. My baby done lef' me an' I'm so all alone. Baboom baboom. I'm just a lonely old houn' dog lookin' to bury his bone. Baboom baboom.*

He looked into the bar. Standing near the entrance, smelling the liquor, he imagined that after two or three double tequilas he'd be saying, what dream? I don't got to show you no stinking dream. A couple more and he'd be in Dolores Park flushing out some China White, the perfect nightmare cure in a little plastic bag.

He had a game lined up in Biloxi later in the week. Maybe afterwards he'd go into New Orleans and blow it out his ear on Bourbon Street. Tonight, he felt obliged to seek justice for Sally. He'd take their money at low hole card wild or any other damned game, and not just their money. He wanted everything they had.

He headed for the elevators. It was a good night to stay inside and play cards. You deal the hand and play the cards, and when it's over only one question is answered, not a cosmic or moral question or a question about the meaning of life, just who wins and who loses.

# 37

No one dared chase after Bobby this time. A muffled Saturday night drifted up from the streets below, but the city no longer existed for the men in the Enrico Caruso Suite. The game had been suspended, the stereo silenced, and the suite was dark; even the light over the card table had been extinguished.

Shocked by the depth of Bobby's contempt, they'd spread out, each wrestling with his own moral quandary. Alex and Charlie lay on opposite couches in the living room, Dean on the plush carpet, and Nelson on a bed in one of the bedrooms. They'd regressed into adolescence, loudly bellowing comments and flurries of conversation back and forth in the dark with long pauses in between, the way they had as kids late at night announcing newly discovered common truths as though they were earth-shattering revelations.

"After all these years, he still hates us," Nelson said.

*Pause.*

"So was it a mistake to bring him here and give him the money?"

"No. It's okay. It'll be a great game, but I can't say I blame him," Alex answered.

*Pause.*

"Who do we blame?" Nelson asked.

"Everyone but Charlie. He was the only one who wasn't crazy with horniness."

"Is that right, Charlie?"

"I was horny, all right, but not for Sally."

"Bobby?"

"Sure."

*Pause.*

"You still feel the same way?"

"No."

*Pause.*

"Are we going to tell him the story?"

"Only if we have to. Maybe we won't, but we probably will."

*Pause.*

"Are you going to beat him, Alex?"

"I haven't lost yet."

"You haven't played Bobby, either."

"I know how he plays, but if I lose, we agreed a long time ago that it would be worth it."

*Pause.*

"Hey, Nelson, did you really paint that '62 the original yellow?"

"I did."

"Cool."

*Pause.*

"Do you believe Sally cheated?" Dean wondered.

"Yes."

*Pause.*

"I wonder how she learned."

"Who knows? It doesn't matter."

"Then what the hell does matter, Alex?"

"The truth matters," Nelson interjected.

"Oh, bullshit," Alex said. "The truth isn't cast in stone. It's only what people say it is."

"Thank you, Socrates, for your wise discourse."

"Fuck you, Nelson."

*Pause.*

"If you were Socrates, you'd drink the hemlock and flip everyone the bird," Nelson surmised.

"Oh, yeah?"

"Yeah."

"Fuck you."

"If the truth doesn't matter, what does?" Charlie asked.

Alex got off the couch, switched on the light over the table, and contemplated the cards and chips.

"Poker matters," he said, peeling a card off the blue deck, the six of diamonds, and speaking to it like an old friend. "Poker is important because it's immediate and uncertain. Poker is an absolute in a world that has rejected absolutes. You win or you lose, and as we know, the best hand doesn't always win but the best player does. It's a perfect escape from reality if reality is too painful, yet poker can be the most painful reality of all. You can lose. You have to risk losing, and you put more than chips into the pot. You wager your soul. You have to make choices on every card, just like in life, and you might be wrong. We made a choice when we were kids, right or wrong, but we made it and lived with it, knowing it would come back to haunt us. And here we are, plagued by a ghost of our own creation. Even Bobby is a ghost, a phantom we've conjured up from the past. It's like resurrecting James Dean or Elvis. And what is our phantom? A mirror in which we see our own reflections. Because of Bobby, we have to make our choice all over again. If we were real men with real character, we wouldn't need Bobby to force us to do the right thing. But we're not, we're thoroughly modern cowards, hypocrites, and liars, and so we need him." His voice trailed off as he picked up the deck and shuffled.

"You're really fuckin' crazy, Alex. You know that?"

"Crazy? Your language is astonishingly imprecise, Lieutenant. As a policeman you should know that being crazy is no longer a crime. It may be the only way to remain sane in a corrupt and oppressive world, especially one of your own making."

*The longest and last pause.*

"He loved her, and that's a powerful force," Alex said, feeling lame and deficient. "He needs to hear the story."

"He might kill us," Dean said.

"So what? We've talked about this a million times, man, and we know that. We have to take our chances."

"*So what?* He says, 'So what?' Bobby is a trained killer."

"He *was*, and that was a long time ago during the war. So were you, Dean, Captain Semper Fi United States Marine Corps. Yea, though I walk through the shadow of the Valley of Death I shall fear no evil 'cause I'm the baddest motherfucker in the Valley. I repeat: so what?"

"You don't forget how."

"You don't forget why, either."

"He has plenty of reasons."

"That doesn't make him a murderer. He's not a murderer."

"Define murder."

"Oh, for God's sake, Dean. Since when are you a lawyer? Every year you get melodramatic and threaten to kill yourself. I'd thought you'd be happy to have Bobby oblige you and put you out of your misery."

Dean raised himself off the floor, walked over to the table and sat down.

"That's just talk and you know it, Wiz."

"But this is real, is that it? Bobby makes it real. Bobby makes you afraid that you might have to pay for your sins."

"You're not afraid?"

"Of course I am, but why dwell on it?" Alex said with a big smile. "I'm a Zen Buddhist. I'll accept my fate."

"Yeah, some Buddhist. If you're a Buddhist, I'm Santa Claus."

Nelson came out of the bedroom and took his place at the table. "You guys can talk more bullshit than a room full of convicts, I swear to God," he said, shaking his head.

"We can still have a hell of a card game," Alex said peevishly. "We've been saving our dough and planning this game for a long time, just for this, to play for millions. What the hell, this is San Francisco, our precious little hometown. Eat, drink, and be merry because tomorrow—" He drew a finger across his throat.

"Afraid of the Big One, Wiz? That why you stayed in New York?"

"Qué será será, amigo."

The discussion was interrupted by a knock at the door. Dean's head instantly jerked toward the foyer.

Charlie roused himself from the couch, flipped on the lights, looked out the peephole and waved at everyone to relax before un-latching the door to let Bobby in.

"Feeling better?" Charlie asked, the solicitous good host.

"Definitely, much better, yeah, thanks," Bobby answered with a convivial grin. "I took a nap and splashed on some fresh cologne like Minnesota Fats, so watch your money, Charlie."

He tapped Charlie gently on the chest, crossed the room, and sat down at the card table. The game was poised in freeze-frame, waiting, the piles of chips untouched.

Grinning, all traces of anger removed like makeup and replaced with a mask of serenity, Bobby poured a glass of soda and squeezed the juice from a wedge of lime into his drink. Taking a sip, his eyes flashed X rays around the table, taking snapshots of four nervous, frightened souls. Only Alex stared back, resolutely recording every twitch, and Bobby weathered Alex's scrutiny by squinting and looking up at the lights.

"Jeez, it's bright in here. You guys must have quit playing."

"We all took a break," Nelson said.

"I can turn down the lights, no problem," Charlie said, reaching for the dimmer.

As the lights came down, reducing the suite to the familiar cone of illumination over the table, Bobby set a blue chip on the back of his left hand and delicately rolled the chip from finger to finger without touching it with his other hand.

Charlie said, "Wow."

Alex chuckled.

Bobby winked.

"Zounds!" Dean exclaimed.

"You like that?" Bobby asked, his voice laced with the gentlest of acids. "Is that what you want? Tricks?" He laughed and held open his coat. "No more tricks, no more fooling around. I know only one way to have a fair trial and pass judgment. If you gentlemen are ready, let's play poker."

# 38

"Let's have fresh cards."

"Good idea."

Charlie broke out two sealed packs of playing cards and gave one to Alex and one to Dean.

"It's still Alex's deal."

"Low hole card wild?" Alex asked.

"Nah."

"Fegiddaboudit."

"Okay," Alex said, thumbing the slick new deck. "Five stud. Cut the cards, Nelson, cut the cards. That's good, okay, a five to Dean, a jack to Bobby, another jack to Charlie, a seven to Nelson, and a six to me. First jack bets. Bobby?"

"Five thousand on the jack."

"Five thousand is the bet. Five thousand, five thousand. Charlie?"

"I'm in."

Bobby lit a cigarette and checked the table. They're just players, he mused, rich amateurs with too much money they're just dying to lose. Except Alex. Dear old Alex had blood in his eye and poker lust in his heart. Tiny creases at the corners of his mouth revealed an undercurrent of anxiety. The Wiz wanted to win so bad he could taste it. Well, Bobby thought, let him have a little taste. Let him have ideas.

Bobby relaxed, smoked, and settled in. He had all night, all day, all week if he wanted. They weren't merely opponents now; they were targets.

"I'm out," Nelson declared.

"See the five."

"I'll see the five and raise five."

"Well, all right, there's a player in this game. Let's get it on."

They played straight poker through the evening and into the night, five stud, seven stud, five draw jacks or better, a little lowball, and a few hands of high-low split-the-pot to spice things up. A stack of vinyl crooners—Ben E. King, Jackie Wilson, Judy Henske, Bobby Darin—serenaded the table from the stereo, a smooth counterpoint to the tension rippling like an electric charge across the green felt. Charlie ordered a buffet spread from room service, and they made sandwiches without stopping play. The game was on, the dream game, the big money game.

"See your twenty and raise fifty," Alex said.

"You raise me fifty grand on that piece of shit?" Dean boomed. "Whoa, mamma, button yo' buttons. You got two measly, dinky nothing pairs showing against my four cards to a queen high straight. Tell you what. You're gonna do the humpty dumpty and fall down go smash all the king's horses and all the king's men ate one hell of a Joe's Special. Eggs, hamburger, spinach, and onion, for your information. I'll see your fifty and raise you one hundred thousand smackers. *Yeah.*"

"A hundred grand? Okay, your hundred and up another hundred."

Two hundred seventy thousand dollars on the seventh card in an ordinary hand. This was big time poker, crazy and wonderful, their teenage fantasy of what a poker game should be, playing for stakes beyond imagination. Even Bobby had never seen anything quite like it.

"We coulda done this a long time ago if you'da showed up, Kimosabe," Nelson said.

"Wouldn't have been as much dough to play with, right? I mean, you guys put more in every year."

"That's true. Twenty-five grand each into the poker pot for twenty years."

"Glad I waited. Ante up, boys. Let's play a hand of seven stud."

"Hey, the wheel of fortune is spinning my way."

"You wish."

Adrenaline city, shrieks and groans, flying cards, chips clinking into the pot, rattling ice, and Judy Henske belting "Baltimore Oriole."

"She was the only woman I ever loved," Charlie exclaimed with a cackle. "Judy baby! Queen of the beatniks."

"I remember," Bobby said. "At The Hungry i with the brick wall and the chicks all in black."

"That was the joint," Charlie reminisced. "I was there the night Lenny Bruce got busted."

"The first time or the second time?" Nelson asked.

"How the hell do I know? There was me and about a hundred cops and Lenny Bruce. He was the first man I ever loved."

"You're a sick motherfucker, you know?"

"Hahaha, at least I know what I like. The real edgy types . . . like Bobby. Hahaha."

"Screw the nostalgia," Alex growled. "Play cards."

Once the giddiness passed, the ebb and flow ran true to form with Charlie and Nelson losing steadily, Dean swinging wildly from ahead to behind and vice versa, and Bobby and Alex winning. They didn't talk about Shanghai Bend; they played cards with a desperate intensity, wolfishly devouring the rituals, the contests of wit and will, the jousting and fencing and laughs. Between hands Bobby was amused by anecdotes from previous years in the Caruso Suite. The fake robbery was re-enacted and embellished like an old family recipe, and the game went on, twenty thousand on a card, thirty, fifty, with so much money in every pot that every card was a legend in spades, hearts, clubs, and diamonds. For a few hours the game was pure poker, five card poetry. Of the 2,598,960 possible poker hands in a straight deck with no wild cards, they saw their fair share.

Slowly but steadily Bobby juiced the game, increasing his bets in small increments, changing styles from hand to hand to confuse his opponents, bluffing, folding, raising, checking, and all the while keeping up a charming patter of jokes. When Bobby felt he had a mission in a game, he babbled an endless supply of short, fast jokes, dirty jokes, clean jokes, ethnic jokes, even elephant jokes.

"What's the gooey stuff between an elephant's toes?"

"I dunno. What?"

"I called your pair. What d'ya got, Wiz?"

"Tens up."

"Slow natives. Bippitty boppitty boom, three sixes, Satan's trips. I think that beats two pair."

"Slow natives? Jesus, enough jokes, already. Let's play cards!"

"Easy, Alex. Cut the deck and keep your hat on."

"I may eat this hat before this night is over."

"Like the time Nelson ate the chip," Charlie said.

"Aren't you ever gonna forget that?"

"Nope."

"Somebody crank up the heat. I'm gonna take off my shirt."

Dean ripped off his red-and-black plaid lumberjack's shirt and undershirt and let his tattoos hang out.

"You don't want any more jokes, Alex?" Bobby asked mildly. "Lost your sense of humor?"

"It's a distraction."

"It's supposed to be. This entire card game is a distraction, but that's okay with me. I came to play and to win, and not for any other reason. How about you?"

Alex smiled and said nothing.

# 39

A few minutes past midnight, Nelson dealing, Bobby caught three jacks—spades, diamonds, and clubs—as his first three cards in a hand of seven card stud. To his left, Charlie's ace of hearts was the high card on the table.

"Ace bets. Lookin' good there, Charlie."

"Ace opens for twenty-five thou."

"Got something there, Fishman?" Nelson asked, looking at a ten. "I'm in."

"I'm out," Alex said.

Dean folded and Bobby silently saw the bet. On the next card Bobby was dealt the ten of clubs, Charlie the king of hearts and Nelson a four, no help.

"Fifty on the ace king," Charlie wagered.

"Adios," Nelson said, turning over his cards. "You got my ten, dude."

"Fifty and up fifty," Bobby said, watching Charlie the way a hawk watches a jackrabbit.

"See your raise and raise you back a hundred," Charlie said, so excited he started to bounce and weave in his chair.

"All right," Bobby said, calm and cool.

"Next card," Nelson intoned. "A nine to Bobby and the queen of hearts to Charlie. Running a straight flush in hearts, ace, king, and queen looking mighty pretty. And Bobby's looking at a straight. Ace still bets."

"Two fifty."

"Wanna be a heavy hitter, hey, Charlie? I'll see it. Two fifty it is."

"Next card, the jack of hearts to Charlie and an eight to Bobby. Ace?"

Charlie stared at his chips for a long time. With two hundred thousand left he bet half.

"Hundred grand."

"See your hundred and raise a hundred," Bobby said without hesitation. "Table stakes, right? That puts you all in, Charlie. You better have cards."

Charlie blinked and blinked again and put in his chips.

"Last card," Nelson said. "Since Charlie's all in, I can flip them up."

"No," Bobby said. "Down."

"Okay, down," Charlie agreed.

Nelson slipped a card across the felt to each player and Bobby peeked at his, the ten of hearts, the card that would have given Charlie a royal flush. Instead, it left Charlie with a flush or straight and gave Bobby a full house, jacks and tens, and a lock on the hand.

"Would you like to make a bet before you turn your cards over, Charlie?" Bobby asked.

Charlie gestured toward the empty green felt in front of him. "I'm all in."

"We can raise the stakes," Bobby said evenly.

Alex, who'd been gazing at the heroes on the wall, snapped around and listened to Charlie's response.

"Raise the stakes to what?" Charlie asked, his voice strained and husky.

"What would you like to bet, Charlie? A million dollars?" Bobby said with a smile. "I'll take your marker."

There it is, Alex thought. Thrilled and exhilarated, Bobby was injecting pure savagery into the game.

"Hahaha, you gotta be kiddin'."

"I'm not kidding. If we flip these cards over now and you lose your stake, you walk away feeling no pain. You bought in for a half million because you could afford it. You lose and walk away thinking you paid for my silence, but it isn't enough. It isn't poker unless it hurts, Charlie. A million would be nice. Hooper Fish would be better," Bobby added.

"*Jesus!*"

Dean started to laugh, and Nelson shook his head and buried it in his arms.

"Isn't that what you came here for, Charlie, to risk everything?" Bobby asked. "To let the cards decide if you deserve what you have? It looks to me like you have pretty good cards."

"You want me to bet my company?" Charlie asked, his heart suddenly racing. "Hooper Fish against what?"

With that question Charlie exposed himself like a fish waiting to be gutted. Alex took a deep breath and nodded, laced his fingers, and rested them on the table.

"Everything I have here," Bobby said to Charlie, passing his hand over his chips. "About three quarters of a mil in chips, plus the one point three I put in the hotel safe. I don't know what you think your company is worth, but that's what it's worth to me. If I win, I'm the fish man. If you win, I'm busted. Finito."

"Jesus, I gotta think about this. You have an eight, nine, ten and jack showing, and if you have a straight, I still have you beat."

"Maybe, if you have the flush. Maybe you have a straight flush, a royal flush. In that case, you can't lose."

"You can just turn over the cards and see who wins, you know," Dean said.

"It's up to Charlie," Nelson reminded, "but if we go beyond table stakes we're setting a dangerous precedent. It's really going for broke."

"Isn't that what the game is all about?" Alex said.

"No limit," Dean added. "The perfect game."

"Perfect for you," Charlie snarled at Dean. "You're not on the hot seat."

"If Charlie's in for everything, it's only a matter of time before we're all in," Alex said. "I say go for it, Charlie."

Bobby smiled, a cold, ruthless smile that came from the bottom of his heart.

"Oh, man," Charlie moaned, sweating.

"C'mon, Charlie. What's it gonna be?" Nelson demanded in his capacity as dealer.

Charlie got the shakes, trembling with such violence that he rattled the chips and had to stand up and walk around the room, mumbling, "Oh shit, oh, shit, three generations, oh, Christ."

"I got a deal for you, Charlie," Bobby said. "Answer me this. How much profit did your company make last year?"

"About eight hundred grand."

"Okay. We can simply turn over the cards now, and maybe you'll win, but if you lose, you're out of the game unless you want to buy in again. Now, you put your company in the pot, and if I win, I'll pay you twenty-five percent of the profits or two hundred thousand a year to run the company for me. I'll give you your two hundred grand for the next year in advance and you can stay in the game and maybe win your company back. That's if you lose the hand, of course. Maybe you'll win."

Charlie's face turned gray. The hilarity and high spirits had disappeared like the Golden Gate Bridge in the fog. Dark shadows surrounded his eyes.

"Do you want a marker?" he asked. "Do you want me to write it out?"

"Your word is good, Charlie," Bobby replied with a smile.

"Shit, I don't know what to do."

"Take your time. Remember, the last time we played, you were the big winner. You won the girl. You might be lucky again."

Bobby calmly laid his cards face down on the table and made a turkey sandwich in the kitchenette. Charlie was such easy prey that he feared he'd gone for the kill too quickly, putting the others on alert and blowing his chances for a real coup. He wanted them to pay for the luxuries they bought with Sally's life, and he wanted them to come willingly to slaughter.

"It looks like you have a hell of a hand, Charlie," Alex said.

"All right," Charlie said, and returned to the table but didn't sit. "I bet the company against . . . against whatever Bobby said."

"I'll call that bet," Bobby replied and took a bite of his sandwich. "Let's see your cards."

Charlie turned over an ace high flush in hearts.

"Very nice," Bobby said. In no hurry, he licked a smear of mayonnaise off his fingers, leaned over the table, and flipped over his hole cards, revealing two jacks and the ten for a full house, a superior hand to any flush. With a groan Charlie sank into an overstuffed chair and buried his head between his knees in a posture of devastation.

Son of a gun, Bobby thought, we finally have a game that means something.

# 40

Dean shook his head and said, "Talk about a hidden hand, Jeez."

"Tough luck, Charlie," Nelson said.

Charlie answered with another groan of anguish. "You finally got your way, Dean," he said. "No limit."

"Bobby had his ten," Alex commented. "It was a lock."

Bobby gathered in the pot, counted out two hundred thousand in chips and pushed them across the felt to Charlie's spot.

"You can stay in the game, Charlie," he said. "That's your pay for a year. It's a lot of dough."

"I'm ruined," Charlie moaned. "I can't believe I'm such an idiot. It happened so fast, I lost my head."

"You didn't lose your head," Dean quipped. "Just your company."

"It's all over."

"It's not over," Alex barked. "You're still in this game. Get your ass over here. You have two hundred G's, and that's not twiddly winks."

"I'll just lose that, too. I always lose."

"Come on, Charlie. Sit down and play cards," Nelson pleaded.

"What's left to play for? Fun? Ha ha ha."

"You're still in this game whether you like it or not. Maybe you can win it back. C'mon," Alex insisted. "It's my deal."

Reluctantly, as though compelled by forces beyond his control, Charlie took his seat and tossed in his ante.

"Seven stud, dealing."

The game had an edge now, not the honed edge of a fine razor but rather the nasty, corroded edge of an old Gillette blue blade. One o'clock in the morning rolled around, two o'clock, two thirty, and with the stakes so high, most hands were decided quickly when players folded without sticking to the end. Bobby's bets were sharp and precise, his play increasingly aggressive and provocative. Dean tried to stay with him and got stung time and again, expressing his frustration by sucking air and grinding his teeth. Nelson played scared, folding frequently, never bluffing, and winning only small pots because when he bet, everyone knew he had good cards and dropped. Charlie folded every hand, trying to conserve his chips and stay in the game although his heart was no longer in it.

Only Alex matched Bobby pot for pot, beating the other players but unable to force Bobby into a showdown. As the night progressed, Alex realized Bobby was merely waiting for the right cards to demolish each opponent the way he'd reduced Charlie to a sniveling puddle of misery. Aware of his strategy, the others were playing like frightened rabbits, but Alex wasn't going to concede the game, not by a long shot.

Caressing the blue deck, ready to deal, he decided to bluff and see if he could bring Bobby down a notch.

"Five draw, jacks or better."

Alex dealt the hand and looked at his cards one at a time in his usual fashion. He had a pair of fives, not good enough to open.

"Dean?"

"Open for ten."

"Bobby?"

"I'm in."

"Charlie?"

"Out."

"Out," Nelson echoed.

"I see the ten and raise fifty," Alex said.

"Shit," Dean said. "Forget it."

"See the fifty and raise fifty," Bobby said.

"See your fifty and fifty more," Alex responded.

"That's three raises," Bobby said. "That's it, okay. I'll take three cards."

"Dealer takes two."

Alex peeled the cards off the deck that lay flat on the felt.

"Your bet, Alex," Bobby said.

"Two hundred."

Bobby grinned and tossed in his cards. "You're pretty slick, pro-fessor," he said with a brotherly shrug. "Take it."

On the next hand Dean dealt the same game and Alex bluffed successfully again, this time taking Bobby for three hundred thousand. In five minutes, a half million dollars had moved from Bobby's stack to Alex's side of the table.

As Alex pulled in the pot, Bobby noticed he didn't stack his chips but left them in an untidy pile.

"I guess you have so much money you don't need to count it," Bobby jibed.

"I feel lucky," Alex said.

"You keep bluffing and we'll see how lucky you are, Wiz."

"You think I was bluffing?"

Bobby chuckled. "Maybe I'm wrong, Alex, but it seems to me you've been bluffing for thirty-two years. And if you can afford this game, you have to be lucky. I know I am. If I wasn't lucky, I'd be dead. Or is it the other way around?"

Patience, Bobby told himself as he scanned the table surrounded by grim faces. These guys are really crazy. How much do they have to lose before they start talking about Shanghai Bend? Maybe it's another setup. Maybe they expect Alex to win it all back so they don't have to say anything.

There was only one way to find out.

# 41

"I've been watching you, old buddy," Bobby said across the table to Nelson. "You puff on those sexy thin cheroots, but you don't drink and you don't smoke Dean's killer weed, and if I were a betting man I'd wager you've never taken a bribe on the job. You're clean as a whistle, Nelson, which is a little peculiar because most cops I know aren't Goody-two shoes, no way. You're different. You must be afraid of yourself when you get loaded. Is that it? Are you afraid you might turn into Crazy Nelson?"

"I left Crazy Nelson behind on the Feather River, Bobby. You must have figured that out by now."

"Nelson has bad genes, that's all," Dean said. "The wrong chromosomes, defective DNA."

Bobby rolled his eyes, his desire to crush them like bugs chafing against his patience. "You became a cop because of Shanghai Bend, yes?" he asked with a grin.

"I don't talk to my shrink about it, but, yeah. That's it."

"What are you really afraid of, Nelson? Losing your pension?"

"Losing face," the policeman answered honestly. "It's a cop thing. If they found out I took all those records, I'd have my ass in a sling. What I did as a kid, well, I was a kid; but what I did as a member of the department, that's different."

"You took the biggest risks to protect everyone by swiping those documents. Did you get anything special for that?"

"Like what?"

"Money. More of the dope profits."

"No."

"Why not?"

"Never occurred to me."

"Invest your money wisely?"

"Oh, sure. Real estate. I live in a little apartment in a building I own, and I don't spend much, except on my cars."

"The Corvette?"

"I have five Corvettes—the '62, a '58, a '65, a '71, all cherried out, and a '91 ZR1 King of the Hill that's my daily driver."

"Holy shit."

"The Plastic Fantastic," Nelson said proudly.

"That's a pretty nice collection, very fancy."

"I like 'em. I have fun."

"C'mon, Charlie," Alex demanded. "To hell with Nelson and his cars. Deal."

"Okay, five stud. Cut the cards, Bobby. There we go. Rolling a seven to Nelson, a queen to Alex, a four to Dean, a three to Bobby, and a six to me. Alex?"

"Check the queen."

"Check the four."

"We gotta have a little action," Bobby said. "A thousand on the three."

"I'm out," Charlie said.

"Let's make it five thousand," Nelson said.

"Good-bye," Alex said.

"Not feeling so lucky?"

"Not this time."

Dean turned over his cards, and Bobby matched Nelson's raise. "Five it is."

"A nine to Nelson and another three to Bobby. Threes bet."

"Ten thousand on a nice little pair of threes."

"See your ten and raise ten," Nelson said, and Bobby knew Nelson had a seven in the hole, giving him a pair.

"Okay, another ten."

Charlie dealt Nelson a second nine and gave Bobby a queen. "Nines bet."

Nelson looked at his hole card, thrummed his fingers on the felt, twisted his mouth around, and counted his chips.

"Fifty grand," he said.

"It's your turn to feel lucky, hey, Nelson? See your fifty and up a hundred."

Nelson took a deep breath and looked at his hole card. His instincts were screaming, "You're up against Bobby McCorkle and you should get out of this hand, get out of this game, get out of Dodge before you get smashed like Charlie," but he really liked his hole card and felt this was the hand that would allow him to make a decent showing in the game.

He took a deep breath, exhaled loudly, pushed a large stack of chips into the pot, and said, "See your hundred and up a hundred more."

"Way to go, Nelson," Bobby said with genuine enthusiasm. "I always like to see a man who shows confidence. I'll see your hundred and I'll raise whatever the value of the Corvette you drove up here."

"The car?" Nelson said. "Dean tried to get the car last night. You want the car?"

"Yeah, and we have one more card to come. What's the car worth?"

"Maybe thirty-five."

"Okay. Thirty-five it is. You in?"

"Shit. Damn. You're playin' with my head, but okay."

"Can't lose, hey Nelson? You don't really want to lose that car, so you must have a good hand."

"Deal the cards, Charlie," Nelson demanded.

"A four to Nelson, no help, and a jack to Bobby, no help. Nines still bet."

"One hundred grand again," Nelson bet, and dropped his chips into the pot.

"Crazy Nelson," Bobby said. "You sure you left Crazy Nelson behind on the Feather River? Wanna get crazy all over again? Is that why you came here, to find Crazy Nelson again, to be Crazy Nelson one more time, reckless and wild and eighteen without a care in the world? Only Crazy Nelson would bet a hundred thousand dollars, right? Lt. Lee of the LAPD wouldn't do that, would he? How much do you have left there, Tonto?"

When they were sidekicks, Bobby had never used the name of

the Lone Ranger's companion. Like the superb poker player he was, he wanted to push that button only once.

He saw the consternation in Nelson's face. Confusion, indecision and weakness made the policeman's voice waver as he said, "I have a hundred and seventy-five thousand in chips."

"Okay," Bobby said. "I see your hundred and raise a hundred seventy-five. And just for fun I'll put up the Hooper Fish Company against the rest of the cars and the apartment building." He clucked his tongue, folded his arms, and sat back.

"You can't do that!" Charlie protested.

"Yes, he can," Alex declared. "It's his, it's on the table and he can do whatever he damned well pleases with it."

"That's my life; it isn't a commodity."

"Can it, Charlie," Alex snapped. "You made it a commodity when you tossed it in the pot. You never gave a damn about the business, anyway. All you ever wanted to do was run around town and spend the money like a big-shot."

"Fuck!"

"I knew it was coming," Nelson said, shaking his head.

"Check it out," Dean said. "If Nelson has two pair, the only way Bobby can win is with three threes, but wait! Nelson might have three nines, or Bobby may have two pair with threes and queens, or—"

"Shut up, Dean," Alex snarled. "We can all see the cards."

"What's it gonna be, Nelson?" Bobby demanded. "You can fold and still be in the game, you can bet the one seventy-five, or you can put it all in. You might win. Wanna be in the fish business?"

Nelson looked at his hole card again and shook his head.

"I fold," he said. "I can't do it."

"Excellent," Bobby said. "Smart move." He flipped over his hole card, a third three that would have won a showdown. "You're still in the game, but I got the car, right?"

"Yeah, you got the car."

"Tell you what, Nelson. I'll trade you the car for the revolver."

"Excuse me?"

"Your big pistola there. I think I fancy that more than a car right now. How about it? Car's worth more, I believe, a lot more. Not a bad deal for you."

"You're crazy."

"Is that an issue?"

"Why do you want the piece?"

"Afraid I'm gonna shoot you? Bang!"

"I dunno, Bobby."

"Don't you want the car back? I'm feeling generous."

Nelson reached under his seat and brought up the Smith & Wesson Model 29 and set it in front of Bobby who let it remain where it lay next to his chips.

"Just like the Wild West, hey, boys? This game is getting serious. I do believe that Paladin and Wyatt Earp would approve. Whose deal? Don't worry, Nelson. You'll get another chance."

# 42

Bobby won several pots in a row, intimidating Nelson, Dean, and Charlie with large bets irrespective of the cards. Showing the three of clubs on the first card in seven stud, he bet twenty thousand and everyone dropped.

Psyched, tormented, his threshold of pain raised to a nearly intolerable level, Nelson exclaimed, "Why don't we just give everything to you and not bother with the cards?"

"That wouldn't be much fun. Aren't you having fun, Nelson?"

"Shit."

"This is your game, fellas. We can quit right now."

No one spoke. No one said: When the game is over, we have to tell Bobby what happened at Shanghai Bend, and we're going to put that off as long as possible, if not forever.

Finally Alex said, "We have to play."

"Why?" Bobby demanded. "It's a hell of a game, but after all, it's only poker."

"We've been planning this game for a long time, and we agreed we needed to do this. It's who we are. The lives we live outside this game just aren't that important."

"Speak for yourself, Alex." Charlie said.

"That sounds like existential Kleenex to me," Bobby said. "Last night you guys made a lot of noise about doing the right thing, but I think you're in this game because you don't have a fucking clue what the right thing is. Nelson, in the laundromat you made a big deal out of the right thing, the right thing. Okay, copper, what is it?"

"Beyond playing the game, I don't know. I don't want to go to prison, the answer is: nothing. Doing nothing is the right thing."

"That's great, that's terrific, that's a comment on our times. You don't know. The great moral dilemma of your life and you don't know what to do except nothing. How about you, Charlie? Do you know? What's the right thing?"

"The right thing would be to call the Yuba County Sheriff and tell him who Sally is," Charlie said nervously. "If it wasn't for Nelson, that's what I'd do. It's what we should've done when it happened, so it's the right thing to do now."

"So, you want to fess up and suffer the consequences. Just what exactly do you think the consequences would be?"

"The case would land in the lap of the Yuba County District Attorney who might not press charges. If he did, he'd probably negotiate a plea. The problem is the records that Nelson took."

"You're afraid Nelson's little peccadilloes might be found out, and you want to protect your friend who protected you."

"Yeah. If all the different authorities and agencies put their heads together, they'll figure it out and Nelson's in the slammer."

"That's truly noble, Charlie. You can say, 'Let's call the cops,' and in the next breath say, 'Well, not really.' You can't have it both ways, pal. You don't know any more than Nelson. Dean, how about you?"

"I agree with Charlie. Call the police."

"Really? Your little wifey will learn how naughty you were."

"Sure, but it's the right thing to do."

"What about Nelson?" Bobby asked.

"I think we'll all go to jail, not just Nelson," Dean answered.

"You must be suicidal or a masochist or some damned thing, Studley. Who do you think you are, Dostoyevski? What is this, *Crime and Punishment* or some crap like that?"

"That's about the size of it, Bobby. I want to clear the air, but I'm afraid I don't have the balls. That's why we're going to leave it up to you."

"Alex?"

"Charlie and Dean think we should call the sheriff, but obviously neither has picked up the phone. Nelson almost agrees, but he has more to lose than they do. They might suffer, but they can walk away from it. Without a doubt Nelson goes to jail, so he's conflicted.

As for me, I would prefer we not call the police. I have selfish interests, of course. I don't want to be publicly vilified, and I'd like to spare our families the pain of our shame. My folks are long dead, but there's Nelson's mom, Charlie's mom, and Dean's dad, the old drunk. Then there are kids and wives. They're innocent, but they'll pay if we turn ourselves in."

"What would you do if everyone except you agreed to call the sheriff?"

"I can't stop anyone from doing that short of murder, and that's absurd."

"Is that what it is, Alex, absurd? Ridiculous? Wouldn't it be another murder to cover up the first?"

Embarrassed silence. Finally, Nelson said, "Look, Bobby, it's up to you to decide," Nelson said. "If you want to call the sheriff, so be it."

"What good would it do me to call the sheriff? How would it help Sally? I have a better idea." Bobby picked up the revolver and pulled back the hammer with a loud click. "Frontier justice. Which one of you killed Sally? Or was it all of you?"

Blanched faces, naked fear. Bobby gently released the hammer, cracked open the gun, and removed the cartridges, weighing them in his hand.

"Shit," he said. "You guys are a bunch of nervous girls. Come on, act like men. Live up to your heroes. Let's play cards."

# 43

After a few more hands Dean fired a joint, and Charlie smoked it with him. To everyone's surprise, Bobby asked for a hit.

"So you're not so pure after all," Nelson said.

With a shrug Bobby said, "It's only weed."

"No, it isn't," Dean declared. "It's Rocket Fuel."

Bobby sucked hard on the fat tube of reefer and then, turning away, used his tongue to force the smoke out his nostrils without inhaling. He finished the deceit with a coughing fit.

Pretending to be stoned, Bobby changed his style and began to play cautiously, folding early on most hands. He stopped badgering his opponents. After moving them from fear to hostility and back to fear, he wanted them to forget about him for a while. Each time someone raised, he folded, removing himself from the action and watching quietly as the others played.

Presently Dean won two hands in succession, the last an impressive win over Alex that put him a hundred thousand ahead. He celebrated with a glass of rum.

"You like that weed, Bobby?" he asked.

"Pretty potent shit, Deano. I can't play cards when I'm loaded, and that weed, man, I dunno. I don't know anybody who can play stoned, but a lot of folks try. How 'bout you, Stud?"

Dean laughed and tossed his ante into the pot.

Your turn, Bobby thought, and said, "My deal. Five stud."

Dean cut the deck and Bobby slowly passed out the cards, dealing sloppily as though he were stoned out of his mind. Blinking, clearing his throat, rocking in his seat, calling out the cards haphazardly. "Nine to Charlie, ah, what's that? A six to Nelson, yeah, a six, and another six to Alex, a queen to Dean—hey, that rhymes, and a jack to me. That right? Yeah, queen is high. Jeez, I guess I'm stoned. Whoa."

"Queen bets five."

"Okay, I'm in," Bobby said and tossed a chip into the pot. It landed on edge and rolled across to Nelson who caught it and placed it in the center of the table.

"I see it," Charlie said.

"Out," Nelson declared.

And Alex, "Likewise."

"Next card, another queen to the stud for a pair, and another jack to me for a pair, and a nine to Charlie for three pairs showing on the table. That's pretty nifty. Queens."

"Twenty-five on the queens."

"Ooo, ladies showing their teeth. Twenty-five it is."

"Too rich for me," Charlie said, and turned over his cards.

Bobby seemed to lose interest in the hand and stared at the photo of Wyatt Earp as though it were the most fascinating image he'd ever seen.

"Bobby, you gonna deal?"

"What? Oh, yeah. Let's see, whose in? Dean and me? Okay. A ten to the queens and a seven to the jacks. Queens still lookin' good."

"Fifty."

"Movin' up there, queenies. Fifty, fifty, okay. Fifty and up one fifty. Jeez, that weed. Wait a minute. Is that what I wanna do? Yeah, what the hell. Up one fifty, Deano."

"You losin' it, man? You okay?" Dean asked.

Bobby chuckled. "I dunno. You gonna see the raise?"

"I'm in."

"Last card. A deuce to Dean and Dean's queen to me. How about that. Your bet."

"One fifty," Dean said.

Bobby leaned over the table and knocked over his stacks of chips. "Shit," he swore. "Maybe I am losin' it, betting into such a pretty pair of queens. Oh, dear, what to do."

He halfheartedly tried to stack his chips again, snorted, cleared his throat and said, "One fifty, okay, and I'll raise—what d'ya got there, Stud?"

"Four eighty."

"Keepin' track, hey? Four fifty? No. Four-eighty."

"And I got my boat."

"Your boat? Oh, yeah, your hot rod boat. You want to bet your boat? What's it worth?"

"Two large."

"Two grand? That's all?"

"Two hundred grand," Dean said. "It's a Cigarette Racing Top Gun with twin Mercury Marine Bulldogs that I tweaked myself, a hell of a boat. I bet my boat." Dean got the giggles. Laughing, drinking more rum, he repeated, "Hell, yes. I bet my boat, the *Queen of Diamonds*."

"Two hundred thousand dollars for a speedboat. That's an expensive toy, Studley. What else do you have? A business, right? Your garage or machine shop or whatever it is. Wanna put that in, too? Against Charlie's business, naturally. You think about it. Here's four eighty plus another two hundred for the boat."

Bobby pushed a huge stack of chips into the pot.

"You're really gunning for us," Dean said.

"It's a poker game, isn't it? I didn't come here to lose, but maybe I will. You in? You see my raise? You aren't chickenshit, are you, Dean? You gonna fold like Nelson? This is a man's game."

Dean's upper lip began to tremble, and with a violent shove pushed all his chips into the pot.

"I'm in, the boat, the shop, everything," and he flipped over his hole card, a ten that gave him two pair, queens and tens.

"Wow, two pair, that's pretty good," Bobby said and turned over his hole card, the jack of clubs for three jacks. "But not good enough."

Shaking, Dean stood, fists clenched, sweat streaming down his temples. "You . . . you, God *damn*!"

"Wanna kiss me again?" Bobby asked, and when Dean leaned over the table toward him, Bobby snatched up the revolver, pointed it at the big man's chest, and commanded, "Sit down, captain, sir."

Nelson dove to the floor, Charlie yelped and covered his face with his arms, and Alex calmly lit a cigarette. Bobby burst out laughing.

"I love this game," he said, eyes locked on Dean's, and Dean realized Bobby wasn't stoned at all. He was sober as a judge.

"Nicely played," Alex said.

"All's fair in love and poker."

Dean sank into his seat, and Bobby put down the gun.

"Is this thing loaded?" he asked.

"Shit," Nelson swore.

"I'm only teasing. I'm pretty sure it's empty." He opened the gun and showed the empty cylinder to Dean, then pushed two hundred thousand in chips from the pot across the table. "I'll give you the same deal I gave Charlie," he said. "You're still in, Stud. Ante up."

# 44

In the dark hours before dawn on Sunday morning the light over the table shined brighter than ever. Bobby tried twice more to goad Nelson into putting everything into a pot, but the policeman was gun shy, as the saying goes, and each time stopped short of risking his fortune.

Where Bobby failed, Alex succeeded. With Bobby dealing a hand of seven stud, after six cards Nelson had four splendid hearts for a possible king high flush, and Alex showed a pair of sevens, a king, and an eight. Everyone else had dropped, and Alex and Nelson faced off, waiting for the final card.

Sweat hung in the air like smoke. Holed by cigarette burns and stained by spilled drinks and gun oil, the dark green felt exuded the raw odor of a battlefield. When the stakes are high enough, poker is war, and cards and chips become tokens for savage emotions.

Right and wrong, crime and punishment, life and death—the grand issues had been pushed aside by the power of the game. Nelson was not meditating on Shanghai Bend as he clenched his teeth and impatiently snapped the corners of his hole cards. He was trying to win the hand, and nothing else mattered.

"C'mon, c'mon, c'mon," he muttered, transfixed.

Alex remained calm, fingers folded on the table. Only Bobby noticed a tiny artery pulsing in his left temple, partially hidden by the frame of his glasses. The Wiz was more anxious than he appeared.

Bobby dealt the last card, intoning the customary chant, "One down for Alex and one for Nelson. Sevens are still high. Alex bets."

Alex glanced briefly at his seventh card and slowly raised his eyes until he met Nelson's. Without looking down, he pushed a tall stack of blues into the center of the felt.

"Two hundred thousand," he rasped, voice harsh and dry.

"I don't have that much," Nelson snapped in reply, blood pressure rising. "You can see that plain as day."

Never taking his eyes off Nelson, Alex asked politely, "How much do you have?"

"Hundred forty-five thousand," came the terse response.

"Okay, one forty-five it is," Alex said, taking fifty-five thousand back.

Face flushed, jaw grinding, cheek muscles twitching, Nelson came out like gangbusters. "I'll tell you what, Alex. It takes a full house or better to beat a flush, and you've been bluffing all day and all night. You ain't the pro from Reno. You don't fool me with your cooler-than-thou attitude. I've seen it before. You're just a smart-ass punk from Alvarado Street and all you have is a pair of sevens, maybe three sevens. I'll put in the one forty-five and raise you my cars and the apartment building—if you have anything to put up against it, like guts."

Bobby saw the muscles in Alex's face relax. The sign of fear, the bluffer's tell, the pulse throbbing in his temple, was gone. An intrepid gambler, the Wiz had caught a hand on the last card and Nelson had walked right into the trap.

"What's the building worth?" Alex inquired.

"Two point one million at the last insurance appraisal."

Alex bent over the table on his elbows and studied Nelson's cards. "We started with five grand, then went to five hundred grand, and now you're betting two million plus on a four heart flush. I never thought I'd see the day. Hallelujah, the poker gods must be appeased."

"Cut the crap, Alex. I'm all in. Whaddaya got that's worth anything? I know you own your fancy New York apartment."

"My assets, let's see," Alex said slowly. "There's the apartment in Manhattan, yes, and the condo in East Hampton, and the stock portfolio, a nice combination of blue chips and high-tech. Pharmaceuticals have been good lately. All together I'd guess I'm worth a little less than two million, depending on the market, but close enough. That sound good enough to you?"

"You'd better not be bullshitting about the stock."

"You pays your money and takes your chances, Nelson. Looks like it's L.A. versus New York. How about it?"

"I'm in," Nelson declared.

"I call," Alex said, and Nelson, hands shaking, turned over the fifth heart.

"Flush, king high," he announced unnecessarily, a grin and a grimace struggling at cross-purposes on his bright, sweating face.

Alex sighed theatrically, adjusted his glasses and turned over a third seven and a hidden pair of aces for a full house.

Bobby lit a Winston, the double snap of his Zippo as sharp as a gun bolt.

There was a tiny delay as Nelson revved from zero to tornado. Eyes popping, face contorting like a Chinese dragon, he snatched up his cards and viciously tore them to pieces. "Motherfucker!" he shouted, gasping for breath. "God damned mother—Rrrrrrrrr!" Flinging the shredded cardstock into the air, he charged into the master bedroom, slammed the door, and a moment later they heard a crash, a thud, and another crash.

Bobby flinched, unsure what to make of Nelson's noisy fit of destruction.

"It's happens when he loses," Dean said to Bobby. "Don't worry about it."

"One of our finer traditions: Nelson loses and wrecks the place," Charlie added. "It's an annual melodrama and usually adds up to about a grand in damages. They'd never let us come back if I didn't know the manager."

"He isn't going to hurt himself in there, is he?" Bobby asked, raising an eyebrow and gesturing toward the bedroom with genuine concern. With two and a half million dollars in cash in the suite, the last thing he wanted was a player launching himself out the window and attracting attention.

Dean shrugged. "You have the gun, Bobby. He'll be all right."

"Nelson!" Alex yelled.

The muted reply: "Go to hell!"

"He's never lost so much before. None of us has," Charlie said.

"Nelson puts on a brave front, but he's an emotional guy. It's hard to say what he'll do. It doesn't feel good to get wiped out. I can testify to that."

"Yea, brother," Dean chimed in.

"Stop whining and feeling sorry for yourselves! This is poker!" Alex shouted, and gathered in the hefty pot. Cooling off, he added in a normal tone, "We need a new deck. Any cards left?"

Dean looked away, embarrassed, and Charlie coughed in his hand.

"What's the matter?" Alex demanded. "It's a card game, not a popularity contest. There's always winners and losers."

"You're a cold son of a bitch, Alex," Charlie said. "You didn't let Nelson back into the game like Bobby did for Dean and me."

"Poker is not a game that rewards compassion. Emotions get in the way."

Easy to say, Bobby thought. Easy to say.

Dean laughed, sputtering in his drink. "You're so full of shit, professor. I'm tired of your pompous fucking pronouncements. You won the hand, good for you. That's terrific. Shut up and show some class."

"I'm giving nothing back, Studley. I came to play."

"Are we gonna play with four players?" Charlie asked.

"We're going to play until there's one player left," Alex snapped.

Bobby tilted his head sideways and slowly nodded his head in agreement. "Last man standing," he said. "The old way. It's okay with me."

Charlie silently tore open a new, sealed deck to replace the one Nelson destroyed, removed the jokers, and began to shuffle.

"Roll 'em, Charlie," Dean said and rapped his knuckles on the felt.

# 45

"Check."

"Check."

"Check."

"Check."

"Checked all around. Nobody's got nothin'. Turn 'em over."

"Charlie takes it with a pair of eights."

"Christ, I'm too old to play all day and all night."

"Let's open the windows and air out the joint."

At 4:00 A.M. they paused the game and ordered breakfast from room service. Sulking, Nelson refused to leave the bedroom and only opened the door to admit a hotel engineer with a new TV.

Dean walked into the second bedroom, pushed open a window, and watched garbage trucks and newspaper vans work the early morning hours.

Poker. Infernal game. How could he explain to Billie that he'd cashed in their life for a pile of chips that was vanishing like their youth? For what? For guilt? For the chance to play with Bobby McCorkle? If he didn't win back the machine shop, maybe he could get a job driving a Chronicle van. He wondered what they paid.

Charlie wandered into the bedroom and stood next to Dean at the window. Below, steam vented from grates in the asphalt, a fortune going up in smoke.

"Are you thinkin' what I'm thinkin'?" Charlie asked.

"What's that?"

"Why'd he let us back in the game?"

"Damned if I know."

"He's torturing us," Charlie said quietly. "He gave us two hundred grand apiece to work for him in our businesses, and if we lose that, we have to work for nothing. We're screwed. You know that, right? We can never beat Bobby. Jesus, we can't beat Alex."

"There's always hope, Charlie. You keep playing and maybe you'll get a hand, but if you think like a loser, you don't stand a chance."

"You can bullshit yourself if it makes you feel better, Dean, and maybe you have a chance in this game, but not me."

"Then you shouldn't play, Charlie."

Charlie thought about his response for a long minute. Finally, he said, "You know I have to play, Dean, Jesus. I'm the king of diamonds, and ever since we got our tattoos, that's been the most important thing in the world to me. You guys—all of us together, and the game, that's my identity. I have to play even if I know I'm going to lose, because if I don't play, it's like denying who I am. I know I'm just a spear carrier, but this year's game was my one shot at the big leagues, to play for real and to play with Bobby again. I had to play."

Charlie finished by shaking his head, desolate and confused.

Dean listened with a sympathetic ear to Charlie's convoluted effort to understand himself. Playing poker in a game destined to be lost was like going to war for your country. Most who were called simply packed their bags and went, irrespective of whether or not the cause was just, and some were born to be cannon fodder. If you were a player, you played. Even if you were a loser, you played.

"I was just standing here thinking about driving a truck, or maybe working as a mechanic," Dean said. "I know engines and you know fish. Maybe you can score a berth on a fishing boat. What the hell, you can always find a game on the fishwharf."

"Losing everything doesn't bother you?" Charlie asked. "It bothers me."

"I knew what I was in for when I sat down, same as you," Dean said, shaking his finger at Charlie. "We'll survive. We're outlaws, remember? And in the end? Well, we'll see. Maybe Alex will beat him."

Over bacon and eggs in the living room Bobby asked Alex, "I hope you like Corvettes. What are you gonna do with five of the buggers?"

Alex shook his head. "Damned if I know. It doesn't make sense to own a car in New York, and when I rent one, I'm a Buick kind of guy. I dunno. I might change my tune."

Alex tipped his hat to a jaunty angle and tilted up his cigarette with his teeth like Franklin D. Roosevelt. A moment later he squared his hat and crushed his smoke.

"Nah, not my style."

"Where would you keep five cars in New York, anyway?" Bobby asked out of idle curiosity.

Smirking, Alex decided on impulse to drop his bombshell. "You know what, Bobby? I don't care because I'm not going back. I'm going to resign from Columbia and the DoD, no matter what happens in the game. I've already written the letters. I'm through with physics, finished with New York, and done with academia and the bloody government."

Coming back into the room, Charlie and Dean overheard Alex's pronouncement, and Charlie squawked, "You're putting us on. You never said anything about that."

"Well, I'm saying it now and I'm not putting you on. I'm walking away from my life. It's different with you guys. With you, it's like pulling teeth, but since Bobby's already taken your companies, you have to walk away whether you like it or not, unless you're lucky enough to win them back. I don't think it's dawned on you yet, Charlie, but we're playing for keeps. Don't you get it? You've been handed a midlife crisis free of charge. We're condemned to be free from our miserable lives no matter what happens."

"What about your wife and kids?" Charlie asked.

"Oh, Christ. My marriage to Joanna has been dead for years. Our kids are in college, and the ex-wife's girls already graduated and have decent jobs. As far as I'm concerned, the kids are okay and the women can go to hell. These modern ladies can take care of themselves, as they constantly remind us. Fine with me. And if I lose the apartment and the condo and the stocks, well, tough shit."

"You're on track to be chairman of the department," Dean said, boggled by Alex's declaration. "You must be out of your mind."

"Hell, yes, I'm out of my mind. I've been out of my mind for thirty years. I planned for this. I knew this game would change our lives. From the moment we walked in here Friday night, we could never go back, win or lose. Shanghai Bend is reality. The game is reality. Losing is reality, because in this game we can't possibly win. Even if we win, we lose because we can't change what we did. All this talk about the right thing is just blather. We did the wrong thing that night, and the only way we can atone for that mistake is by giving up our lives and starting over. Sally's bones are real and Bobby is real, but we're fakes, Dean, you and Charlie and Nelson and me. We're phonies, we're bullshit, and we have to pay no matter what Bobby does."

"Win or lose," Dean said.

"That's right. It's the game and nothing but the game. The rest of it doesn't matter in the slightest."

"If you quit your job, what're you gonna do, Wiz?" Charlie asked.

Alex grabbed a deck, shuffled and fanned it. "Play cards," he answered with a stony face. "Straight poker, no wild cards."

A tiny smile flicked across Bobby's face. "You want to turn pro, Alex?"

"That's the idea, yeah."

"Think you're good enough?"

Alex closed the fan, popped four eights off the top of the deck, and flipped them into the middle of the table.

"We'll find out."

Bobby picked up the eight of hearts, held it up to the light, and, squinting, examined it on both sides.

"You should already know," he said with a smile.

# 46

With seventy-eight thousand dollars in chips, Charlie didn't have to scan the table to know he was low man on the totem pole. Dean had about a hundred thousand left, and Alex and Bobby had well over a million apiece.

"At a thousand bucks a pop, how long would it take me to lose it all if I tossed in my antes and dropped out of every hand? Ha-haha," Charlie wondered out loud.

" 'Til about noon, if you could stay awake that long," Bobby answered. "Why wait? I'll make it easy for ya. Twenty-five grand on my sixes. You in, Charlie?"

The game was five stud with Alex and Dean out. Bobby had a pair of sixes on the first two up cards and Charlie showed a king and queen.

"What the heck. I'm in."

"Rolling," Alex said, dealing the hand. "A four to Bobby and an ace to Charlie."

"Runnin' a straight there, boy," Bobby said. "Hotsy totsy. Twenty-five more."

"Gotta stay in," Charlie said, counting out chips and dropping them into the pot. "Deal."

"A deuce to Bobby and a ten to Charlie," Alex announced. "Looking good, Charlie, four cards to a straight, ace high, but the sixes still rule the table."

"Check," Bobby said.

Charlie laughed. "That's an old trick," he scoffed. "Check to see if I have the nerve to bet my straight. Want to see if I really have it? Suppose I don't have a straight. Maybe I have a pair of aces or a pair of kings. Any of my cards paired up will beat your sixes. It'll

246 THE WILD CARD

cost you to find out." Charlie pushed the rest of chips into the center of the table. "Twenty-eight thousand," he declared, and held his breath.

Bobby hesitated. "What do you think, boys? Does he have it? Does he have a hot card in the hole, or is he trying to buy the hand?"

Alex lit a cigarette and Dean gazed at the heroes. Neither Dean nor Alex nor the heroes said a word. Like the others, Bobby had seen Charlie looking at his hole card and silently mouthing, "Nine nine nine nine," repeatedly.

Counting out chips, Bobby said, "Okay, twenty-eight. And I'll tell you what, Charlie. If you win, you can have your company back. And if I win, you tell me which one of you killed Sally."

Charlie went white. Barely audible, he mumbled, "I can't do that."

"Why not? Is it a secret?"

"It's not for me to say."

"Don't you want your company back? One word, point your finger, and you're back in business."

"You can't turn us against one another, Bobby. We're the royal flush."

"Now, that's loyalty," Bobby said. "I'm impressed. Tell me this: Was it you?"

"No."

"Want to make the bet?"

"No."

"Then it's table stakes. What do you have?"

Charlie turned over his hole card, the nine of hearts.

"Hahaha hahaha, shit. I thought you'd pack it in. Oh, my God."

Charlie's exit from the game was more dignified than Nelson's. He silently went into the bedroom and took a long, hot shower.

# 47

"You want me to be judge and jury," Bobby said to Alex and Dean, "but I don't have all the facts, do I?"

"When the game is over, you will," Alex said.

"It may never end," Bobby said. "It could turn into a marathon and go on forever."

"That would be okay with me," Alex said. "Let's play."

"Five draw, anything opens," Dean announced.

"Not jacks or better?" Bobby asked.

"Nope, not with three players. Anything opens. You can open on guts if you have any."

"That's a game for a desperate man," Bobby commented.

"Listen, at Khe Sanh sometimes artillery rounds were coming in every twenty seconds. Boom! Boom! Made it hard to sleep, spilled the coffee, guys getting wasted all over the place. But the worst was, one day these other officers and I were trying to play cards, and we didn't get to finish a hand because a shell landed on our bunker and two guys in the game got blown up. Now that's desperation."

"Spare us the war stories, Studley," Alex complained. "Just deal the cards."

"You play much poker in beautiful Southeast Asia, Bobby?"

"I never talk about the war, Dean. That's my rule."

"Don't you ever pull out those Silver Stars and read the citations?"

Bobby gave Dean a long, cold stare. A drowning man, clinging to anything that might keep his head above water, in the last thirty-six hours Dean had been drunk, hungover, drunk again, stoned, lucid, incoherent, crazy, sane, and now, desperate, reaching for anything that might keep him in the game.

"I don't talk about the war, and I don't like to repeat myself.

Since you really want to play this out to the end, let's stick to poker. Deal, *por favor*."

With a grimace, Dean pushed the deck across the table. "Cut 'em, Wiz."

Alex symbolically cut the deck by touching the top card with the tips of his fingers, and Dean swiftly dealt each player five cards.

Bobby picked up his cards and watched Alex and Dean perform their rituals. Poker, he thought, is monotonous, routine work, paying attention, remembering details. Alex looked at his cards one at a time, and, showing no reaction, a clue that he had nothing in his hand, left them on the felt. Dean picked up his cards and moved them around in his hand, trying this configuration and that as though he wasn't sure of the best way to play the hand. Bobby didn't play the hand; he played the players.

"Check," Bobby said.

"Check," Alex echoed.

"Open for twenty," Dean wagered.

"See your twenty," Bobby said promptly, "and bump it twenty."

"Fold," Alex said and pushed his cards into the center of the table.

"I'm in," Dean said. "I'll see the raise."

Bobby looked at Bret Maverick and then at Dean who grinned back and stroked his beard.

"One card," Bobby said.

"Dealer takes two."

"Your bet, Deano. You opened."

"Check."

Bobby shook his head, his tolerance for Dean's sloppy play at an end. By taking one card, Bobby had convinced the big man that he had two pair or four cards to a straight or flush. Bobby's mind was as clear as a cold night in Reno, and he knew Dean had a low three of a kind. If he had three aces, he'd bet more, or raise, but he did neither. By checking, Dean sealed his fate.

"You should have about one fifty," Bobby said, counting chips. "That's the bet. One fifty."

To Alex, watching Dean make the final plunge was like watching a suicide jump off the Golden Gate Bridge. Dean was a complex human being whom Alex never completely understood although he loved the big man like a brother. He never understood Dean's tattoos or wild streak or why Dean lived so close to Shanghai Bend, but Dean lived his life according to a closely held code, a renegade's code, and Alex understood that. Dean was faithful and true, but in the end, he couldn't control his guilt. He wanted to jump off the bridge, and there was nothing Alex could do to help him.

"You've been drawing one card all night and then bluffing that you caught a hand," Dean said and pushed all his chips into the pot. "I call."

"You can bet more," Bobby said, "like the truth against your machine shop."

"Fuck that. That won't work with me any better than it did with Charlie."

"You sure? If your cards are worth one hundred and fifty thousand dollars, surely they're worth an answer to a simple question. Who killed, Sally, Dean? Was it you?"

"Just show your cards, Bobby."

"Three tens," Bobby said and laid his cards face up on the felt. "Read 'em and weep."

"Holy shit."

Dean sighed and tossed his hand willy-nilly onto the table. Alex spread out the cards and revealed three fives.

Bobby tensed, expecting a violent explosion from the big man.

Dean's eyes fluttered around the table, from the cards to the chips in the pot to Alex to Bobby and landed on the revolver, still on the table next to Bobby's chips.

Reaching into his pocket, Bobby drew out a single cartridge, tossed it in the air and caught it. Prudently, he removed the gun from the table and placed it under his seat.

"It's a cruel game," Alex said.

"I need a drink," Dean said and reached for his bottle of rum.

"You lost your business but not your house," Alex commented dryly. "You still have something to play with."

"Do you want everything, Wiz, down to the last nickel?"

"I'm just a player, Dean. If you want to play, we'll deal you in. I don't give a shit one way or the other."

"The house isn't mine. It belonged to Billie before we got married, so the answer is no. I'm tap city."

The second bedroom door opened and Charlie emerged in fresh clothes, hair dripping from the shower.

"What's going on, guys?" he asked.

Bobby didn't glance up. Alex turned around briefly to look at Charlie, then focused intently on the cards in Bobby's hands.

Dean pushed himself away from the table, cleared away his glass and ashtray, and daintily swept the felt with his hands.

"What's happening is what we all suspected would happen," he said to Charlie. "A shootout at the OK Corral."

Charlie and Dean pulled their chairs away from the table and settled in to watch, the pain of their losses tempered by the sheer excitement of the confrontation. Their lives had become chips in somebody else's game, a peculiar situation that wasn't too far removed from the world beyond the Enrico Caruso suite. At its best, poker is a facsimile of the human condition, charged with vigor and energy, fraught with whimsy and unexpected twists, and always ending in sudden death. The best man didn't always win, but the best player, no matter what his character, almost always took the final pot.

"I guess it's time to go fishing," Charlie said to Dean.

"Looks like."

Bobby and Alex paid no attention. All that existed for them was a deck of cards, two immense piles of chips, and each other.

# 48

"Just you and me," Alex said. "Heads-up."

"I'm glad you can count to two, Alex," Bobby said. "Let's put that mathematical talent to work. What do you say we raise the ante?"

Alex lit a Lucky and smiled. "Sure. Anything you like."

"Ten grand?"

"Sounds right, like bare knuckles."

Alex was as dangerous as any player Bobby had ever faced. By now the Wiz had picked up one or two of Bobby's tells that gave him an edge in certain hands. A superior player like Bobby exhibited few signs that gave away his cards, but some tells always existed: if nothing else the autonomic physical response that dilated and constricted his pupils. Observant and astute, Alex was watching everything, and Bobby believed that if he continued to play his aggressive game, he'd lose.

"Your deal," Alex said.

Bobby slowly and methodically shuffled the cards, no longer pretending this was just another game. Sultans and tycoons didn't play for these stakes. With two and a half million dollars in chips and millions more in property on the table, it was not only the biggest game he'd ever played in, it was the biggest game he'd ever heard of. Ironically, because of Shanghai Bend, news of the million dollar game played by the boys from Noë Valley would never travel beyond the hotel suite. No legend was in the making here. The losers would find ways to explain their losses without revealing the truth, and the winner would do the same. It occurred to Bobby that if he lost everything, including the money downstairs in the hotel safe, he'd drop no more than the original five thousand dollar buy-in, not too steep a price for an interesting session at cards, but it meant he had little to lose while Alex had his life on the line.

Across the table, the immediacy of finally squaring off against Bobby McCorkle severely tested Alex's remarkable cool. Sweat glistened on his forehead, and ashes spilled down the front of his shirt. Unlike Bobby who was used to playing for days at a time, Alex's stamina was near the end. Running on pure adrenaline, he was close to exhaustion. Furthermore, three decades of relentless anticipation were taking their toll. He'd played this game in his head so many times, it was hard to clear away all the possible scenarios and concentrate on the game at hand. He blinked, trying without success to steady his mind. Ghosts swirled around the table, his grandfather, Sally, the Cincinnati Kid. This game, right now, was the focal point of his life, and he was terrified.

Bobby noticed Alex's sweat and ashes; looking deeper, he saw Alex's fantasy in which the Wiz was the greatest poker player on earth living out his dream here in the Enrico Caruso Suite. If Alex won, he'd go straight to Binion's Horseshoe in Las Vegas, and with a stake of millions he'd be the toast of the town—until he lost. The scary thing about Alex was that he knew what would happen, win or lose, and didn't care. At the end of the line was a Nelson Algren nightmare, a seedy life of cheap hotels and two-dollar games. Trapped in a midlife identity crisis, Alex desperately sought *la nostalgie de la boue*; he wanted to wallow in the low life, and in his warped perception of the universe, that had to cost him millions. He was afflicted with the fatal flaw of every poker junkie who ever lived, including his father and grandfather. At the very bottom of his twisted heart he needed to lose. Bobby knew the only question was when: now or later.

"Been thinking about this game, Wiz?" Bobby taunted, and when Alex produced a tiny smile, Bobby clucked his tongue and asked, as if admiring a voluptuous woman, "The million dollar game, wow. Does it give you a hard on?"

Alex blushed. "What if it does?"

"Then you're a player."

The blush told Bobby that Alex did indeed have an erection, and in that moment Alex's marvelous poker face was stripped away to reveal the fear underneath.

"What are you going to do if you win, Alex? You'll have a hell of a bankroll, and all this property and businesses to run."

"I'll sell it all. Cash it in. Not a problem."

Bobby observed that neither Charlie nor Dean reacted to this callous declaration.

"That's a hell of a thing to do to your friends."

"We all knew the risks when we sat down to play."

"Are you sure? I didn't," Bobby contradicted. "I came down here for a five thousand dollar game. I had no idea this was a setup for you to rip off your friends. Just a friendly little game among old pals, my ass. You conned these guys into throwing in a half million each of their hard-earned dope money, plus their property, just to fatten your kitty. I bet you keep a book on everybody, a secret book that describes every game you ever played, the habits of the players, and all their secrets. You've been doing it for years, just to prepare for this game. What do you think, Dean? Does Alex keep a book?"

"I wouldn't be surprised."

"Well?" Bobby asked Alex.

"I keep a book, yes. There's nothing wrong with that."

"But you never told anyone, did you?"

"No."

"Winning is really important to you, isn't it?"

"This isn't a gentlemen's sport, Bobby. It's not how you play the game that counts, it's whether you win or lose."

"And every year you set up these patsies so you can inflate your ego, right?"

"The wild card is never a patsy. You're certainly not."

"Would you cut the cards right now for a million dollars?" Bobby asked sharply, pushing the deck into the middle of the table.

Alex didn't hesitate before he said, "No."

"Why not?"

"It's not poker."

Bobby laughed quietly. A genuinely good player, intensely focused and confident of his skill, Alex could be psyched and beaten by making him think too much, thus turning his strength against himself.

"Well, I hope you read your old notes on me. When I was eighteen, I used to light a cigarette every time I got good cards. Do I still do that? Gee, I don't know. C'mon, Wiz, let's play seven stud. Cut the cards."

Alex won the first hand when Bobby folded on the second card, and Bobby won two in similar fashion, bang bang. Then Alex won three, bang bang bang, then Bobby five, bang bang bang bang bang, with no hand taking more than thirty seconds. Heads-up poker is quick, the betting fast, the atmosphere auction-like in its cadence.

"Ten on the queen."

"Your ten plus twenty on the jack."

"See your twenty and bump fifty."

"Fold."

The game ebbed and flowed like the tide in the bay, back and forth, back and forth, each player looking for the tiny advantage that would break the game open. After fifteen minutes of furious action, Bobby started a streak in which he checked or folded on the first card for twenty-three hands in a row. Calmly smoking Winstons and saying nothing except, "Check," and "Fold," the tactic called "no-stay" in poker parlance frustrated Alex who tried raising and lowering his opening bet to no avail. Nothing kept Bobby in the game. Five stud, seven stud or draw, Bobby folded and conceded a ten thousand dollar ante each time. As the streak continued, Alex's biological poker computer began to melt down trying to guess what Bobby was trying to do. Was he simply waiting for an exceptionally good hand? That had to be it. Bobby folded high cards and low cards, and when he folded an ace on the first card in five stud, Alex shook his head, mumbling, "What's the matter with you? I thought you wanted to play."

Bobby shrugged and remained silent.

A few minutes before first light, Alex dealt a hand of seven stud, and when Bobby looked at his hole cards he had a pair of tens to go with a queen up against a king up for Alex.

"King bets twenty thousand," Alex said, expecting Bobby to drop again.

"See your twenty and up twenty," Bobby said.

"So you're finally going to play a hand? See your raise and raise another twenty."

Bobby knew Alex had at a least a pair of kings if not three. "Call," he said.

"Next card. A seven to Bobby and a nine to the dealer. Dealer bets fifty."

"Fifty and up fifty."

"See your raise and raise a hundred."

"I'm in," Bobby said.

"Next card. A queen for a pair to you and a seven to the dealer."

"Queens bet a hundred grand," Bobby said.

"I'll see your hundred."

"Not going to raise me, Alex? All right. Roll 'em."

"An ace to you and a queen to the dealer."

"You got my queen," Bobby said.

"It's my queen now."

"Since you got my queen, I'll only bet a hundred grand again."

"See your hundred and raise two hundred."

Without a doubt Alex had three kings. Bobby was ready to rock and roll with a full tilt bluff. He pushed three hundred thousand in chips into the pot.

"Okey dokey smokey, deal."

"A six to Bobby and a jack to the dealer. One more card to go. Queens bet."

"Hmmm," Bobby said. "One million dollars."

Charlie gasped. Dean popped his lips and uttered, "Wow!"

Bobby watched the tiny muscles twitching in Alex's face that revealed tension. Alex truly didn't know what Bobby had, but he knew Bobby knew he had kings. No one bet a million dollars into three kings unless he had a better hand. Alex concluded that he had to improve his hand on the last card to win, but it would cost him a million dollars to buy that card.

"Call," he whispered, and put ten bumblebees into the pot.

"Last card, down."

Alex dealt the cards, and Bobby watched his opponent hesitate, his eyes lingering a split second on the back of his final card before he glanced up to check out Bobby. You never should have taken your eyes off me, Bobby thought, and he knew Alex needed that card to make his hand.

Relaxed, Bobby watched the artery pumping in Alex's temple. When he finally raised the corner of his card, the pulsing blood vessel remained steady.

Bobby counted out the rest of his blues and reds and put them into the pot. "I have three hundred thousand here, and I'll toss in Dean."

Under his breath, Dean exclaimed, "Jesus."

Alex was losing control. His breath was constricted, his face flushed. He looked like he was about to wet his pants. Uncharacteristically, he picked up his hole cards and studied them.

"Fuck no," he swore, throwing down the cards. "I fold."

Bobby deliberately turned over his tens. "Two pair, queens up."

Alex began to tremble, took a deep breath, and quickly gained control of himself. He'd been bluffed into folding a winning hand, three kings, and lost over a million and a half dollars.

"Still think you're good enough, Wiz? I'd love to see you in Vegas swimming with the sharks. C'mon, ante up. It's my deal."

# 49

Alex's stake had been reduced to his property, the property he'd won from Nelson, one short stack of reds, a few blues, one bumblebee, and the whites in reserve. If poker can be compared to bullfighting, Alex was unaccustomed to playing the role of the bull. Across the table Bobby was poised like a fearless killer of *toros*, a matador sighting down the length of his sword, taking aim for the moment of truth.

Alex tried desperately to maintain a Buddha-like façade, but the inside of his mouth was dry and his eyes watery and red. Reviewing the last hand, he realized he'd psyched himself on the million dollar bet. Just play the odds, he told himself. Just play the odds and ignore anything the son of a bitch says.

Bobby leaned back in his chair, raised his glass of soda and lime and said, "A toast, gentlemen, to the royal flush in diamonds. Your loyalty to one another is astounding."

"Wait," Dean said, holding up both hands. "Let me get Nelson."

Dean banged loudly on Nelson's door, shouting, "Come out here, Chinaman. Open up."

After several more bangs and shouts Nelson opened the door. Half asleep, naked to the waist, he asked, "What?"

"Bobby wants to make a toast. It's just him and Alex left in the game."

"What?" Nelson blinked and rubbed his eyes.

Dean cupped his hands over Nelson's ears and pulled out a pair of rubber plugs.

"I was asleep," Nelson said, yawning. "Is the game over? What time is it?"

"It's a few minutes past five. Bobby's going to make a toast."

"Hey, Crazy Nelson," Bobby said, raising his glass. "Alex, Charlie, Dean, to the royal flush, the hand that beat the Cincinnati Kid."

Charlie stuck a glass in Nelson's hand and they all raised their drinks in salute. No one except Bobby looked festive, and their hollow voices almost groaned, "To the royal flush in diamonds. Hear hear."

"Hear hear."

The room was quiet, the stereo off, the hotel dormant in the wee hours. Alex was flexing his finger muscles, adjusting his glasses, and fiddling with his chair.

"Let's get on with it," he urged.

"Tell you what, Alex," Bobby said. "Let's let Nelson deal."

"Why not? Sure," Alex replied.

"That okay with you?" Bobby asked the policeman.

"I don't know if I'm awake yet."

"I'll get you some coffee," Charlie said.

Bobby pulled out Nelson's chair, saying, "Sit down, make yourself comfortable. You'll be all right."

Nelson took his seat, picked up the blue deck and started to shuffle.

"My cut," Bobby said. "The Wiz gets the first card."

"What do you want to play?" Nelson asked.

With a grin, Bobby said, "Let's play low hole card wild, just for old time's sake."

"Oh, shit, Bobby, no," Alex protested.

Bobby leaned over the table and said directly to Alex, "Just in case there's some confusion, let me ask you why we're here. Is it because they dug Sally's bones out of the riverbank, or for some other reason, to resolve your identity crisis, perhaps?"

Incensed, Alex retorted, "We're here for a poker game, and we don't play wild cards."

"Ah, so, pure poker, no wild cards. Such symmetry, such elegant simplicity. What nonsense. You were willing to play low hole card wild earlier, but if you're not now, too bad. Game's over." Bobby pushed back his chair and stood up. "Cash me in and we'll call it a night."

Alex hissed, "You bastard."

Bobby smiled. "I'm not greedy," he said. "I've got millions here, more than enough to keep me playing cards for at least a month. I have a game in Biloxi on Wednesday with a crowd of Cajun gun runners, Panamanian dope dealers, and politicians. I really like those guys, and I'm going to be in Mississippi no matter what happens here. It's up to you, Alex. Either we play the old game, or we quit, and you get to start talking."

"Bobby—" Charlie started to say, but Dean cut him off.

"Shut up, Charlie."

Bobby started counting his chips.

"Alex, for God's sake," Charlie pleaded.

Bobby looked around at the four men, riveting each with a glance, and calmly said, "You knew this would happen, didn't you? You all believed it would come down to Alex and me, and you made a deal. He wins and gives it all back and you pay him off, or something like that. I'm not big on conspiracy theories, but you guys have had a long time to work it out. Trouble is, maybe Alex doesn't want to keep his end of whatever deal you made. If you make a bargain with the devil, well then, good luck. I don't give a damn. I'm happy to quit winners."

"All right," Alex snarled. "Nelson, deal a hand of low hole card wild."

"We're gonna play?" Bobby said, delighted.

"Yeah, we'll play."

"Excellent."

Bobby sat down, cut the cards, and Nelson, awake now, dealt two hole cards to each player, calling out, "This is low hole card wild, gentlemen. The lowest card in the hole and all like it are wild. An eight to Alex and the queen of spades to Bobby."

Alex and Bobby looked at their hole cards and then at each other.

"Let's make this short and sweet," Bobby said. "Fifty thousand on the queen."

Alex had two deuces in the hole, the best possible way to start a game of low hole card wild, a hand that could only improve.

"I call," he said.

"Next card. A deuce to Alex and a nine to Bobby. Queen still bets."

"Hundred thousand on the queens."

Jesus, Alex thought, three deuces and my deuces are wild, I'll have four eights at least. He said, "I see your hundred and raise a hundred."

"We have a game here, Wiz. That deuce must have done something for you. Glad to see it. I'll go easy on ya. I call."

"Fifth card, a queen to Alex and a six to Bobby. Queen nine still bets," Nelson said.

"You got my queen again. I check," Bobby said cheerfully.

Four queens, Alex thought. Four mother loving queens.

"I have a hundred and ten in whites, seventy-five in blues, and one thirty in reds," he said. "That's the bet, three fifteen."

"Alrighty."

"A four to Alex, no help, and a five to Bobby, no help. The queen nine still rules."

"Wanna see the last card, Alex? The down and dirty last card? Gee, what can we put in now? You don't have any chips left over there, Wiz, so let's have some fun. I'll bet the boat against the cars," Bobby offered.

"Fair enough. Deal."

Nelson dealt the last card, bellowing out the ritual, "Down and dirty!"

Before Alex could look at his card, Bobby said, "I'm not going to look at my last card, Wiz. I put in Dean and Charlie against you and Nelson. All in, Alex, everything."

Alex studied Bobby's cards, the queen of spades, nine of hearts, six of clubs, and five of diamonds, and figured the only possible hand that could keep Bobby in the game was three or four of a kind or a hidden flush. What could beat four queens? The odds! The odds! To hell with the odds. Bobby was bluffing again, like the last hand.

"I call." Alex turned over his cards. "Four queens."

Everyone leaned forward to see Bobby's cards.

"What can beat four queens?" Bobby asked, and then turned over a natural full house with three sixes and two queens. Six was his low hole card, and with three wild sixes, he had five queens.

The fifth queen, the wild card, the ghost of the queen of hearts.

# 50

Alex closed his eyes and drew a deep breath, struggling to accept his loss. He failed. Paralyzed, his mind went blank.

Nelson, Dean, and Charlie looked at their hands, chewed their lips and stared at the shuttered windows as though they were open. Bobby recognized them from a thousand games, the forlorn, sagging, sad faces of the defeated.

"Oh, my God," Charlie said.

Bobby rubbed his hands together and paused to admire two and a half million dollars in fine ceramic chips. He selected one blue and put it in his pocket with the six rounds from Nelson's revolver. Encountering the bullets, his fingers began to have ideas.

"Unless you have something else to play with, it looks like you boys are wiped out," he said, standing up to stretch.

"Game's over," Alex mumbled.

"No, it isn't," Bobby said.

Stunned, awkward silence.

"Oh, God," Charlie moaned.

"You have everything," Dean said.

"No, not everything," Bobby replied with an edge in his voice.

"What do you want?" Alex asked, mumbling, "As if I didn't know."

"I came to play for five thousand dollars, and that was fine. And when you raised the stakes to a half million, that was fine, too, because it was cash. But then I raised the stakes again and you lost a lot of property that I don't see. The first question is: how do I collect?"

"Don't you trust us?" Nelson asked.

"Since you ask, the answer is, no sir, I don't. Poker like this is illegal in California, and gambling debts are damned near uncollectible."

"You want markers? IOUs?" Dean asked.

Alex said, "Our word is good. We'll sign over the property, at least I will."

"I'm sure you will, Alex, because you want to walk out on your life, anyway. Dean and Nelson and Charlie, I'm not so sure about. No matter what you say now, you can wake up tomorrow and think, that guy can't prove he won my building or my company. You'll begin to get ideas. Just like Shanghai Bend, you can pretend this didn't happen. No way. I want a lawyer to draw up papers," Bobby said.

"A lawyer!" Dean exclaimed. "Jesus." And Nelson added, "It's five o'clock on Sunday morning, Bobby. Not too many attorneys are at work."

"Oh, I know an ambulance chaser who'll take my call. Reno is full of 'em. And if I don't call a lawyer, what can I do to collect? Should Charlie and I go down to the fishwharf right now and tell his boat captains I own the fleet? How about you, Dean? Want to go up the river and give me the keys this morning? Any way we do it, you'll have to explain why some guy is claiming he won your goods in a poker game. Your secret goes public, whatever it is. You're exposed for what you are. Think about it. Want to go down to the wharf, Charlie?"

Prolonged silence. Gray faces.

"Charlie?"

No answer.

"Dean? Nelson? You didn't think this through, did you? You don't know what to do. Well, I have an idea. I don't really want to call a lawyer, but I will if I have to. The same thing goes for the Yuba County Sheriff. I don't want to call him, either, but I will. On the other hand, I'd prefer to sort this out in this room right now."

Jingling the six fat .44 magnum cartridges in his pocket, Bobby reached under his seat, brought up Nelson's pistol and laid it on the table.

Undisguised horror.

"Okay," Bobby said. "You have a little common sense left, so here's what we'll do. We'll let the cards decide. I think that's only fitting. We'll play five card no peeky heads-up one at a time, and the best hand wins. If I win, you tell me the truth about Shanghai Bend and I give you back your property. Not the money, I'm keeping that. And if *you* win, you can have your stuff back and say nothing. If you want to keep silent forever, you have to win, and all of you have to win. One loser and he talks. If you don't want to play, I'll start making phone calls. I'm making it easy. I don't want your buildings or businesses or cars, and I sure as hell don't want some damned silly boat. You want your lives back? Play cards, or by God I'm taking everything and holding you to it, and I'll call the Yuba County Sheriff for good measure and you can tell him who cracked Sally's skull. Who's first?" Bobby snapped. Snatching the red deck, he began to shuffle.

"You want to play cards for the truth?" Alex asked.

"Why not? First I hear all this bullshit about the right thing, and it turns out you don't know what the right thing is. You think the right thing is to let sleeping dogs lie, to keep quiet, say nothing, do nothing. But you feel guilty enough to pay me off with all this dope money and the cash you lost in the game, but it went farther than you expected. The game got out of control and you forfeited everything you've acquired by pretending all these years that Sally never existed. You're all respectable members of society, substantial citizens, men of means, but you know you're frauds, and I know you want to continue being frauds. Fine. We're going to decide everything on the turn of a card. If you don't like it, we can do it the other way with lawyers and cops and the whole nine yards. Let's cut the crap. Who's first?"

"And if we lose and tell you what happened, then what?" Nelson asked.

"It depends on what you say. You've had a long time to work on your story, so it better be good."

"We haven't worked on the story," Charlie said. "We—"

"Shhh," Bobby hissed. "Who's first?"

No one moved.

"What do I have to do?" Bobby asked, picking up the gun. "Put a bullet in someone's knee?"

"We can't all win. You know that," Alex said.

"Stop stalling. Enough bullshit. What are you afraid of?"

"You," Dean answered. "We're afraid of you, Bobby."

"You're afraid of what I might do when I learn the truth?"

"Yes."

"What's the worst I can do? Call the sheriff? Shoot you with this gun? You'd better think about what's gonna happen if you don't play. I spent many years planning revenge on you people, but I put it behind me. I grew up, but now you're pissing me off, stalling and trying to buy me off. I'm going to hear the truth, one way or the other."

With a long sigh Alex said, "What the hell. I'll play."

"Then cut the cards."

Alex lifted half the deck and covered it with the bottom half. Bobby set down the revolver, swiftly dealt five cards to Alex and himself, then turned over his first card, a ten.

Alex turned over an ace.

Bobby turned over a second ten.

Alex turned over a second ace, and when all the cards were turned, Alex won with a pair of aces.

"You're a winner, Alex," Bobby said. "The life you want to abandon is now yours again. You don't have to say a damned thing. Who's next? Who wants his stuff back the most? Charlie? Nelson?"

Dean took his seat at the table, reached over and, hands trembling, cut the deck. Bobby scooped up the cards and dealt two more hands.

"No need to prolong the agony. Just flip 'em over," Bobby said.

Dean turned over all his cards and revealed a pair of threes.

"A pair, that's good," Bobby said, and turned over his cards one at a time.

"A seven, a king, a ten, a deuce, and another seven. Sorry, Stud, you lose. Want your business back? Start talking."

Dean looked at the others, still uncertain.

"Go ahead," Charlie said. "Tell him. There's no way around it."

Nelson nodded and Alex stared at the heroes on the wall.

"I thought," Dean began, and faltered. "I was so drunk I thought—she—"

"I saw her in the river," Charlie stammered. "I woke up and everyone was gone, so I went through the woods and I saw Dean and Nelson and Alex hiding in the trees, and then I saw her naked in the middle of the river near the rocks by the falls. Buck naked and a little chubby."

The story began to spill from four voices at once.

# 5 1

"It isn't fair that Bobby gets the girl all to himself," Dean said, expressing his envy by drop-kicking a beer can into the river.

"Boy meets girl, girl meets boy, happens all the time," Alex said.

"Let's go give 'em a scare."

"What? You're nuts."

"The boogie man, the boogie man, woo woo."

"You're drunk."

"So what, Wiz? So're you. Where's Nelson? Hey, Chinaman!"

"What?"

"Wouldn't you like to stick your dick into that girl?"

"I wanna go to sleep."

"Sleep? With pussy aroun'? Whatsa matta wit' you? Maybe you should crawl in with Charlie and fuck him."

"You're an asshole, Studley."

"Well, at least I ain't queer. Shit, I'm goin' over there."

"You'll be sorry," Nelson warned. "Bobby will kick your ass, and you know he can."

"Bobby this, Bobby that, Bobby Bobby Bobby. Fuck 'im."

Dean hopped off the boat onto the shore and started tramping through the woods.

"Christ," Alex said to Nelson. "We'd better go after him or we're gonna have big trouble."

"Bobby was right this afternoon," Nelson said with deep remorse. "We never shoulda let her on the boat in the first place."

"Too late f' that. Let's go."

"Shit, Alex. Bobby can take care of himself. Dean'll get what he deserves."

"Come on, Nelson. We gotta stop this pervert before he starts a riot."

Awake in the forward cabin, Charlie waited until Alex and Nelson left the boat before following them unseen into the woods.

Lurching drunkenly through the woods, Alex and Nelson caught up with Dean behind a thicket of underbrush near the far end of the island. The moonlit night was clear, warm, and buggy, the tent silent and still, the river steaming with foam from the falls.

"Come back to the boat, Dean," Alex whispered as loudly as he dared.

"Shut up, fool."

"What're you gonna do? Knock onna door and ask Bobby's permission?"

"I just wanna give 'em a scare."

"I don' think Bobby'll be scared by anything you can do. You're trying t' pick a fight 'cause you're drunk and stupid and jealous. Grow up."

Dean seemed to waver in his resolve, grinning sheepishly. "I'm the boogie man," he said without conviction.

"Yeah, right."

"I don't hear nothin'," Nelson said. "Maybe they're asleep."

"Come on. Let's go back t' the boat'n play cards."

"Shh. I hear something. Look, the zipper in the tent."

Alarmed, Alex whispered hoarsely, "Back up! Back up! Let's get outta here! If Bobby sees us, holy shit."

Hidden in the foliage a hundred feet from the tent, Alex, Dean, and Nelson watched Sally emerge nude, radiant, a river nymph, and their hearts raced and their cocks got hard. They remained stock still and waited for Bobby to come out after her, but he didn't.

"Lookit. Damn."

"Shh."

She stepped gingerly over the rocks and sharp clam shells and waded into the water up to her knees, her back to the woods. She was singing, not any particular song, merely trilling la-la-la la-la-la and splashing water into her face and over her body. Then they noticed she had a deck of cards in her hand that she began flipping into the river one by one.

"La-la-la la-la-la."

"It's like a painting," Alex whispered, overcome by the beauty of the scene. "You know, one of those old paintings in the museum."

In the throes of rampant lust, Dean growled, "It don't look like no painting to me. It looks like pussy."

"If Bobby comes out, he'll be pissed if he finds us," Nelson said, trying to keep his head while his dick jumped around like a snake inside his pants.

"Like I give a shit," Dean said.

They stared, imaginations pumping enough hormones into their bloodstreams to put all the rules of civilization to the test.

"This isn't right. We shouldn't be doing this," Alex said, embarrassed and confused by the power of his emotions, yet he couldn't make his legs carry him away. His eyes were nailed to the waif in the river as she turned, giving them a full view of her budding adolescent body.

"Oh, Jesus," Nelson moaned, trying to squeeze his eyes shut which they refused to do.

Alex sighed, knowing he'd never have the charisma of a Bobby McCorkle to attract a girl like that. Just wasn't in the cards.

Water streamed between her breasts and between her legs. The falls behind her creamed white and hissing as though the river had felt her presence, become aroused and was ejaculating all around her.

"Whaddaya think she'd do if I jumped inna water with her?" Dean snickered.

"I don't know, but I know what Bobby'd do."

"I can't stand it!"

Nelson grabbed his dick and came in his pants, gasped, and thrashed off into the woods running right past Charlie without seeing him in the bushes. Charlie saw the stain on the front of Nelson's Bermuda shorts and watched him rush to the boat and jump in the river away from the others.

Sally neither saw nor heard their shenanigans and continued to sing and splash in the water now up to the middle of her thighs. The liberated deck of cards spread out in a long line like uprooted water lilies drifting downstream. Delighted, she watched them float away, then spread her arms wide, threw her head back and thanked the stars for giving her this moment, the end of innocence and the beginning of love. A little woozy from the beer, she was glad she hadn't passed out like Bobby. Boys did that, she'd noticed. They just drank themselves silly.

"She can't swim," Alex said. "She shouldn't be out in the river like that."

"Look a' those titties," Dean said. "Look at the hair on her pussy."

"Dean, you're just drunker'n shit, so shut up."

"I'm gonna go get her."

"No, you're not."

Alex abruptly walked out of the woods and across the rocky beach to the edge of the water.

"Sally!" he shouted as loud as he could. "Get out of the river! It's dangerous!"

With the falls directly behind her, Sally couldn't hear. All she saw was Alex gesturing wildly for her to come to him, and then she saw Dean walk out of the woods behind him. They were getting a good look at her in the moonlight, that was for sure, so instead of shrieking like a dizzy bimbo and trying to cover herself, she waved, did a little dance, and wiggled her ass. Alex started to laugh, but Dean was ready to rip off his clothes and plunge into the river.

"God *damn*!" Dean gasped. "Look at that. It's Lady fucking Godiva. Maybe I better go in after her."

"Cool it, Deano. Bobby's gonna be out here any minute."

Alex waved again, blushing as his eyes devoured Sally's stirring beauty. He took a step into the water.

Not feeling threatened but having no intention of getting any closer to the boys, merely wanting to tease, Sally cocked her wrists on her hips, elbows akimbo, and jiggled her tits like Gypsy Rose Lee.

"She wants me," Dean hissed, tearing off his pants.

"Dean! Christ."

"Hey, baby!" Dean hollered, and ran into the river, stiff dick swinging, screaming, "Geronimo!"

Appalled, Alex froze, unable to decide whether to go after Dean or run to the tent and wake up Bobby.

"Oh, shit, now I've done it," Sally blurted as she watched the big, naked kid rushing toward her in a tornado of white water. She shouted, "Bobby! *Bobby*!"

But Bobby couldn't hear. Dean, pounding nearer, clearly heard her call for help, which at first only fueled his jealousy. Resentment of Bobby poured out of him like sweat, but the water slowed his progress enough for him to think: Jesus, if Bobby comes out of the tent, there's gonna be a fight.

Confusing signals battered through the alcoholic haze in Dean's brain. Fuck or fight or what? Sunburned knees pumping through the water, he glanced down and saw his flopping red penis just as the abrupt chill of the river sent a jolt of sobriety through his nervous system. It dawned on him that a lifetime of friendship was being tossed like detritus into the river. Was it worth it? Maybe it didn't matter. Maybe what he wanted was to kick Bobby McCorkle's ass and beat him at something.

He looked behind him and saw Alex on shore, agitated and hopping up and down, and the tent, unchanged, with no Bobby in sight. Then he looked up and saw only revulsion in Sally's face, her lips pulled back in a grimace, eyes bulging, and her body, so inviting from a distance, trembling and covered with goose-pimples. He'd expected to be received with open arms and open legs, and when he saw that wasn't the case his confusion deepened.

Capable of defending herself, Sally was more afraid of the water than of Dean. She knew that if she aimed a kick at Dean's crotch, she'd lose her balance, so she braced to hit him in the nuts with her fist.

Sloshing toward her, grinning at her defiant stance, he faltered on the slick bottom, slipped, and belly-flopped with a loud splash. For a few seconds, he drifted like a pink whale in the current.

Starting to laugh, Sally checked herself, thinking laughter might provoke the drunken fool. Instead, she began to take tiny steps on the treacherous bottom to distance herself from the crazed and naked Dean.

He found his footing, stopped his drift, raised himself to his knees, and shouted to Sally, "You're beautiful."

She shouted back, "You're crazy and drunk."

From shore Alex, still immobilized, could see them shouting inaudible words. Farther back in the woods, Charlie watched the scene in the middle of the river as if it were a silent film in slow motion. He saw Sally backing toward the strange, pitted rocks and gesturing as though she were trying to push Dean away.

"Leave me alone," she yelled.

Dean rose unsteadily to his feet, wobbling in the current, and took a step toward Sally, who continued to retreat. Finally compelled to intervene, Alex charged through the water, tackled Dean from behind and started a clumsy, slippery wrestling match. Enraged and confused, thinking Bobby had awakened and attacked, Dean flailed madly at Alex, who clung to his back, arms wrapped around Dean's chest as he tried to drag the bigger boy toward shore. Alex managed only to pull Dean over on top of him and then had to let go to keep from drowning.

Gasping for air, Alex broke the surface, startling Dean, who barked, "Alex! I thought you were Bobby!"

"I'm not gonna let you do this, Studley. You're out of your mind. Leave her alone."

From his knees Dean launched a roundhouse punch that missed by a foot and toppled him into the water. Feeling braver by the second, Alex charged again, thinking: I should get a medal for this.

Dean got his fight, whether he wanted it or not. With Alex and Dean entangled in a drunken brawl, Sally moved away from the struggling boys, inching downstream between a pair of rock formations.

These stupid boys are fighting over me, she thought as they churned the water a few feet away. Should I be flattered or appalled? Then she noticed that with every step the water was deeper and the current stronger.

Suddenly, Dean broke free from Alex and lunged again for Sally just as she stretched to grasp a rock for balance. Fueled by adrenaline and alcohol, Dean's football instincts took over and he slammed her with a linebacker's body blow that drove her head with tremendous force against the rocks.

Sally collapsed like a popped balloon. An instant of shock, too quick for pain, and she was gone. The river closed over her like a green cloud, and she began to drift away.

Dazed, Dean whirled to face Alex, who was kneeling in the river, coughing up water and muttering, "You bastard."

"She's a fucking *tease*, for chrissake!" Dean screamed. "What the fuck is the matter with *you*?"

When Alex didn't respond, Dean turned again and saw only the river. Baffled, he mumbled, "What the fuck? Where'd she go?"

Only Charlie in the woods saw Sally go under. One moment she was there, arms and legs flailing, and the next instant Dean hit her and she vanished. She'd fallen into a dredged-out hole in the bottom of the river, and when Charlie saw the top of her head bob to the surface ten yards downstream, she was drifting face down toward the other end of the island. Then she went under a second time, and neither Alex nor Dean, intent on each other, had seen what had happened.

Charlie rushed out of the woods. "Get Sally!" he shouted, pointing downstream. "She's drowning!"

"God *damn*!"

Alex waded toward the deeper middle of the stream, and when the top of her head appeared again on the surface, he dived in and within a few stokes found himself being swept downstream in the current. A step slower, Dean stumbled on a rock and opened a cut on his shin. Swearing and bleeding, he thrashed toward the middle of the river as Charlie arrived on the beach. The tragedy unfurled in curious silence, without shouts or screams, only the bubbling of the river and hiss of the falls.

When Alex reached the spot where Sally had gone down the third time, at the other end of the island near the boat, he discovered the water was only waist deep and stood up. Immediately, he saw her milky white body no more than ten feet away, unmoving, caught on an underwater snag. He brought her to the surface and a wide-eyed, terrified Nelson watched from the *Toot Sweet* as Alex pulled her from the water.

Blood seeped from the side of her head. Limp, lifeless, she'd drowned so fast Alex wasn't sure if she was breathing or not. Frantic, he tried mouth-to-mouth resuscitation, and when that didn't work, he turned her on her belly and pumped her arms and pushed on her back. The truth lay naked on the beach. A few feet away, frozen stiff, mouth agape, Nelson worked his jaw but no sound came from his throat. A moment later, Dean swam ashore and fell to his knees at Sally's side, sobbing.

"Is she all right? Is she okay?"

Alex looked away, shaking his head.

"What happened? What happened?" Nelson demanded.

Charlie rushed up, took one look at Sally's bleeding head and motionless body, and collapsed in a heap.

An owl hooted. Mosquitoes attacked. The moon sank behind the levee, and the night darkened over the eerie falls at Shanghai Bend. The four boys surrounded the dead girl and looked at each other, their scrambled minds teetering between paralyzing shock and the white abyss of true panic. The body that scant minutes before had provoked so much excitement and wonder now inspired only dread.

Flies settled on the corpse. Playing cards floated along the shore of the island, trapped by eddies behind the weird rocks. The remainder of the plastic-coated cards drifted with the current, and over the next week the entire deck would stretch from Shanghai Bend to San Francisco Bay. One card, the five of diamonds, would make it out the Golden Gate and ride the Californian Current three hundred fifty miles south to Los Angeles and wash up on the beach at Santa Monica, the only piece of Sally's soul to make it home.

A red-tailed hawk hunting above the falls would have seen beyond the levees to the farmland, alfalfa to the east and peaches to the west. Only the bravest and most desperate creatures were moving around in the dark. Three hours before dawn the closest human beings were a family of migrant Mexican farm workers camped in trailers in a peach grove a quarter mile away. A sleepless young mother feeding her newborn heard shouts from the distant river.

*Saligetatadariveritsdeincheros.*

*Gadam.*

*Jebebicheronimo.*

*Bobibobi.*

The barely audible sounds were rendered in unintelligible English of which she knew not a word, and she forgot about the exchange a minute after she heard it.

Four miles north in Marysville the lone deputy assigned to patrol that section of Yuba County was booking a drunk driver. It was the still of the night, the dark and quiet hours. Traffic on Highway 99 was light, with only truckers and travelers who wanted to beat the heat on the road.

A train hooted through a level crossing miles away. Above, the hawk dove toward a field mouse, made her kill and flew away. Upstream, the Feather spilled over the falls, and downstream the placid river flowed into the Sacramento, the Carquinez Strait and the great bay, past cities and towns and the millions who lived along the shores. The boys clustered around Sally as though to shield her from those millions of eyes. Sudden death was beyond their experience, and they didn't know what to do. Or rather, they knew what to do—tell somebody what happened—but were deathly afraid of the consequences.

Whatever grace had existed in their lives was gone. Frightened, still drunk with hangovers rapidly approaching, burned by adrenaline, sick and traumatized, they began to understand that what happened next was up to them.

"What're we gonna do?" Nelson asked.

"We have to tell Bobby first," Alex said.

"Tell him what?" Dean demanded.

"What do *you* think, Dean?" Alex snapped. "We have to tell him something."

"He'll kill me," Dean said, only beginning to realize what he'd done. "He'll say it was my fault."

"It was," Alex declared, nodding his head.

"It was an accident," Dean insisted.

"Horseshit. You'll have to tell him you were in the river and what you were doing there. Her head's busted open, and that doesn't look like an accident," Alex said.

"I was . . . confused," Dean mumbled. "I still am."

"You're drunk. We all are, and this is really fucked up."

There was a long moment of silence while they all stared at Sally's body. Dean convulsed once, violently, from misplaced lust and genuine fear, and lay down on the beach, moaning. Nelson's stomach turned over and he thought he was going to be sick. Charlie closed his eyes and rocked on his haunches, feeling only pity and sorrow for the dead girl he'd hardly spoken to. It just wasn't fair, he thought. I won her and maybe I should have just gone off with her and talked.

"Fishermen are going to show up here before dawn," Alex said quietly. "That's not too long from now."

"What did you see, Nelson?" Charlie asked.

"I was near the boat. I saw Alex swim down the river and pull her out of the water."

"That's all?"

"That's what I saw, Charlie. What about you?"

"I saw Alex and Dean fighting in the river, and then I saw Dean hit her and smash her into the rocks."

"In the water?" Nelson asked, "Dean? Why?"

"I thought she wanted to fuck me."

"She didn't," Alex said sharply.

Nelson croaked, "Oh, Christ. You did this?"

Stricken with grief for himself and for Sally, Dean could only nod.

"Keep your heads together," Alex rasped harshly. "You can't ask your mommies what to do. We're the royal flush, and we have to stick together, including Bobby. Whatever we tell Bobby, we have to tell the cops the same thing."

"What cops?" Dean asked, a spike of terror lighting up his eyes. "We're in the boonies. We don't even know where we are."

"They have cops or a sheriff or something. Every place has cops," Nelson wailed.

Suddenly their parents, humiliated and ashamed, loomed large in their imaginations, and behind the scolding moms and dads were cops, courts, judges, and prison guards. Terrifying headlines danced in their heads.

Alex thought for a long minute and then said, "No matter what we tell them, the cops will think we raped her, and they can prove it because Bobby fucked her. That's for sure. She's not eighteen, and that's rape in the state of California."

"We're screwed," Charlie mumbled.

Alex continued, "They won't believe it was just Dean. Look, we can tell Bobby she slipped and fell. He doesn't have to know anything else."

Dean looked up and stared hard at Alex. "You'd do that?" he asked.

"She's dead and we can't change that," Alex whispered hoarsely as he began to understand the magnitude of the situation. "We have to protect ourselves. We have to come up with a story and stick to it."

"Like hell," Nelson said. "I don't have to protect myself. I didn't do anything. This crazy fuck killed this girl."

"Nobody will know that unless we tell them, Nelson, and then you can say good-bye forever to Studley, and probably the rest of us as well."

"Maybe we should put her back in the river and let her float downstream and get the hell out of here," Charlie said, desperate.

"No way, man," Alex said, shaking his head. "If we do that, when they find her, it won't be long before they find the guy at the marina in Sacramento, and our ass is grass."

"Then we can tell them we saw her float by the boat, and when we got to her, it was too late," Charlie suggested.

"No matter what we say, Bobby will think we screwed her and killed her," Dean said, voice low and full of despair.

"He'd be half right," Alex said.

They all looked at Dean.

"I'll tell Bobby I did it and turn myself in. It's the right thing to do."

"No," Alex said. "Too risky for all of us."

"What do you want to do, Alex?" Dean asked, his voice almost breaking. "Put her on the boat and take her with us? What the hell would we do with her?"

"Cops," Nelson said.

"Parents," Charlie moaned.

"San Quentin," Alex said, and the name made them shudder.

"They can't put us there," Charlie protested.

"Oh, yes they can. We're eighteen. Rape and murder. That's why they built the gas chamber. It's Caryl Chessman time, boys."

Dean started to weep, and within a minute they were all in tears.

"I think we should tell the truth," Nelson said.

"They won't believe us," Alex answered.

"Why not? They have to believe us."

"No, they don't. They don't have to do shit."

"Alex is right," Dean said. "They won't believe us. Bobby is going to jail for rape and me for murder. Or we all go."

Another long silence, punctuated by more tears.

Alex looked away from Sally toward the woods in the center of the small island, then back at his friends and said, "We can bury her."

"What?" Nelson screeched. "That's really crazy."

"Bury her. Make her disappear. She's a runaway from down south. She said she had no family, so she won't be missed, or at least they won't be looking for her here."

"We can't be sure of that," Nelson protested. "We don't really know anything about her. We don't even know her last name. Maybe her name isn't Sally at all."

"It's our only chance," Alex insisted. "There's a shovel on the boat. I saw it."

"That's the same as admitting we killed her," Nelson said. "If they dig her up, we're fucked."

"That's a chance we have to take. Otherwise, it's the gas chamber for sure," Alex reasoned. "And look, even if they do believe us and let us go, everybody will know. Suppose we have a trial and we're acquitted, it'll hang like a cloud over us for the rest of our lives. We'll become pariahs. The colleges won't let us in. Our parents will kick us out. I know my dad will. We'll be fucked. We didn't do anything, but if we bury her and keep quiet, no one will ever know."

"Unless they dig her up," Nelson said. "With a broken head, it will look more like murder than if we just tell them now."

"We'll dig deep. None of this shallow grave in the woods bullshit."

"I don't know," Charlie said. "It just doesn't seem right. It's not fair to her."

"Nothing is going to bring her back."

"But we're innocent," Nelson said. "We didn't do anything. Especially Charlie."

"We wanted to."

"That's not a crime."

"It's not what we did," Alex said. "It's what they'll think we did."

"You're a cold son of a bitch, Alex," Charlie said. "I mean, she's dead, it was an accident, but what about her? Maybe she has a family, or friends. If we bury her, she's gone forever and they'll never know."

"We can't do anything for her, Charlie," Dean said. "Not now."

"I don't know. This is fucked."

"Alex is right," Dean said. "We have to put her in the ground."

"What about Bobby? What do we tell him?" Nelson asked. "Bobby's our friend, man. We can't lie to him."

"Yes, we can, and we have to," Alex said. "He won't want to screw up the rest of his life any more than we do, so let's not give him the chance."

"This is really fucked up," Nelson said.

"We'll bury her and go home and nobody says anything, ever."

"The right thing," Nelson said. "The right thing is to tell the truth."

"If the world was a fair and decent place, then yes. But it isn't," Alex insisted. "Caryl Chessman died in the gas chamber, and he didn't kill anyone. What do you think they'll do to us?"

"We have to stick together, whatever we do," Charlie said.

An airplane droned overhead, lights blinking, heading for Sacramento. The river flowed. Insects buzzed.

Alex said, "Charlie's right. We're the royal flush. Bobby, too. He'll understand we have to stick together. We have to decide what to do and then do it. I don't want to go to jail, I don't want to talk to cops, and I don't want to ruin the rest of my life because somebody has a big mouth. We bury her and say it was an accident. Dean?"

"Okay."

"Charlie?"

"I guess so."

"Nelson?"

Nelson looked at his tattoo, rubbed it, and said, "I don't know."

"C'mon, Nelson," Alex prodded. "Don't you want to go college and live a normal life?"

"It's not normal anymore, not after tonight, and it will never be normal again. This isn't just another prank, Alex."

"But you didn't do anything. Why pay for what you didn't do?"

"What about her? What's fair to her? If we bury her, then we are guilty of something."

"Yes. Saving our own lives. If we talk about this, your mother will be so ashamed of you, Nelson, she'll never get over it."

Nelson slowly and solemnly nodded his head, acknowledging that truth. "All right, but you and Dean have to tell Bobby what happened."

"Okay, we're all agreed," Alex said. "And no one ever talks about this, right? To anyone, ever. No parents, no friends, no one for the rest of our lives."

"That's going to depend on Bobby, isn't it?" Nelson said. "We can agree but if Bobby doesn't, there won't be anything we can do about it."

"I'm scared," Charlie mumbled, and began to weep again.

"We're all scared," Alex said, punching Charlie in the shoulder, "but we can't sit here crying all night. The sun is going to come up and there'll be fishermen."

"Look, we have to tell Bobby, so let's do it," Dean said. "Let's pick her up and take her over to the tent."

Awkward and embarrassed, each boy took a limb and they carried Sally's body into across the island. On the way Dean stumbled and dropped her and fresh blood from the cut on his leg smeared across her forehead. They had to stop again when Dean was overcome with nausea and had to vomit. By the time they arrived at the tent they were in tears again.

Alex went in and shook his sleeping, snoring friend.

"Bobby? Bobby, wake up."

"Huh? Wha—"

"You'd better come outside."

"Where's Sally?"

"Outside."

"What's going on, Wiz? What time is it?"

"Still dark. Come outside."

"Ow, my head. Christ, let me put on my pants."

Grinning, Bobby guessed maybe they'd figured out she'd cheated at cards and were calling him out for a showdown. The deck was stacked, fellas, and I'm sorry 'bout that but them's the breaks. Let's have a beer for breakfast.

"Sally?" he shouted. "What's happening, babe?"

When she didn't answer, he looked at Alex, whose tear-streaked face was barely visible in the dark interior of the tent.

"Alex? What's happening?"

"Come outside."

She was cold, turning blue, dead, with blood streaked across her forehead and matted over her right temple. Bobby's upper lip began to quiver and muscles in his face began to twitch.

The first thing he did was rip down the tent and cover her. Then he walked away a few yards and sat down on a rock and remained very still, looking at them, evil thoughts crashing through his mind like a stampeding herd of wild horses. He didn't want to talk to them or hear what they had to say. He wanted to kill them and was trying to decide how.

The four stood together muttering among themselves.

"You have to talk to him, Alex," Nelson said.

"Go get the shovel, Nelson. We gotta do this quick."

Nelson ran off toward the boat, and Alex took a step toward their stricken friend.

"Bobby, we're sorry," he said.

Bobby continued to stare, saying nothing, then looked away, gazing over the falls and the river gurgling at his feet. A card bobbed in the water, the seven of hearts, and he watched it break loose and float away.

He was certain one of them had hit her and smashed her head, and that one had to pay. Which one? Dean? He could catch Dean, maybe knock him out and drown him, but the others would get away. Maybe he could run one more down, but not all of them. He felt sick. The violence welling up inside him turned his stomach, but he forced down the rising bile and refused to give in to the impulse to throw up.

"Bobby, we have to do something," Alex said.

After a long pause, voice choked with venom, Bobby said, "Looks like you already did."

"It was an accident, Bobby. She was dancing naked in the river, and we saw her and tried to get her out of there, but she slipped and hit her head."

"Charlie, what happened?" Bobby demanded.

"Just what Alex said."

"Dean?"

"When Alex pulled her out of the river, she was already dead."

The detonation, the psychic grenade. Bobby's mind ripped loose from its moorings. Past and present and future disappeared in a blaze of white heat. Belief vanished. Right and wrong evaporated. Friendship atomized and disappeared. Love died. They were lying. All that remained was hate and violence, biology without humanity. They took Sally away from him, in body and in spirit. His life shattered like a race car slamming into a brick wall. Deranged, with all his senses gone awry, he saw his friends as unspeakable monsters.

"You're a lying motherfucker."

With a roar he leaped off the rock and attacked Dean, swinging wildly and landing a punch to the nose, which started bleeding again before Alex and Charlie pulled them apart. Bobby collapsed on the ground, pinned by Alex and Charlie and writhing with rage.

Just then Nelson returned with the shovel and asked, "What's going on?"

"Bobby went nuts," Charlie answered.

"What're you gonna do with that?" Bobby demanded of Nelson.

"Up in the woods, I think," Nelson said to the others. "The ground is softer, not so many rocks."

"What the fuck are you gonna do?"

"We're going to bury her," Alex said. "We have to."

"You cocksuckers. What do you mean you're going to bury her?"

"We can't tell anybody, Bobby. They'll put us in jail. They'll say it was rape and murder."

"They'll put us in the gas chamber and kill us no matter what we say," Dean said.

"Good idea. You first, Dean."

"Bobby," Alex said. "We've known each other since we were little kids. We're the royal flush. We have our entire lives ahead of us. We didn't do anything, but we know no one will believe us. We have to bury her and get out of here right now."

"You didn't do anything? *You didn't do anything?* Don't tell me you didn't do anything."

"Bobby—"

"Shut the fuck up, Alex. You pricks. You can't get away with this. You can't go back to San Francisco like this never happened, like Sally never existed. She was—"

Clenching his teeth, his mind exploding into incoherent fragments, he couldn't go on.

"Yes, we can," Alex said. "We have to. Even if they believe us, our lives are ruined if we tell anyone."

"He's gonna tell," Charlie said.

Nelson dropped the shovel and walked away, banging himself in the head and swearing to himself that he'd never drink again as long as he lived.

"Do you really want to turn us in?" Alex asked. "Do you want to go to jail?"

"No," Bobby snarled. "I want to kill you, and if I don't get out of here right now, that's exactly what I'll do. *Get off of me!*"

Alex and Charlie let him go and he stood up, eyes red as rubies, his mind on fire. Sally's essence still clung to him, and he shuddered and felt his skin go cold.

Without another word Bobby stepped over to the collapsed tent, lifted a corner and took one last look at Sally. Her eyes were open but he didn't touch her. He grabbed his shirt and tied it around his waist, took a deep breath, and jumped in the river. Without turning back he swam to the other side, pulled himself up on the bank, climbed the levee and disappeared into the peach orchard.

# 52

"And after you went over the levee, we didn't see you again for thirty-two years, until last night," Charlie said, his voice breaking under the strain.

With the burden of silence lifted, the mystery of Shanghai Bend revealed, the mood in the Caruso Suite was tense and subdued. The tale had gushed out in bits and spurts, the bulk of the narrative supplied by Dean and Charlie with frequent additions from Alex and Nelson.

Silent and attentive during the telling, when the story ended Bobby lit a cigarette, poured a fresh glass of soda and methodically squeezed in some lime juice He considered laughing in their faces.

He remembered sitting on the curb for two hours across the street from the Marysville Police Department. The building was small, he recalled, made of gray stone and constructed in such a way that it tried to look bigger and more important than it was. The Yuba County courthouse next door was more imposing. Blind justice and her scales were carved into the cornice. His vivid imagination conjured up Dean being strapped into the green gas chamber at San Quentin.

The cops coming to work early in the morning looked like deer hunters. He saw a judge, or a man who looked like a judge, enter the courthouse. The judge wore a suit and straw hat and was skinny and dignified, a symbol of all that was right and good and law-abiding.

She was dead and no judge could change that. Oh, Jesus, did they kill her? What really happened? He could never be certain. Should they die? What was justice? Who should decide? The cops? The judge? Him? He'd never see her again, never show her San Francisco, never sit with her in a café talking to beatniks.

He believed they'd get away with what they'd done if he didn't tell the police, and telling wouldn't bring her back. They wanted to pretend nothing had happened, but he couldn't pretend. If he told, he'd be part of—what had Sally called it? The system. She said he was part of the system, and the system was right there across the street. He didn't want to be part of any system, and he didn't want to go to jail, either. If he walked into the police station, he wouldn't walk out.

He wasn't a snitch. After a lifetime of friendship, he owed them that, but he couldn't be their friend anymore, not after this. Sally had showed him another world, and he wasn't going to find it in Berkeley or any place else he knew. He wanted to be on the other side of the world—the French Foreign Legion occurred to him— and never see anyone he knew ever again.

He walked away, stuck out his thumb on the highway, and a truck driver told him about the induction center in Oakland. He didn't have to go to France. He could join the Army and get a free ticket to West Germany. That sounded far enough away.

In the Enrico Caruso Suite, Bobby snapped out of his reverie, and after a long minute picked up Nelson's revolver and paced around the room, reloading the gun as he spoke.

Click, one round.

"So it was you," he said to Dean.

"Yeah. It was me."

Click.

"And you pulled her out," Bobby said to Alex.

"I tried to save her. I failed."

Click.

"What have you guys been saying? If we hang, we hang together. How noble. Summary executions all around."

Click.

"Very dramatic, just like in the movies."

Click.

"Would the world be better off without you in it?"

Click, the sixth and final cartridge. Bobby shook his head. "The world could care less. We're just card players. Me, I've got something to live for, a game in Biloxi on Wednesday night. As for the rest of you, you lost everything, and if you want to kill yourselves, or me, or each other, be my guest." He looked at Nelson and said, "This is a ridiculous gun."

With a hollow chuckle Bobby stopped pacing and laid the big Model 29 on the table.

"Anyone want a bloodbath?" he asked, backing away from the table and throwing up his hands. "Anyone want to cover up one murder with another? Anyone think I'm such an asshole for beating you that I deserve killing? Want to make me pay for *my* sins?"

No one moved.

"You sure? Dean? Here's your chance to end your guilt forever, but I'm not going to do it for you."

Dean buried his head in his hands.

"Don't you think your story is self-serving?" Bobby asked.

After a long pause Charlie replied, "I imagine it is, but it's still the truth. Alex pulled her out of the water and tried to resuscitate her, which was more than the rest of us could do, but her head was busted open. If we'd known what we were doing, we might have saved her. None of us was a paramedic."

"You've had thirty-two years to spin your tale. 'Dean was drunk and crazy and hit her and killed her, but it was an accident. He didn't mean to.' I'd say that's a weak defense for a charge of homicide."

"There was no homicide," Charlie protested. "We're not murderers."

Bobby glanced at Nelson. "There's a name for it, isn't there, Kimosabe?"

"Felony manslaughter," Nelson replied. "That's homicide, all right."

"And for that you were afraid of the gas chamber."

"Oh, God, yes," Alex answered. "We didn't think anyone would believe us."

"I don't know why anyone would believe you now. Your story doesn't prove your innocence. It's just a story, but burying her indicates guilt."

"The story is true," Dean insisted. "It was me and I'm admitting it. It's not easy."

"But you did kill her, Studley, and I'd hate to put that to a jury, if I were you."

Bobby took a drag on his cigarette, blew smoke at the ceiling and gazed at the heroes. Hey, Paladin, he thought to himself, if you rode into their town in your black leathers, would you believe them, or would you kick their asses to kingdom come? He remembered how much he'd wanted to kill them that night, and how many times he'd thought about it since. Now, a different urge was rising inside him. Justice. Mercy. He'd been a better man than them then, and he was a better man now.

"I can guess the rest," he said without emotion. "You dug a hole, dumped her in, tossed in the queen of hearts, covered her up and placed stones and logs over the grave. You were smart enough to clean up the campsite and as many beer cans as you could find, collect her clothes and radio and suitcase, then you hopped in the boat and went back to San Francisco and started telling lies."

"That's right," Nelson said. "That's what I told you in the cab last night. I saw your mom the next day when she came over to our house to ask where you were, and I told her I didn't know, which was the truth. I said you had a fight with Dean and took off. We were really afraid that you went to the police, and it was a huge relief a couple days later when we heard you joined the Army."

Bobby sipped his drink. He couldn't undo his life. Knowing the truth didn't do him any good at all. The truth had not made him free, but it had made him rich and that was good enough. He could afford to be charitable.

"So do you believe us?" Charlie asked.

Bobby laughed a wicked little laugh that came from deep inside.

"Why do you care whether I believe you or not, Charlie? You lost your company in a card game and won it back with a nice story.

I think you should be more concerned with what that means rather than whether I believe you or not. Ask yourself this: Are you paying for your sins, your bad judgment, or simply your poor ability as a poker player?"

# 53

Five canvas bags full of money were stacked near the door. The boys from Noë Valley sat around the card table, desolate and silent. Cards and chips lay scattered over the felt, devoid of meaning.

Bobby leaned over the felt and towered above them, eyes blazing like an Old Testament prophet. "You're responsible for what happened to Sally, but not for what happened to me. I ran away from Shanghai Bend, not you. If I'd stayed, things might've turned out differently, but we'll never know. Now, there's no reason for your lives to be destroyed except you got in over your heads in a card game.

"So be it. You made me the judge, but the jury was the fifty-two cards in the deck. The cards gave you back your lives, and now you're condemned to live them.

"Dean, you're going to live the rest of your life on the Feather River with your guilt. You'll suffer more at the scene of your crime than on death row in San Quentin.

"Alex, you'll have to go back to New York and face whatever mess you left there. And you're forbidden to play poker anywhere except this room.

"Charlie, you poor son of a bitch, I don't think you'll have any heirs, so rewrite your will and leave Hooper Fish to these guys. And do yourself a favor: don't play cards for serious money.

"And Nelson, Kimosabe, I want you to be the Lone Ranger. I want you to transfer to the missing persons division of your department and spend the rest of your time as a cop tracking down teenage runaways."

He gestured toward Nelson's briefcase full of documents and continued, "If I were you, I'd burn those papers. And if you want to play next year, you have my number. I'm always up for a game if there's enough money in it."

A knock on the door punctuated the end of his speech.

"Be right with you," he hollered, and added, "No hard feelings, hey, fellas? It was only poker. See ya 'round."

He didn't wait for any sign of agreement. He sauntered over to the table, spread the blue deck, picked out one card, and left the Enrico Caruso Suite with a wink and a wave.

He stopped at the front desk and collected the last of the canvas bags. Outside, as the bellhop piled the bags into a taxi, the rising sun caught snowcaps in the Sierra two hundred miles away. Bursts of silver and gold flashed across the red sky.

With a friendly wink Bobby tipped the bellhop an old silver certificate C-note.

"Thanks!"

"Where to, pal?" asked the driver, a young black man with a beret and gold earring.

"I'm gonna make your day," Bobby said, climbing in. He leaned over the back of the front seat and fanned four hundred-dollar bills and the ace of spades.

"How'd you like to take me to Reno?"

Looking out the window, Dean watched the cab pull away from the hotel, took a deep breath, blinked, exhaled, bent over the stereo and put on the rock and roll classic "Jim Dandy" by LaVerne Baker.

"Okay?" he asked, popping his fingers to the snappy beat.

"Okay," Alex answered. "It cost damned near four million dollars, but okay. It was worth it. What a rush. Thanks, Charlie. You hung in there like a champ."

"You're welcome."

"Nelson?"

"He'll never talk. It's okay."

"Boy, he really had me sweating," Charlie said. "I was sure he was going to blow us away, even after we told him."

"Maybe we should make sure none of us talks," Nelson said, snatching up the revolver. He aimed the long, menacing barrel across the table at Charlie, whose eyes popped wide in a moment of sudden terror. Nelson shifted his aim to Alex and then to Dean, still crouched over the record player.

"Nelson? What the hell are you doing?"

Dean backed against the wall. Nelson pulled the trigger three times and there were three loud clicks and nothing else. Blanks. No gunpowder.

"Oh, Christ."

Laughter, tears, shaking heads.

"You're still crazy."

Dean had the presence of mind to pour four shots of rum and pass out the glasses.

"To the royal flush."

"The royal flush."

"To Rocket Fuel."

"Rocket Fuel."

"And next year's wild card."

"The wild card."

"Long live the game."

"The game!"